Kenya closed her eyes and let him work, following in her mind the ever-widening circles he was making against her skin. Feet were a funny thing. Although, as a rule, she valued her weekly pedicure back in New York, the touch of her aesthetician was brisk, clinical. It was a job that needed doing, and so it was done well. But this, this was different. Although he touched nothing but her feet, her whole body felt at ease. She was barely aware of having sighed.

When he spoke, she had to shake herself to focus on his words: "Take heart, Kenya. We can do this."

Dear Reader,

Arabesque is excited to publish the Ports-of-Call summer series for 2005, featuring four romances set in exotic locales, including Venice, Italy; the Fiji Islands; Trinidad; and Accra, Ghana, in West Africa.

In Sandra Kitt's *The Next Best Thing*, April Stockwood tags along with her friend Stephanie on a business trip to Italy, but finds herself stranded in Venice when her passport and wallet are stolen by a pickpocket. When handsome Hayden Callaway, a foreign-service agent and old high school acquaintance from Philadelphia, comes to her rescue, April finds her holiday fling involves more than just sightseeing.

Set in Fiji, *A Taste of Paradise* is the backdrop for Marcia King-Gamble's steamy island romance. When hotel acquisitions director Jillian Gray is sent to the South Pacific to buy a run-down old property, with plans to turn it into a luxury resort, she doesn't count on sexy African-American transplant Benjamin Fuller getting in her way. But he has other ideas about the old hotel and Jillian.

When actress Kenya Reese visits Trinidad in Simona Taylor's *Then I Found You*, she thought it would be under different circumstances. But with the threat of blackmail and extortion, the rising star is forced to hire security advisor Damon St. Rose, a handsome and imposing figure. Despite their disagreements, the two find suspense and romance a potent mix amid the excitement of Carnival.

In a sequel to *Once in a Lifetime* and *After the Loving*, Gwynne Forster's *Love Me or Leave Me* follows Drake Harrington, the youngest of three successful brothers who own an architectural, engineering, and construction firm. When the Harrington brothers take a trip to Ghana to view a potential project, Drake invites local TV anchor Pamela Langford to come along. Although both enjoy the cultural and historical sites in and around Accra, the trip to West Africa also pushes their love to the limits.

With best-selling and award-winning authors Sandra Kitt, Marcia King-Gamble, Simona Taylor, and Gwynne Forster contributing to this series, we know you'll enjoy the passion and romance captured in each exotic destination.

We welcome your comments and feedback, and invite you to send us an e-mail at www.bet.com/books/betbooks.

Enjoy,

Evette Porter
Editor, Arabesque

Then I Found You

Simona Taylor

ARABESQUE
BET
BOOKS

BET Publications, LLC
http://www.bet.com
http://www.arabesquebooks.com

ARABESQUE BOOKS are published by

BET Publications, LLC
c/o BET BOOKS
One BET Plaza
1900 W Place NE
Washington, DC 20018-1211

All Kensington Titles, Imprints, and Distributed Lines are available at special quantity discounts for bulk purchases for sales promotions, premiums, fund-raising, and educational or institutional use. Special book excerpts or customized printings can also be created to fit specific needs. For details, write or phone the office of the Kensington special sales manager: Kensington Publishing Corp., 850 Third Avenue, New York, NY 10022, attn: Special Sales Department, Phone: 1-800-221-2647.

First Printing: August 2005

10 9 8 7 6 5 4 3 2 1

Printed in the United States of America

Then I Found You *is dedicated with love and gratitude to Mrs. Jean Howe, for being a third grandmother to my son, Riley.*

Chapter 1

Men.

Huh!

It was impossible to live with them, and it would hardly be feasible to scrunch them all together on some huge ice floe in, oh, say Antarctica, with enough sports channels, beer, chips and guacamole to last a good long time.

But at least that particular ice floe fantasy, which Kenya seemed to be having more than usual these days, was now serving to keep her sane as she endured the prolonged ranting of the man pacing before her.

"Do you have any idea what you're doing?" Ryan Carey asked for the tenth time in the past few minutes. He was a fairly tall man, with a florid, freckled face that competed for attention with his thicket of carrot-colored hair. His anxious green eyes bugged out as he frantically sought to distract her from the task at hand, and his Adam's apple bobbed in his throat as though he had choked on an oversized chunk of fruit. "Do you? Do you?"

"Packing." Kenya tried to sound calm, but her shaking hands belied the flippant nonchalance of her answer. To illustrate the point, she folded a pair of jeans and crammed it into her ivory-colored suitcase. It wasn't a very large suitcase and it was already bulging at the seams. But she hadn't thought to buy a larger one, because she wouldn't need much clothing where she was going. She wouldn't be gone long—or so she hoped.

"You're in the middle of rehearsals! You can't just walk away!"

"I talked to the producers. They're willing to let me have some time. A little time, that's all I need."

"Oh, I'm sure that must have made them very happy," Ryan countered sarcastically. "Having you walk out on them just as they had decided to take a chance on you. Just when they'd invested so much in you." He looked at her as though she'd just given away state secrets to the enemy.

"Of course, they weren't *happy*." She hung her head a little sheepishly, fully aware of the enormity of her effrontery. She was a minnow asking favors of whales. Her new employers—a large East Coast film company—really had invested a lot in her, treating her with great respect, doing everything to make sure she was comfortable. Even the hotel room in which they stood was paid for by the studio—and here she was, absconding. "But they're willing to let me take time off."

"Suicide," Ryan intoned darkly. "You've gone and killed your career just as it's begun to take off. Just as you've made something of yourself."

She hoped he was wrong. *Please, let him be wrong!* Her career, her art, meant so much to her. For as long as she could remember, acting was all she'd ever wanted to do. Being able to cloak yourself in someone else's persona, being able to become someone else, was what she lived for. Was she really going to lose it all if she made this trip?

She sat heavily on the edge of the hotel bed with her make-up kit on her lap and, for want of something to do with her hands, toyed with the brass clasp, opening and closing it, opening and closing. *Click. Click.* In spite of the incessant, muffled roar of the Manhattan traffic, which penetrated even the closed window, the tiny sound echoed in the otherwise noiseless room like the chatter of nervous teeth.

Sensing a moment of weakness, he leaped on it and drove in the wedge. "Think of how hard you've worked to get where you are. Think of all the bit parts, the crowd scenes, the 6 A.M. casting calls, the rejections . . ."

"I know," she murmured.

"Think of the shifts you spent waiting tables and slinging hash browns in one greasy spoon after the next, just to pay for your tuition. Julliard's an expensive school."

"I know, Ryan! But I'm telling you—"

"Even if you're willing to turn a blind eye to the enormity of the opportunity you're putting at risk—and as your manager, I beg you, *implore* you, not to do so— think about it this way: this job alone will pay off your entire student loan, and you'll still have more than enough to move out of your parents' house and buy yourself a nice place of your own. You could even . . ." He waved his arms expansively in the air, trying to illustrate the chance she was giving up. "You could even get better help for your father—"

"Now, that's enough!" Her sharp response was enough to halt Ryan's spiel, if only temporarily. "Don't talk about my father! I'm doing the best I can for him. And my mother. I know they need the money. I know we could get better attention for him if I stayed, but this . . . I need to do this. I need to go."

"To Trinidad?" Ryan was incredulous. "Who *needs* to go to Trinidad?"

"*I* do." She forced her fingers to cease their agitated fiddling with the clasp on the make-up case and set it down carefully on the bed. There were things Ryan didn't know and couldn't know about her trip. She was forbidden to tell anyone, even those she trusted.

Although Ryan had been her manager for a mere three months or so, she supposed she did trust him—at least, as much as she could trust anyone—considering the debacle that her relationship with her last manager had been. The mere thought of Tobias, in all his spiteful, evil beauty, made her wince, and the weight of anguish and regret that she had been carrying around in the pit of her stomach ever since their breakup made its presence felt.

Toby, public relations genius, career planner extraordinaire, devil incarnate. Toby had taken her from part-time gigs in small dinner theaters that were too far from Broadway to even be considered Off Off Broadway, to walk-ons on network soap operas. It was only a matter of time before his charm, connections, and influence had won her small speaking roles in minor independent films . . . and then those speaking roles had grown larger.

In that astounding way in which careers in the movie industry rose like meteors in the night sky, suddenly she'd become *someone*. Not a celebrity, surely, not a star, she always reminded herself modestly. But someone that people who knew movies, people who made movies, were interested in. She'd actually landed a role in a major film, the kind that played in first-run theaters. It was a supporting role, with maybe twenty minutes of screen time total, but it was the kind of role that most actresses prayed for all their careers and never saw materialize. Her name would appear in the opening credits, way after those of the lead players, of course, but in the *opening* credits, remaining on screen for several seconds before fading and not, as it usually did, quickly scrolling upward in tiny print at the end of the movie, with character titles such as "girl on bus" or "woman in red hat."

There weren't many good supporting roles for young black women, at least, not very many positive ones. While both the East and West Coast film industry abounded with parts for women like her as corpses, addicts, and prostitutes, Kenya had sought and achieved more, and it was all thanks to her former manager.

Toby had won her a chance of a lifetime. Then he'd cut out her heart—not cleanly, with the accuracy of a surgeon—but brutally, mercilessly, leaving her torn and bleeding.

She had allowed him to manage not only her career, but her image, her life, and her relationships. At the time that she had met him, he had been forty to her twenty-three. He had known more about living well than she could have ever dreamed and had set about teaching her with Pygmalion's intensity. He'd dictated how she should style her hair: permed, in a warm chestnut rinse with a hint of fiery highlights, and precision cut into a pixie style, which suited her small, oval face. He'd told her how to dress: stylish and sexy, but not outrageously so. He'd taught her about wine and fine cuisine.

And then, he'd begun to dictate whom she could and could not see, and how she should spend her weekends. Where she should party, which friendships she should maintain, and whom she should excise from her life. She'd been awed enough by him to think that she loved him, and, damn him, he'd been content to nurture that illusion to further his aim of exerting total control. Extricating herself when the suffocating confines of his tender mercies had become too much had taken determination, and the firestorm that had followed was too much for her to think about. Especially now, when there was so much more on her mind.

Kenya rubbed her hand over her brow. Even the dim hotel lights burned much too brightly for her. In just two days she was flying out to the island of Trinidad, not for a sudden, impetuous Caribbean getaway, as Ryan thought, but on a matter of life and death.

A mission of mercy.

Ryan was still staring at her, arms folded now, waiting for her to say something, anything, to clarify her position, justify her actions. "I have to go," she repeated stubbornly.

Ryan sighed the sigh of a man defeated. "Very well. Let me come with you, then."

"No!" she said hastily. What she had to do needed to be done privately. Quietly. "I'm going alone."

"You can't fly there by yourself. And besides, it's February. Isn't there some kind of Mardi Gras thing going on down there?"

"Carnival," she acknowledged. All her life, she'd heard stories about Trinidad, and in those stories, the annual Carnival festival was featured prominently. She'd always yearned to visit, to see with her own eyes the stuff of fairy tales. But there would be no time to appreciate the beauty and excitement that awaited her. This was not a vacation.

"Isn't it going to be crazy? People and parties? All over the street? What if something happens to you! You're due on the set in two weeks! Suppose you get hurt?"

"I won't get hurt." She tried to sound convincing. "I'll be all right." To be honest, she was scared out of her mind. Off to meet a stranger, a hostile stranger, to strike a bargain with unknown terms. That didn't meet her definition of being "all right," but she had to try. "Besides, you can't come with me. I'm not your only client. You have other clients to tend to."

"You're my most promising one," he said softly. "You

have a door wide open to you that very few even approach. My job is to make sure you cross the threshold."

Kenya got up from the bed, uncurling her stiff legs from under her, and walked across the soft carpet to touch him on the arm. "I'll be fine, Ryan," she assured him. "You don't have to worry about me."

His anxiety abated with her plea. "I *am* worried about you, Kenya. If you don't want me with you, at least take a friend."

"I don't know anyone to take." That admission alone took a great deal of strength. Between the demands of her career, managing her father's illness, and Toby's merciless culling of her relationships, she had precious few friends left. And none were close enough to confide in in her time of need, much less follow her to the Caribbean on a whim.

Ryan gave her a long, searching look before he sighed again, this time in defeat. "Very well, Kenya. Go ahead. And God be with you." He reached beyond her to the mantel, sweeping up her airline tickets and travel itinerary, giving them a long, hard look before replacing them. Then he retrieved his coat and hat from the back of a chair where he had thrown them and prepared to leave.

"I'll call you," she promised. At least it would give her a friendly voice to look forward to. "Soon as I get there."

Ryan responded with a non sequitur. "You won't be alone."

She looked perplexed. "What's that?"

"There'll be someone watching over you," he said. It was more an assertion to himself than a response to her question.

An uneasy sensation ran down the back of Kenya's neck. Surely, he was talking in the spiritual sense. *Tell me*

he's talking about angels. But then he had to be. What else
could he mean? Who else could be watching over her?

Even though Ryan's departure meant that his attempts at persuasion were over, Kenya was sorry to see
him go. Once he left, she would be alone again in this
big, empty, cold hotel room. As she watched Ryan let
himself out, shrugging his heavy coat on as he did so, she
felt an almost panicked urge to call him back, sit him
down, spill the beans, ask for advice, and plead for help.
But she steeled her nerves, did her best to look him
square in the eyes, and wish him a good evening.

He nodded and left without another word.

Alone again.

Always alone. It wasn't too bad, she reminded herself, as
long as you found something to fill the time with. There
was little left to pack and an entire night and day to get
through before her flight was due to leave. There were books
and magazines on the side table, and the ever-present television that seemed to watch her with jaded eyes.

Instead of entertainment, she was drawn—with the
same fatalistic attraction of a small insect toward the
bright, yawning mouth of a Venus flytrap—to a large
white envelope that she'd hastily shoved into the drawer
of the nightstand beside the Gideon Bible when Ryan
had shown up unannounced.

She removed the contents of the envelope and laid
them out on the bed. Over the few weeks that these
papers had been in her possession, not a day had passed
when she hadn't taken them out and pored worriedly
over them. The several sheets of paper were worn soft by
her constant handling. On the face of it, they didn't
amount to much: a few faxed documents and four or five
handwritten letters, their accompanying envelopes festooned with brilliantly colored Trinidad and Tobago
postage stamps featuring exotic wildlife. The faxes were

blurred, but not so much that she could not decipher the coat of arms of the country and the information that they purported to support.

Information that could destroy her family.

She read them over again, even though she knew each word, each punctuation mark, by heart. The letters were meticulously written, couched in pleasantries that made it hard for her to believe that they contained, in essence, a threat that could only be averted by a visit to the letter writer. The fact that this person had taken the time to congratulate her on her success and inquire about the weather, her well-being, and the health of her parents made the demand for her presence all the more frightening. A cold, bald, simple missive would have been less creepy, easier to swallow.

"I hope you know what you're doing," she said to herself as she refolded the pieces of paper and inserted them carefully into her handbag. Just how she would meet up with him once she got there was anyone's guess. There was no return address on any of the letters and no contact number anywhere to be seen. With luck, once she arrived in Trinidad, she would be able to sit down and think hard about what she would do next. It was not like her to be that reckless. But all choice had been snatched from her hands.

Putting her bag aside and clearing away the suitcase and debris of her packing, Kenya stretched out on the bed, above the covers, and stared up at the ceiling, trying a few deep breathing exercises in an effort to relax. It was just as well that she had nothing to do tonight. She needed all the rest she could get in preparation for what was to come.

It wouldn't be pleasant. Blackmail never was.

Chapter 2

Damon Saint Rose had a headache. It wasn't one of those "take two aspirin and have a nap" kinds of headaches. It was more like one of those "hit between the eyes with a sack of potatoes" kind of headaches. Some cruel and unjust god was reaching down, grasping the tight bundle of nerves that sat at the point where his massive shoulders met, and wrenching it upward in twisted, tortured handfuls, sending shards of pain dancing inside his skull. The conversation he was having with his cousin, Leshawn, wasn't helping much, either.

"I've been either in the air, in an airport, or getting to and from an airport for the past forty-eight hours, Leshawn," Damon protested.

"I know."

"And of those forty-eight hours," Damon continued wearily, "I've had three, maybe four hours' sleep, tops."

"I know. I know you're tired. Why don't you sit down? For a little while, at least. Hear me out." Leshawn sounded sympathetic, almost sheepish, making Damon feel rotten for complaining.

He took a long, controlled breath. The fact that he was in a lousy mood wasn't Leshawn's fault, he reasoned.

The tendons in the base of his neck cranked pressure up a notch, sending streaks of searing pain down his back, legs, and into feet that were swollen in their shoes, making him realize that sitting might not be such a bad idea. He released his grip on the enormous army green duffel he still held in one hand and let it drop to the floor. The bag was so huge that he often joked that it would have been a handy way to dispose of bodies, if he was so inclined. Aside from his laptop computer and the occasional carry-on, he always travelled with just that one bag. He had little use for suitcases, especially the kind with wheels. If a man couldn't carry all his belongings in one hand, he believed, then he just had too much stuff.

"Point the way," he said wearily. "Talk to me, but talk fast, while I'm still conscious."

He shucked off his heavy winter coat, still damp from the mild flurries that had greeted him the minute he'd stepped outside at JFK International Airport an hour and a half ago, and had persisted all the way to Leshawn's Brooklyn apartment. Tiny flakes of snow had long since melted in his crisp, black, close-cropped hair, leaving it glistening. Damon wasn't one for hats, even in the most severe weather. He found them irritating and preferred the cool, moist kiss of melting snowflakes to the confines of leather or felt. He was about to toss the coat aside but remembered that these days Leshawn was no longer the messy, carefree bachelor he had once been. Out of deference to the mistress of the house, Damon carefully hung his coat on a hook in the hallway where they were standing.

"It won't take five minutes to plead my case," Leshawn assured him.

"Good," Damon replied in a valiant attempt at patience. "Because it won't take five *seconds* for me to say no."

"It's only two weeks out of your life," Leshawn began. Obviously, he was planning on appealing to Damon's usually reasonable, logical nature. "Three, if that many."

The problem was that Damon was too tired to be either reasonable or logical right now. "The next two weeks I was planning to spend getting over the last *five months* of my life. I'm tired, man. I was counting on some R & R."

"The Caribbean's a really restful place," Leshawn countered. Never having been there, he added. "So I've heard."

"It's also a very *sandy* place," Damon retorted and added sarcastically, "so I've heard." He followed Leshawn into the living room and headed for his favorite chair. It was a padded leather recliner with overstuffed arms and back, and it swung out easily to allow him to put his feet up. It was one of those rare pieces of furniture that readily accommodated his huge frame. A man of his size would have been a fool not to have taken advantage of the comfort it offered compared to standard-sized furniture, which aside from being uncomfortable, always made him feel ungraceful and overgrown. The fact that it was also Leshawn's favorite piece of furniture, and that he was now depriving him of its use, gave him no small measure of satisfaction.

He winced in pain as he sat, and his right knee groaned in gratitude as he took the weight off of it.

Leshawn saw the grimace. "Knee bothering you tonight?" he asked sympathetically.

Damon nodded. He'd simply spent too much time flying for one day. Even first-class seating on most airlines wasn't roomy enough to provide relief from the pain he still endured, even now, after the damage his leg had sustained ten years before, when his pro football career had come to an excruciating and humiliating end.

He'd been one of the highest draft picks that year, even after resisting pressure from pro scouts to leave college before graduating to join a top-ranking NFL team. Instead, he had talked them into allowing him to finish his degree on the advice of his mother. You always had to have something to fall back on if "this football thing," as she called it, "didn't pan out."

Prophetic words, indeed. In his fourth year in the NFL as one of the league's leading young linebackers, during one fateful game where everything had been going right, suddenly everything had gone wrong. A small but crucial mistake, a lapse in concentration, and a player the size of an iceberg had tackled him out of nowhere, blowing out his knee, and shattering forever his dreams of football glory.

Learning to stand and to walk had been acts of sheer will, a medical miracle that was more a testament to his own stubborn refusal to give in to life with a disability than to anything else. Reclaiming his physical mobility had taken two years, and by then his promise of athletic success had melted away into memories kept alive only by a handful of photographs and articles torn from the sports pages.

Also ended was his fallback career in law enforcement. His intention to join Leshawn on the police force would never become a reality; there was no way he would ever pass a police physical. Determined to succeed in life, Damon invested everything he had earned during his football career into his new security business and had lured his cousin into joining him with the promise of travel and adventure. In retrospect, perhaps it had taken tragedy for him to find his true calling in life. As far as he was concerned, even the NFL could not have made him as content as he was now.

But they had been talking about sand, hadn't they? He

drove his point home. "Five months in Saudi Arabia, my friend. Five long months. Four and a half of those, sum total, roughing it in an oil field. In one of the sandiest places in the world. I've got sand in every stitch of clothing I own. I've got sand between my toes, sand in my ears, and sand in places I don't even want to think about. I don't think I've ever been this happy to see snow. Right now I feel like running outside and lying down in your front yard to make snow angels."

"This is Brooklyn," Leshawn reminded him. "We don't have snow. We have slush."

"Slush angels, then." The idea amused him. "But be that as it may, a beach is the last place I want to be."

"But Trinidad isn't just a beach. It's got mountains. And cities. And . . . um . . ." Leshawn scratched his head, searching his limited knowledge of the island for another selling point. Damon almost felt sorry for him. His geography was slightly better than his cousin's. He was sure that if pressed, he would be able to deliver at least a two-minute lecture on the southern Caribbean island's wealth of oil and natural gas, strong tourist industry, and smattering of sugar, rice, cocoa, and coffee. But he didn't offer to help.

Leshawn persevered gamely, turning his eyes upward and focusing on some invisible point on the living room ceiling in an effort to recall what he had read about the island. "And it's Carnival time. I know. I looked it up on the Internet. And Trinidad is ground zero as far as Carnival is concerned. That means music, and food, and girls wearing almost nothing at all. Party all day, party all night."

Damon harrumphed. "Except I'd be going there to work, not to party. Even if the client wants to party, *I'd* still be on duty."

Leshawn disappeared into the kitchen, which was just

left of the living room, switching on the light as he did
so. He did his best to carry on the conversation from
inside without shouting. His wife, Marilee, was asleep
upstairs with their baby, and she didn't take kindly to
being awakened at what she called an ungodly hour.
"Work, yes, but easy work. Piece of cake."

Damon had to resist rolling his eyes. After seven years
in business together, Leshawn still labored under the
delusion that an "easy" job actually existed. "There's no
such thing," he reminded him, "Not in our line of work."
In the security business, there really was no such thing as
a "piece of cake." If someone had made the effort to hire
him, that meant they were expecting trouble, and that
meant that he had to be on alert twenty-four hours a day.
His clients could party, running around like cackling
chickens, pulling whatever crazy, dangerous, and ill-
advised stunt wandered into their heads, because they
knew he'd have their back. As a matter of fact, half the
time they seemed to court danger, almost as if they were
testing him, or as if the fact that they had someone like
him in their court made them reckless.

Leshawn came back, a steaming mug in each hand.
He offered one to Damon. "Decaf," he said reassuringly.
"I know you're just about ready to head home and crash,
so I'd hate to keep you up."

"Thanks." Damon took it gratefully, tipping his head
way back and drinking half without hesitation. "Good
idea." He slept badly, frequently spending several nights at
a stretch in a hollow-eyed quest for sleep, and his cousin
knew better than anyone that this was his Achilles' heel. The
interference of caffeine was the last thing he wanted. His
cousin knew him well. It was just the way he liked it: black,
with enough sugar to stand the spoon upright in the mug.
He had a sweet tooth that would not be denied.

"And there's enough sugar in there to put a rhino into

a diabetic coma," Leshawn added, as though Damon hadn't noticed.

Damon grinned for the first time tonight, his fatigue unable to prevent the warmth he felt for his cousin from overcoming him. Leshawn *really* knew him well.

The sons of twin sisters, they'd grown up almost as brothers, so close in age and physical appearance that they reminded Damon of some old television show his mother used to watch, the one about identical cousins. The name of it always escaped him, but as far as he could recall, it was about these two cute little girls, played by the same actress, who were always getting into trouble.

Identical cousins, yeah, that was them. Both men had the same dark skin, the color of Brazil nuts in the shell; the same quick black eyes; clean shaven good looks; and large, well-shaped features. Until a few years ago, their builds were nearly identical, except for the fact that Leshawn was almost two inches shy of Damon's towering six-foot-six frame. Now, however, after three years of his wife's cooking, Leshawn exceeded Damon's two hundred and fifty pounds by an extra twenty, most of which had settled around his middle. In spite of Marilee's skill with sweet potato pie, though, Leshawn's upper torso and arms were just as bulging as Damon's, with hard, defined ridges of pure muscle. Side by side, they looked like a pair of young bulls, and for people who didn't know their gentle nature, they were almost frightening to behold.

When Damon finished his coffee, he set his mug down carefully on the small cork tile that Leshawn had thoughtfully provided to prevent rings from the hot cup from forming on Marilee's wooden coffee tabletop. The change in his cousin was a frequent source of amusement for Damon. He'd transformed himself from a man who kept enough beer cans, pizza boxes, and trash lying around his bachelor pad to keep a recycling plant operational for a week to one who kept coasters in his minibar and knew how to use them. Damon hid a smile and restrained himself from giving Leshawn the ribbing that he deserved.

Somewhat soothed by the warmth that now suffused his chest, he was willing to hear Leshawn out. Hearing him out, he reminded himself, didn't necessarily mean he *had* to take the job. He still reserved the option of saying no.

It wasn't as though they were hard up for money. The security consulting business was doing well. So well, in fact, that they now had over a dozen agents scattered across some of the most dangerous parts of the globe, from southern Africa, to volatile Latin America, to the war-weary Middle East, providing personal protection services to some of the most vulnerable and wealthy people on their small but important list of clients.

Their security services went far beyond those of a bodyguard. Any thug with a gun and half a brain could do that. He and his employees saw themselves not as guards or mercenaries, but as experts skilled at identifying the kinds of risks that their clients might fall victim to, such as kidnapping, extortion, fraud, and hostile attacks on their businesses or personal finances. Their clientele ranged from energy company executives to developers and contractors involved in building bridges, roads, and pipelines in far-flung places. It was not a job for someone who disliked travel or discomfort.

Damon, Leshawn, and the men in their employ were physically suited to the job but knew that it required more brain than brawn. It required foresight, instinct, a quick mind, and a nose designed to detect even the slightest whiff of trouble. Every single employee is an expert in his field. Damon's company charged exorbitant sums of money for their services—and they were worth every penny.

That very same nose for trouble was twitching right now. Damon knew that whatever new assignment Leshawn had signed him up for was going to be out of the ordinary. That he didn't mind. The extraordinary kept you alert, alive, and avoiding danger. But just how extraordinary would it be?

"Okay," Damon finally conceded. "I've got a stomach full of sugar, so I'm feeling mellow. Shoot."

"As I said," Leshawn began, "This one is going to be easy. Honestly, you may even enjoy this assignment—"

"Skip the sales pitch, my man. Just give me the 411. Who've you got me tangled up with?" In spite of himself, Damon could feel a tiny tingle of anticipation building deep inside. Ever the adventurer, he was intrigued by the promise of mystery. The still, clear voice that kept him out of trouble in some of the world's most dangerous places was speaking to him now, and it was telling him that if he were to accept this challenge, whatever it was, he was in for a ride.

That tingle of anticipation made him glad that unlike his cousin, he was still active in day-to-day field work. Since getting married, and more so since the baby had come, Leshawn had taken on fewer of the personal and overseas assignments. Over time their roles changed; Leshawn had become the manager of sorts, involved in making personnel assignments; booking flights, accommodations, and rental vehicles; and handling the numerous legalities that running such a business entailed. His only overseas trips these days consisted of filling in in an emergency for employees, or surprise audits where Leshawn would drop in to ensure that everything was progressing smoothly. Before, most of those tasks had fallen under Damon's purview, and he had been relieved to give them up, preferring to be in the field.

The catch, though, was that he, like all of the other

agents, was expected to accept whatever assignment he was given. Though, of course, they had the right to refuse if they really had strong objections. So far, Damon had never done so.

Would he be refusing tonight? "So, who's this guy? Is he an activist? An oil man? Oh, wait. Don't tell me." He put his fingers to his brow like a fairground psychic receiving an incoming message. "The President's gotten bored with his Secret Service bodyguards and is looking to subcontract."

The smile that had been playing about Leshawn's lips faded. "Damon," he began, and stopped. He looked down into his mug of coffee as though expecting to find a script for his next words floating on the surface.

An uneasy suspicion arose in Damon's mind, like a groundhog popping out of its hole, but then, restless, disappearing below the surface again. Leshawn couldn't have done what Damon thought he'd done. Not when he knew Damon was dead set against it. Not when he knew how important it was to him.

The coffee mug brought forward no answers, so Leshawn lifted his head again. "You're the only agent who can take this job," he began, trying his best to make the way smooth for what he was going to say next. "There isn't anyone else free."

The nasty suspicion arose again, and this time it was bolder. Once aroused, it stayed put. "Don't tell me you did what I'm thinking you did," Damon said. "You didn't."

Leshawn was on his feet seconds before Damon was, but just barely. "Yes, but—"

"You got me a female client." Damon's statement was level and without emotion, but his heart was pounding. "A woman."

"Just this once." Leshawn was equally calm, but

Damon knew him well enough to detect his apprehension. "I didn't have a choice."

As if it had never been there, the control in his voice was gone, giving way to incredulity and disappointment. "You had a choice! You could have said no!"

Instead of debating the issue, Leshawn tried to placate Damon. But in doing so, his words buried themselves deep into wounds that, though four years old, were still raw. "It's not going to happen again."

Damon stalked out of the room without a backward glance. "You're right about that, cousin," he said over his shoulder, "because I'm not taking that client." It was time to leave. In his confusion, he wondered where he'd left his coat. If need be, he'd leave without it. He just wanted to get out.

"Don't do this to yourself," Leshawn pleaded. "Let it go. That's all in the past. Please, let it go. Forget it, and move on."

That stopped him cold, like a seven-point moose stopped dead in his tracks by a hunter's bullet. "Forget it?" He echoed. "Say that again?"

Leshawn slapped his head in self-castigation. "No, no. Poor choice of words. I know you can't *forget* what happened. Nobody expects you to. But you *can* move on."

In spite of the cloud of anguish that blurred his vision, Damon found his coat and put it on. In his haste, his hands became entangled in the sleeves, and they bunched up on his shoulders, making him feel awkward and foolish. He could feel Leshawn's grip on his upper arm, trying to restrain him more by persuasion than force. It was love for his cousin, and that alone, that stopped him from wrenching away.

"Just give me a few moments, man. That's all I ask. Don't leave like this."

He dearly wanted to leave. He wanted to continue on

his trajectory toward the door, and put some space between him and the conversation that had triggered such unexpectedly sharp pain. But the gash in his chest had already been reopened, and leaving the house wouldn't dull the hurt. That pain was something he was condemned to carry with him for the rest of his life, like the corpse of an albatross slung around his neck, filling his nostrils with the stench of his own miserable failure and its mortal consequences.

Damon's shoulders drooped under his cousin's hands, signalling his defeat, and Leshawn was able to lead him without effort back into the living room and steer him gently back into the embrace of that huge leather chair.

Damon clasped his hands and rested his chin on them, staring into space for an immeasurable span of time, until his surging emotions subsided. Leshawn, knowing his cousin well, said nothing. He sat motionless across the room, trying to soften the sound of his own breathing lest it become intrusive.

Damon realized that his top teeth had been worrying the skin on the back of his wrist, and he stopped the nervous gesture. Slowly, reason returned, lingering on the threshold of his mind, as timid as the prodigal son returning to his father's doorstep. Maybe Leshawn was right. Maybe it was time to confront his anguish, rather than hide behind some stupid, self-imposed exile of female clients. His lips pursed wryly. "So this is therapy? This is your idea of forcing me back onto the horse I've fallen off of?"

Leshawn shook his head emphatically. "No, no. You know I'd never do that to you. You don't need me to force any kind of therapy on you, especially not something as ham-handed as this. I really didn't have a choice."

Damon exhaled deeply through his nose, and with

that, all resistance seeped out of him. "Okay. So tell me. Who is she?"

"Her name's Kenya Reese." Leshawn watched his face closely, waiting for a reaction to the revelation.

If it was a reaction of recognition that he was waiting for, he didn't get one. Instead, Damon rubbed his chin thoughtfully. "Kenya Reese. I know that name. I know that I know that name."

"She's an actress," Leshawn prompted.

That didn't help much. "You know I'm not big on the whole celebrity thing, but somehow—"

"If you don't know it now, you will soon. She's new, but she's going to be hot."

"And she needs—" Damon hesitated, "—someone to watch over her."

"Yes. Protection."

"From what? Is she being stalked?"

Leshawn shook his head. "Not according to my brief. Don't think so."

"Paparazzi?"

"Nothing more than usual, it seems."

"What does she want, then?"

"It's not what *she* wants. It's what her *manager* wants. He's the one hiring us."

"Why? Is she shooting a movie over there?"

"No, actually, she's supposed to be shooting a movie over *here*—in New York. From the sound of it, she just suddenly decided to go. It was the weirdest thing. Two days ago she's in rehearsals; yesterday she announces that she's taking a few weeks off to fly to the Caribbean." Leshawn snapped his fingers. "Just like that."

"Capricious," Damon mused. "Risky." Capricious clients, the kind who upped and did whatever popped into their heads, were hard to protect. Especially during Carnival, when they would be smack in the middle of one of the biggest street parties in the world, with a few hundred thousand people roaming around drunk and in masks through the streets. If he *were* willing to climb back on the proverbial horse, was this the kind of female client he wanted to take on?

"Maybe she has good reason."

"Possible." Damon rubbed his chin thoughtfully. "Maybe she's running from something. Maybe she's running *to* something."

"Who knows?" Leshawn was eyeing him sharply, trying to deduce whether he was becoming more or less inclined to take the job as the conversation progressed. "Or she could just be needing some time off. Everybody needs a break sometimes."

Leshawn's words tapped insistently at Damon's skull, like raindrops from a cloudburst drumming against a windowpane. Everybody *did* need a break sometimes. Even he did. Suppose he cut himself a little slack? What if he set his guilt aside instead of cradling it in his arms like some stray animal, nurturing his own shame and heartache?

Leshawn read the surrender in Damon's face, reached over to a nearby table, and picked up a large manila envelope. "She's flying out tomorrow afternoon," he reminded him and handed him the envelope. "Here's your ticket, car rental, hotel booking. She's leaving out of JFK. Check-in's at four-thirty. Can you do it?"

Could he? As tired as Damon was, he was glad that there would be so little time before this new assignment began. Less than twenty-four hours didn't give him time to do much more than take a shower and get some long-deserved sleep before he needed to get up, do his laundry, and pack everything back into that huge duffel bag. There were battle-weary soldiers home on furlough who had more turnaround time than that! In a way, though, the rush would do him well. Less time for his own cowardice to sucker punch him into backing out.

He took the envelope, nodded in silent acceptance, and with a mixture of curiosity and resignation, opened it. Ignoring the travel documents for the time being, he reached in and pulled out a standard publicity head shot of the client he had now promised to protect.

"Hello, Kenya," he said. He tilted his head to one side and examined her critically. It was a good photo. Someone obviously had spent a great deal of money on the lighting, clothing, hair, and make-up. He wondered almost idly if she would look as good in person as she did in the photo. After all, with enough money and a talented stylist, anyone could glow like the woman in the photo did. Her hair, the color of which vacillated between a rich chestnut and a warm burgundy, was relaxed and styled in a precise but casual pixie cut that framed her small, delicate, oval face to perfection. The haircut made her look no more than twenty-five, and her startlingly large, brown eyes completed the image. Her make-up was artfully done, leaving her face with a healthy, vibrant glow while giving the impression that she was wearing little, if any at all. Straight, white teeth were just visible beyond the upper curve of her full lips.

He put the photo down. Accompanying the photo was a group of clippings from newspapers and magazines, arranged in chronological order, with the most recent at the back. He rifled through them idly, noting a brief but varied list of credits. Then, suddenly, the clippings became more lengthy, ripped out of gossipy tabloids rather than legitimate publications. And this time the subject was not her work, but her private life.

Damon's brows lifted as he read. Leshawn studied him, trying to gauge his expression, but said nothing. The lady had been busy, at least—if all this was true. He was not a movie fan, but he knew enough about how the world of film and Hollywood worked to take everything that was said with a grain of salt. He checked the dates scribbled in the margins of these latest clippings. The newest was a mere week old. If what these stories said about her was true, no wonder she was so anxious to leave the States for a while.

He picked up the photo again and stared at it. "Hello, Kenya," he said once again, softly. *This* was the woman who so scandalized the gossip sheets? Without comment, he slid the photo back into the envelope. Eventually, he said, "Tell me one thing, though."

"Sure."

"We've never taken on a job like this. We work for business people, not movie stars. Why did you say you didn't have a choice?"

Leshawn shrugged. "It's sort of a favor for an old friend."

"*She's* an old friend?" Damon found that hard to believe. " Of *yours?* In what universe?"

Leshawn took the teasing with good humor. "Not her, her new manager. She just signed with him a few months ago. As you can see from the gossip sheets," he pointed at the envelope Damon was still holding, "she had a problem with her old one. We go back to my days on the force, Ryan and me. He begged me for help, and I promised him. . . ."

"An ex-cop who manages starlets?" Now that was one he hadn't heard before.

"Why not? I'm an ex-cop who manages ornery old grumps like you."

Damon couldn't stop himself from smiling at that little barb. "Well, at least that stands to reason."

"Not really. Both are a pain in the butt." Despite his teasing, Leshawn's face reflected nothing but relief and gratitude that Damon seemed resigned, almost optimistic about his new assignment.

Damon was sure that the anticipation of his refusal had caused Leshawn a good deal of anxiety, and that alone made him feel better about what he was about to do. The two men had always been there for each other. If Leshawn needed a favor, he'd certainly give it. He swung his legs down from the footrest on the huge chair and rose heavily to his feet. He bore the pain of his football injury with the dignity of one who had long ago become used to it. Leshawn hurried to help, picking up the heavy bag Damon had earlier abandoned, and followed him to the door.

Outside, the snow had disintegrated into a miserable drizzle, but Damon didn't feel it. He fished in his pocket for the keys to his car, which Leshawn usually kept parked safely in his garage for him whenever he was out of the country. As always, his cousin had faithfully kept it clean, shiny, and ticking; with one click of the remote, the headlights came alive, and the car hummed its welcome.

He knew deep in his aching bones that he would regret this decision. But a promise was a promise, after all, and he couldn't let Leshawn break a promise to his friend. "Tell your old buddy from the force not to worry," he informed him as he took the bag from his cousin and tossed it into the waiting truck. "I'll look out for his Miss Reese. I'll do whatever it takes to bring her back home in one piece. You have my word on that." He wasn't sure if that promise was for Leshawn's benefit or for his own.

"Your word is good enough for me," Leshawn said softly.

Chapter 3

In spite of the cold, dismal February weather outside the terminal at JFK International Airport, Kenya was hot and itchy. It probably had something to do with the wig. She would be the first to agree that it wasn't a very *good* wig. She had borrowed it from a sympathetic wardrobe assistant, even though, technically, she wasn't supposed to take such items off the set. The fact that *she* wasn't supposed to be off the movie set either made her feel less guilty about taking the wig.

Surreptitiously, she slid a hand up to adjust the offending half-pound of braided hair, the tail ends of which kept slipping down the back of her sweater and driving her mad. She hadn't worn her hair long since she was seventeen, and it felt odd. The mass of fine, serpentine braids, each tipped with an assortment of cowrie shells, hair ornaments, and filigree clips certainly wasn't her style, either. But, she supposed, that was what made it a disguise. Between the wig, the large denim hat, and the reflective sunglasses, she hoped that she would be allowed to stand in the check-in line in one of the busiest airports in the country and not be recognized.

She was less embarrassed by the ugliness of the getup

she was wearing than she was by the fact that it was necessary to wear it in the first place. She wasn't that famous. Not A-list famous, certainly. Not even B-list. Most of the time, she managed to blend in with the crowd almost anywhere in New York without being spotted, except for a few encounters with fans of the soap opera she'd been on before her lucky break on the big screen. And even some of those just stopped her to tell her that she looked like "that Kenya lady."

But all that had changed in these past few weeks, and not for the better. Damn Tobias. Double damn him. In being foolish enough to love him—or to think that she had—she had allowed him access to her private world, unknowingly providing him with the ammunition he needed to avenge his offended pride after she had realized that their relationship had become too uncomfortable.

Once she explained to him that their professional relationship as manager and client and their relationship as lovers created an uncomfortable place to be, his vengeance had fallen upon her like an iron fist, shattering the one thing she held most dear: her reputation. Hell, Kenya had discovered, hath no fury like a self-centered man scorned. With the same meticulous care and attention he had paid to building her name as a new, up-and-coming actress, he had set about destroying that good name.

Now, she couldn't visit a supermarket without reading a tabloid headline about herself, dripping with malicious lies. Toby's well-planted seeds of scandal and gossip that the press had fallen for catapulted her into tabloid notoriety. So, yes, she was hiding. Maybe she was being overcautious. Maybe she was fooling herself about her own importance in the greater scheme of things, but once there were reporters willing to go through your garbage, call up your old high school friends, and harass your parents, it paid to be careful. Didn't it?

The line at the check-in counter moved up. Kenya shook herself to quell her anxiety, closing the gap ahead of her. There were only two or three persons between her and the counter. That was a relief. In five, maybe ten minutes, she would be on the other side, in the relative comfort of the departure lounge, where at least she could have a seat and a cup of coffee, and bury her face in a newspaper until her flight was called.

"Excuse me." A deep voice rumbled at her elbow, not addressing her, she sensed, but someone nearby. There was a rustle of movement right behind her, and instinctively, she shifted her position to allow whomever it was to pass.

She tried retreating into her thoughts once again, shutting out the activity around her. But something was stopping her, something weird, almost eerie. Like a fork stuck into an electric outlet, something was intruding, interrupting her thoughts, leaving them sputtering, crackling, and chaotic. But what? A shiver ran through her, starting at the top of her head, wig notwithstanding, rippling down the back of her neck, spreading to her front, along her breasts and belly, down her arms and into her fingertips—wave after wave—and down her legs and into her toes. The hair on her body stood on end telegraphing messages—on and on it went until every nerve ending within her resonated.

The message was: *Danger nearby!*

There was something huge right beside her. No, not some*thing*, some*one*. Someone was a little too close for comfort. She flinched, pulling her jacket a little tighter around her in an attempt to protect herself, and looked up . . . and up.

A mountain of a man was putting an enormous

army-green duffel bag down on the floor right next to her, exhaling deeply as he did so—as though it hurt to bend over. The hand that held the straps of the bag was so huge that the handle looked fragile enough to snap in his grip.

The skin on his hand was rich and Hershey-bar chocolate. And try as she might, Kenya could not stop her eyes from following it to the point where the sleeve of his bottle-green flannel shirt met his wrist, and from there, up along his arm to his chest, which looked as deep as it was wide.

Stop it, she reprimanded herself. *Stop staring.* A line jumper was a line jumper, and this man who was trying to insinuate himself next to her had certainly not been in the line a moment ago. She hardened her features into her best scowl without making any eye contact. In New York, eye contact could be dangerous business. "The line forms at the *back,*" she said pointedly.

The mountain didn't move.

This time she did not hesitate to let her annoyance show. "Look," she began, "we're all in a hurry. We've all got the same flight to catch. But I'm sure if we just do what we need to do in an orderly fashion—" She stalled. In her irritation, she had done exactly what she had been trying to avoid: lock eyes with this huge, offending stranger.

And what eyes they were! Implacable, unwavering, as unblinking as a cat's. Dark . . . blacker than black . . . and fixed steadfastly on her.

She shivered again, as the sense of danger that had rippled across every inch of her skin seconds before made another circuit, this time penetrating beneath her skin, running through flesh and bone, sounding an alarm louder than before.

She struggled to tear her eyes away from his but succeeded only to find her gaze riveted to the rest of his face. His features were large and well formed, elegant in spite of their size. His brows were dark, thick, and winglike; his nose long; and his cheekbones high, broad, and well-defined. His mouth was unsmiling but far from hostile. His lips were full, wide, and exquisitely shaped. There was something about them that brought an inexplicable craving for chocolate bubbling up from deep within her consciousness. Without realizing it, she ran her tongue across her bottom lip. She could even *taste* the chocolate!

Maybe just this once, her muddled brain struggled, *I can just let him slip in before me. There's still time to catch that flight. . . .* She half smiled, ready to let him slip past her if he wished. He didn't step into the space as it opened up before them but remained at her side.

"Miss Reese," the stranger began, just loudly enough for her to hear him, but not so much that anyone else around them could.

Visions of steaming cocoa were banished in an instant, and with them, any goodwill she had fleetingly felt toward the man who was still insinuating himself closer. He had called her by name! The danger signals that had rippled through her body became alarm bells clanging in her skull. He knew who she was!

That could only mean one of two things, neither of which—in her frame of mind—was she in any mood to deal with right now. She chose the least offending option first. "No autographs," she whispered. "Sorry. Please, not right now, okay?" Normally, with autograph seekers, she always obliged. It was part of an unwritten contract that any performer had with her fans: they showed her their appreciation, and she gave them the respect and time they were entitled to. To be honest, every request for an autograph made her feel warm inside. It told her that she was doing something right.

But she couldn't. Not today. "Please," she repeated. "Normally, I would be more than happy to, but today . . ." She trailed off, feeling guilty, touching her hand to the dark glasses that obscured her eyes, cursing them for being what was now obviously a useless disguise.

"I'm not here for an autograph," the man beside her said, speaking as softly as he had before. He sounded almost apologetic. "I'm afraid you've misunderstood . . ."

She had indeed! Her whole body drew tauter still. If he wasn't an autograph seeker, then the second, less pleasant option came into play. He was a reporter. Either he had gotten wind of her trip and followed her here, or he was an opportunist who had spotted her in the crowd and was now sidling up to her to squeeze out a story by hook or by crook.

"No stories," she told him sharply. This time there was no trace of guilt. "No quotes. No interviews." She looked anxiously around her, searching for an escape route and finding none. The firmness in her voice was betrayed by a note of pleading. "I've said all I have to say. Over and over. Why can't you leave me alone?"

The man was silent, his dark eyes still on her, holding hers for so long that she had to tear her gaze away, focus it elsewhere, anywhere but within his uncomfortable thrall.

Eventually, he spoke. "I'm not a reporter." The statement was decisive, without a hint of irony or deceit.

She looked at him again, wanting to believe him, if only for her own peace of mind. For what it was worth, he had an honest face. But, unfortunately, honesty could be feigned. What else would he want from her, if not another tawdry story? She searched her mind for any alternate explanation but failed to find one. She made a small, disbelieving sound and begged urgently, "Whoever you are, and whatever you want, please, leave me alone.'

His brow furrowed slightly, and his look became more piercing, more wary, as though he was afraid that she might lash out or, worse, burst into tears. "Miss Reese," he finally said, "I'm your escort."

She couldn't be hearing right. "My what?"

"Your security escort." Then, he added slowly, as though the words pained him even to speak them, "Your bodyguard."

An incredulous gasp escaped her. "My bodyguard? Are you joking?" What reason did she have to believe him? In the past few weeks, she'd had one reporter pose as a chambermaid in her hotel, and another as a handyman on the set. She wasn't prepared to be lied to like that again. She glared at him, summoning as much skepticism as she could and allowing it to show in her face, hoping to intimidate him into backing off. The effect, unfortunately, was diminished by the fact that she stood barely five feet to his six feet . . . plenty. She felt like a cornered cat hissing at a tiger.

He was nowhere near intimidated, but a puzzled look did cross his features. "You mean you're not expecting me?"

"*Expecting you?* How could I expect you if I don't even know who you are? And for your information, this is just about the lowest, dirtiest stunt any reporter has pulled to date. Bodyguard! Huh!" She all but spat out the word. "Did you really think I'd fall for that one?"

He looked so perplexed, it would have been comical, had she not been so upset. "Really, I am—" he floundered.

"Ahem!" A short, bespectacled man in an ill-fitting, off-the-rack business suit coughed ostentatiously into his fist and nodded at the check-in counter, where the clerk was now patiently waiting for her. She had been sidetracked by this bold-faced reporter and his trumped-up story that she had failed to see the front of the line was completely clear.

Having said all she needed to say to the con artist—
and half suspecting that he probably was wired for
sound, and that anything else she had to say would wind
up verbatim in some gossip column or on the Internet—
she clamped her jaw shut, hitched her carry-on bag
higher on her shoulder, and stepped up to the counter.

The creep stepped forward with her. Kenya's jaw
dropped in amazement. "Look," she began, abandoning
any attempt at being tactful, "I'm on to you, so drop it.
Don't expect me to take your stupid, sophomoric bodyguard nonsense for anything other than what it is: an idiotic, lamebrained lie. And it won't get you a story. So if
you don't mind—"

"I'm *not* a reporter," he said again. His voice was as
level as it had been the moment he first addressed her.
"I told you who I am. I'm your escort. My name is Damon
Saint Rose, and—"

"Saint Rose? I don't know anyone by that name."

"Ryan sent me."

The name made her stand stock-still. She watched him
with cautious suspicion.

He tried again. "Ryan Carey. Your manager."

"I know who Ryan Carey is," she snapped. "And I don't
believe you."

His logic was implacable. "How else would I know his
name?"

"You could have looked it up," she countered. "On the
Internet, or somewhere. You could have asked someone.
A friend of a friend."

"I didn't."

"You could have"—she floundered, waving her arms
for emphasis—"bribed someone."

"Like who?"

"Anyone." To be honest, she had no idea who he
could have gotten to. But she was sure that information

on anyone was out there, if someone knew where to look. "I don't know. Another actor. Another reporter. Anybody. You people know how to get information when you want to."

"*My* people?" He gave her a quizzical look. "And who would 'my people' be?"

"Reporters!" She spat out the word as though a bug had flitted into her mouth.

"I'm going to say this only one more time. I am not a reporter. Look, let me show you my ID." Before he could reach for anything, there was a sound behind them. They both turned.

"*Ahem!*" Once again the little man behind them gestured impatiently at the check-in counter, which was still empty. The clerk was still there, waiting for Kenya, her welcoming smile having faded somewhat. "Miss," the man said. "Could you please!" He jerked his thumb at the long line, which had come to a halt behind her. People were standing on tiptoe and peering up front, trying to see what the holdup was.

Irritated by the tall, pushy intruder, Kenya strode to the counter and slapped her travel documents down on it. The check-in clerk gave her a quick once-over, pausing briefly when she read the name off the ticket, and then squinted a little at her face, trying to put the name to the bewigged and behatted woman who now stood before her.

To Kenya's despair, the mountain tagged along, slapping his own documents on the counter beside hers with equal emphasis. "We're traveling together," he informed the clerk.

Kenya's jaw went slack. *The nerve of some people!* She protested vigorously to the clerk, who had accepted Mr. Saint Rose's papers, but who was still looking quizzically at her for confirmation of his claim. "I most certainly am not traveling with this man! I don't even know him!"

"I'm escorting the lady," he reiterated firmly to the clerk, who was now glancing bemusedly from Kenya's indignant face to his adamant one. To her further horror, the man leaned forward and, in a highly audible whisper, confided in the check-in clerk, "I'm her"—he paused for effect—"*protection. You understand. Studio business.*" He reached into his inside jacket pocket, pulled out a wallet, and flipped it open, showing the ticket agent something that Kenya couldn't see but had no doubt that it was some kind of fake identification. And then the creature actually gave the woman a wink!

The ticket agent looked thrilled at having had real-life show business intrigue dropped into her lap on what had promised to be a mundane shift. She grinned broadly, and even broader still when he put a finger to his lips and continued, "It's confidential. Could you oblige?"

To Kenya's dismay, the agent's scarlet-tipped fingers flew as she proceeded to accept his seating requests without so much as another glance at her for confirmation.

Kenya sputtered. "Protection? *I* need protection? Says who?"

"Says your manager, Mr. Carey, as I have just been explaining to you."

She was beginning to get a sinking feeling that maybe he really was what he said he was: a rent-a-thug of some sort. This did not make the situation any more palatable. "He wouldn't do such a thing," she declared. Then, she reminded herself that Ryan Carey had been in her employ only a few months, since she had gotten rid of the snake in the grass who had, up until quite recently, been managing her business. She trusted him as much as she could, considering the circumstances. But how well did she know him? Doubts assailed her, and she questioned her own confident declaration out loud. "Would he?"

"He could, and he did." Once again he slid his hand into the inside pocket of his jacket, which seemed large enough to hold any number of objects, withdrew a manila envelope, and handed it over to her without another word.

Kenya took it from him, ripped open the envelope and took out the contents. There were a handful of documents: a contract signed by her manager, a number of travel documents and itineraries, a receipt representing an advance for the man's fee—the figure on it made her brows shoot up—and a glossy stock photograph of herself. Even though it was the type of photo she routinely autographed and delivered by the hundreds to her publicist, the knowledge that this stranger had this last item in his possession made her uncomfortable.

"Believe me now?" He didn't try to retrieve the envelope and its contents but regarded her face intently for signs of a change of heart.

Kenya didn't know what to say. Quitely, she handed the papers back over to him, and into his pocket they went once again. By now, the check-in process was complete, much to the relief of the people standing impatiently behind them, and he scooped up the travel documents on the counter, both his and hers, and prepared to leave. Sheer fear of losing sight of her passport and tickets sent her scurrying after him.

As he walked, she noticed that he favored his right leg, as though he was recovering from an injury of some sort. It looked like it hurt. She briefly felt sorry for him, but then she squelched her compassion. He'd probably earned himself a muscle strain perpetrating whatever mayhem he was usually hired for. As a matter of fact, she was willing to bet that what he had been doing wasn't legal. His type neither knew nor cared much about niceties such as the law.

His careful, deliberate gait did nothing to slow him down, as the length of his legs—easily twice as long as hers—more than made up for the slight limp. He was walking quite quickly to the security checkpoint now, and she had to hurry to keep up with him. He didn't even have the courtesy to slow down for her benefit. Even so, she glanced down at the leg he favored and wondered if it was as painful as it looked.

He caught her glance. "Old war wound," he said dryly. "Don't worry, it only hurts when I'm really tired. I'm in top physical condition. You'll have all the protection you require."

Protection might not be such a bad idea, she thought wryly, considering the fact that she hadn't the foggiest idea what she was going to encounter once she landed in Trinidad. But a sense of pride prevented her from admitting that to him, or even to herself. Instead, she countered, "I'm not worried, and your physical condition . . ." She was going to say "couldn't be less interesting to me," but that would be a lie. In spite of his limp, this man's physical condition was *well* worth *any* woman's second glance. So, instead, she asked sweetly, "Got it on the job?"

He gave her a quizzical look, so she clarified herself. "Kicking someone around? Beating someone up over a bad gambling debt?"

He took the taunt without flinching. "That's not within the scope of the services I provide."

"Which part? The kicking around part, or the gambling debt part?"

"Neither."

"Ah, so you just ride around with actresses all day?"

He was still moving quickly, intent on reaching the security gate, but took the time to throw over his shoulder,

"No, you're my first. I usually have more important people as clients. People who do *real* work."

Ouch, she thought. *That stung.* It took someone who knew nothing of the business to assume that acting wasn't "real" work. She hated to be dismissed like that. In retaliation, she lashed out. "Well, at least I don't run around airports shanghaiing people for a living!"

Now he stopped. Suddenly, right in front of her. In her haste, she was unable to slow her forward momentum and slammed into his huge chest like a stock car hitting a wall along the deadman's curve on a racetrack. The wind whooshed from her lungs on impact, and she felt her bag slide from her shoulder and hit the floor with a thud.

Instantly, his arms came up to encircle her as she felt her knees buckle, and before she could join her carry-on bag in an ignominious heap at his feet, he caught her with as much effort as he would a pillow tossed at him from across a wide bed.

"Don't," she began and stopped. There it was again, that tingle breaking over her body like an electric wave. But this time the premonition of danger was overwhelmed by something more exquisite. She could smell him—not a single, definite odor, but a handful of separate scents all layered over each other. Jacket, shirt, hair, skin, each warm and distinct, but each derived from or dependent upon the other. The result was like a swig of brandy that looked innocent enough in the glass but that proved to be insidious, putting her off guard and leaving her brain buzzing.

He towered over her, looking down at her as she struggled to regain her balance and composure, and the previously inscrutable face reflected something that she would have sworn was surprise. The dark, piercing gaze deepened even further, and instead of releasing her, he let his eyes move slowly over her face, as though seeing her for the first time.

"Don't," she said again, though not as emphatically as before.

He let her go at once and stooped to collect her fallen bag, leaving her feeling abandoned. "Sorry," he mumbled. "I was just . . . I thought you were going to fall there."

Embarrassed by her clumsiness, and even more so by her sudden, unexpected reaction to his helpful embrace, she snatched her bag from his grip and clutched it against her chest like a shield. "I wouldn't have," she insisted, unwilling to admit, even in the face of all evidence, that she would most certainly have done exactly that, here, in front of all these people, had it not been for his intervention.

A smile almost allowed itself to play across his lips. "If you say so," he said, but it was obvious he didn't believe her for a second.

She had the grace to be ashamed of her churlishness. She'd almost sent herself sprawling, and he'd saved her from scraped knees and injured pride. The least she could do was thank him. "Sorry," she conceded. "Maybe I would have, after all."

"Maybe you would have." Again, the smile considered making a brief appearance but seemed to think the better of it, leaving Kenya slightly disappointed.

"Thank you," she allowed herself to say.

The enormous shoulders lifted slightly. "Just doing my job," he responded gravely.

The words brought her crashing back to reality. His job. To protect her. Because her brand-new ex-cop manager—who in the world, other than her, would land themselves an ex-cop for a manager—deemed it necessary. What a laugh. "That, it's not," she said irritably, her guard back up again.

"What's not what?"

"Protecting me," she explained patiently. "It's not your job. It's not anyone's job. I look after myself."

The near smile that had been hovering around his mouth ran for cover, leaving behind a thin, grim line. He patted the breast pocket of his jacket and reminded her, "I've got a whole sheaf of papers, including a signed contract for my services, that says otherwise."

"*I* didn't sign them," she pointed out.

"You didn't have to. Your manager has power of attorney to manage all your business affairs. And this, Miss Reese, is business."

"It's not," she retorted. "It's personal. I'm going to Trinidad for personal reasons. And they're none of your business, so don't even bother asking."

"I will, and you'll tell me." He looked about to say more, but then a thought occurred to him. He lifted his hand and peered at his heavy watch. "We have fifteen minutes until boarding, and you know how long it takes for security screening these days."

She looked down at her own watch, although she knew before doing so that it would corroborate his statement that time was running out on them. Her mind raced. This man wasn't giving up. Whether she liked it or not, he was getting on that plane. She could choose not to fly, but that would put an end to her mission before it had even truly begun. Or she could go with him, appear to go along—and ditch him at the earliest opportunity.

What to do? What to do?

Before an answer could come to her, he let a bombshell drop. "And I have my gun to check through."

"Your *what?*" Her face registered her shock.

"My gun." His tone was matter-of-fact, as though he were talking about a wallet or a cigarette lighter. "It's licensed, sealed in a steel case, and it's coming with us.

And it takes time to go through the security check, so we'd better—"

"Do you need it?" She wrinkled her nose in distrust, eyes sweeping up and down over him, half expecting him to draw some huge, cartoonish device from a hidden pocket and brandish it about. It was bad enough she was saddled with this enormous stranger. But one who was armed and didn't seem to think that was any big deal? She didn't like it one bit.

"Do you want to be *without* it?" he countered.

"I was going to, before you turned up," she retorted.

Damon glanced down at his watch once again. They were really cutting it close. "Let's put it this way," he told her. "The way I see it, you're stuck with me. And I come with a gun. It's in your best interest."

"Guns are never in anyone's—" Then, Kenya halted. She was going to a country she had only heard of, to meet a man she didn't know. A man whose correspondence was nothing short of threatening. As much as she disliked the very real spectre of violence that a gun presented, it just might be a wise idea. She hung her head.

"Good." He recognized her capitulation for what it was and seized the opportunity before she could change her mind and rebel anew. He motioned to her. "Hurry up. Let's go."

She didn't move a muscle. "I'm not sure I—" she began.

He cut across her. "We'll talk about it on the plane." He held his hand out to her. "Come."

No one could have been more surprised than she when she followed him.

Chapter 4

"You can take it off now, you know."

Kenya looked at the man seated beside her, his long legs just barely accommodated by the space assigned to them. She'd been trying her best to ignore him for at least an hour, since they were airborne, and he seemed happy to allow her to do so. As a matter of fact, she'd become convinced that he'd fallen asleep on her, as he'd closed his eyes as soon as he'd buckled himself into his seat. She had the sneaky feeling now that although he'd been resting, he was alert, watching her every move from beneath heavy lids.

She dragged her attention away from the guidebook on Trinidad that she had been intently reading. "What's that, Mr. Saint Rose?"

"First off, the name's Damon. Surely, you don't plan on calling me Mr. Saint Rose the entire trip?"

If she were honest, she didn't want to be calling him *anything* the entire trip. She didn't even want him *on* the trip. But she was too polite to say so. "All right," she said grudgingly, "Damon it is, I suppose." Good manners also forced her to reciprocate. "Then I guess you can call me Kenya."

"Good. That's a start, Kenya." He placed a slight emphasis on the last word, as though just having her concede permission for him to call her by her first name represented a minor victory for him. Indeed, having her knuckle under and allow him to accompany her onto the plane must have been victory enough, and he seemed quite pleased about that. With good reason: he didn't look like the kind of man who enjoyed losing.

The sound of her name on this man's lips brought her the same feeling of disquiet that had assailed her at the airport when she'd seen her photograph in his possession. It was so casual, and yet so . . . intimate. Briefly, she regretted allowing him to use her first name. That alone was a crack in the shield she'd vowed to erect between them to compensate for his having intruded upon her. It was a situation that she was determined to endure only as long as it would take for her to call Ryan the moment they landed in Trinidad and get him to call off the overgrown guard dog he'd sent to shadow her.

Saint Rose, or, rather, *Damon,* didn't know it yet, but he didn't have more than a day or two left to use either of her names, first or last. She supposed she could put up with him that long.

"So, are you going to?" he was asking.

She struggled to focus on what he was saying. "What?"

He was patient. "I was asking if you were going to take it off now. The disguise." He glanced pointedly at the mess of braids that was still perched atop her head.

Kenya felt her face flush. She'd all but forgotten the silly idea she'd had that her wig, floppy hat, and glasses would divert any unwelcome attention at the airport. It certainly hadn't fooled him. Self-consciously, she put her hand up to touch a stray braid. "Didn't work, did it?" she said, embarrassed.

"No, not exactly. Not with me, anyway. But then again, I was looking out for you. No one else at the airport," he encompassed the inside of the cabin with a vague sweep of his arm, "or in this plane, is expecting you, so you could easily be spotted without any problem."

"It's worked before," she said defensively.

"I'm sure it has. And I understand why you felt you had to do it. Believe me, I sympathize with you. You're entitled to your privacy." His voice was kind, so kind, in fact, that she had to watch his face carefully for signs that she was being patronized—she still hadn't forgotten that nasty crack that he'd made about her work not being "real" work—but found none.

He went on, "But you can take it off. You'll feel a lot more comfortable, and it's going to be a long flight. Don't worry, if anyone recognizes you and tries to give you a hard time, I've got you covered."

"I'm sure you do," she said testily. "That's what Ryan sicced you on me for, isn't it? My own personal pit bull."

He didn't even flinch. "Yup. If you need any kneecaps busted, just whistle."

Her eyes flew open. "You'd *do* that?"

He didn't miss a beat. "Not for what Ryan's paying me. Kneecaps are extra."

Kenya failed to hide her shock. "What?" she said, aghast. Her gaze flicked to the huge hands that were resting idly on thighs that were even larger, and her fertile imagination was immediately rife with images from every bad mob movie she'd ever seen—ones where tire irons were weapons of choice and dark back alleys teemed with men like him.

This time he honestly and truly did smile, and his whole face changed. The full lips pulled back to reveal large, white, straight teeth, and creases appeared around his weary eyes. It was a struggle not to feel herself warming to him. When he smiled, she almost forgot how big and scary he really was.

"I'm just kidding!" Mischief danced in his black eyes. "Kenya, Kenya . . ."

Oh, he was saying her name again!

"I don't break kneecaps. I don't beat people up, for a fee or otherwise, at least not unless my safety, or my client's, is immediately threatened. I'm not a thug, or a bouncer, or a debt collector, or anything else you seem to have bubbling up in that brain of yours. You've got me all wrong. I'm a man of peace."

Part of her wanted to believe that, if only to make her feel less threatened by his presence. "Strange profession," she countered, "for a man of peace."

"I like to think of it as keeping the peace."

Kenya's doubt was palpable, even though she chose not to say a word.

"You don't believe me. I can see it. I wish you . . ." He stopped, seemingly distracted by a thought, and then exhaled deeply though his nose. "You know what? I think the source of the problem between you and me is—"

There's no "you and me," she wanted to say, but before she could, he continued.

"—that we got off on the wrong foot. Back there, at the airport. I know I startled you. I thought you were expecting me, and you weren't. I know my presence can be a little overwhelming—"

She couldn't prevent herself from exclaiming, "You can say that again!"

His laugh was as deep and gusty as she would have expected from a man his size. "I know! I intimidate people just by *breathing!* But I'm nowhere near as scary as I look." He leaned a little closer to her, and when his face was just inches from hers, she realized that his eyes were not as black as she had first thought them, but that they held, in their depths, a hint of warm brandy. They drew her in, pinning her down like a moth in a collecting tray.

"So let's start over, Kenya. I need to introduce myself properly, not just come barrelling in on you like I did before. We haven't even shaken hands. We should, like civilized people." He held out his hand, and Kenya surprised herself by taking it without hesitation. She tried not to think of how warm it was, and how it engulfed her own as a baseball mitt would a doll's hand. It was several long seconds before he released her. She had to resist the urge to rub her tingling hand with the other.

"My name is Damon Saint Rose. I was born and raised in Brooklyn, and I have a degree in criminology. I'm a security consultant. I'm part owner of a company with my cousin, Leshawn. We have twelve people in our field staff and one beleaguered, overworked secretary. Most of the members in the field are overseas at some time or another. We advise American nationals in volatile foreign countries how to protect themselves and their businesses from terrorist attacks, kidnappings, insurgency, and a handful of other dangers specific to each country, most of which never really take place. In most cases, whenever the threat to my clients becomes too real, or imminent, the first course of action I usually advise them to take is to remove themselves and their families from the source of the problem. I believe that prevention and evacuation are the better part of valor."

He stopped in the middle of the longest speech he'd made since he'd met her to take a swig of his tonic and soda, and then he went on. "But while that may be the best course of action, sometimes things . . . happen."

"Bad things," Kenya said slowly.

He nodded. "Yes. Bad things. And when the circumstances demand it, we stay and fight."

"I'll bet," she murmured, and now it was his turn to

search her face for signs of meanness. She hastened to assure him that she meant nothing untoward in her statement by urging him to tell her about his clients. "So, what kinds of clients do you have?"

As he shrugged, the coarse green material of his shirt pulled taut against his chest and then relaxed. "It varies. Oil executives, mainly, and developers, architects, and so on. A few researchers and journalists. People whose jobs take them right into the eye of the hurricane, so to speak."

"People with *real* jobs." She couldn't resist reminding him, "unlike me."

His face flushed under his dark skin. "Sorry, Kenya. That just slipped out. I wouldn't have said it, but"—he rubbed his eyes with one hand—"I'm tired. I flew in yesterday from a long, difficult assignment in the Middle East, planning on getting at least a month or so off before another job came in, and then this cropped up. No turnaround time. It was all I could do to catch a few hours' sleep, do my laundry, and repack. I haven't spent more than one night in my own apartment since last summer. So forgive me if I was short with you. I honestly didn't mean what I said."

What people say often holds a grain of truth, thought Kenya, *even if they flatly deny it later.* "Out of the fullness of the heart, the mouth speaketh," she quoted.

He smiled ruefully. "Not this time."

"Not even just a little? Are you really telling me that you think my work is as valuable a contribution to society as that of your oil executives and your architects?"

"It's an honest living," he said with equanimity.

"Have you . . ." She wasn't sure how to ask this question without seeming to be fishing for compliments. Asking "Have you seen me?" sounded presumptuous and egotistical, so, instead, she phrased it as "Have you seen my work?" Bizarrely, she found herself wishing he had and, even more, hoping that he had liked what she'd done.

He looked rueful. "No, honestly, I haven't. I just haven't got the time to go to the movies much, and I hardly ever watch television, except for the news. But Leshawn's really good at research. Whenever we take a job, we try to collect as many write-ups on the client as possible. So he's provided me with some. . . ." He hesitated, looking as uncomfortable as a man would if he had suddenly opened a bathroom door and surprised a woman in a private moment. "I've read some articles about you. . . ." He looked like he was about to say something more but then drew his lips taut.

So he'd read stories about her. *Those stories.* Curse Tobias and his vicious slander. He'd known her so well, known that her reputation was the one thing she held most dear, and as a man acquainted with the way things worked in the industry, he knew just how to destroy it. She knew exactly what he had read by the way Damon now avoided her eyes, so different from the confident, almost taunting way he had held her gaze just moments earlier. Everything within her wanted to cry out, *Lies! Lies! It's not true! None of it!* But pride wouldn't let her.

Why should she justify herself to him? He didn't mean anything to her. His opinion of her didn't mean anything. So what if he believed them? So what if he, like her most gullible fans, had swallowed all that gory tabloid fiction like dime-store candy? She was an actress, and a good one, and if he wanted to believe the worst about her, well, too bad. It came with the territory.

She stiffened and withdrew, pressing her spine into the back of her seat, and began flipping through the book in her lap, trying to find her page. But her fingers slipped on the glossy surface.

He wasn't letting her off that easily. "I can promise you,

Kenya, that what you do for a living, and how you lead your personal life, have no bearing on how I treat you. You're a client, and like any other client, you are entitled to a hundred percent of my attention. You're no more or no less important than anyone else. Understand?"

"Gosh, thanks," she said dryly.

He was still anxious to minimize any offense that he had caused her. "Please, I'm sorry for that crack back at the airport. I apologize. Being tired is no excuse. I was rude, and I'm sorry. I should have known better." He paused, waiting for a sign that his apology was accepted.

She nodded, more out of a yearning to bring the whole tiresome subject to a close than anything else.

"Now," he said. "Take off that wig and those glasses. Relax. Be yourself. Nobody's watching: everyone's minding their own business, just enjoying the flight. No one's even looking our way. Go ahead. I promise you, you're safe with me."

With little more than a surreptitious glance around to confirm that even in such a public place, she might as well be alone, she slowly took off her dark glasses, let her hand creep up to remove the wig from her head, and then stuffed the items into the carry-on bag at her feet, next to the floppy hat she had discarded on boarding.

When she was done, she ran her fingers through her short, feathered hair, glad to feel coolness on her head again, lifted her eyes to his—and froze.

He was staring. His eyes, so tired and bleary a few seconds before, were riveted, focused on her face with the intent, appraising stare of an art collector eyeing a piece that he had seen before only in print. His gaze began at the top of her head, taking in her warm mink highlights and wispy locks, and travelled to her eyes, clear as honey, and unprotected by the two darkened lenses.

"What?" she asked defensively, embarrassed by the bold-ness of his stare and the frank admiration in it.

He didn't answer. Instead, his gaze moved downward, along her short, straight nose; dipped swiftly farther still to her pointed chin; and then lifted once again, coming to rest at her mouth, which she had gnawed free of lipstick. His glance was a touch, and she clasped her lower lip between her teeth, drawing it in like an anemone responding to an absentminded brush by a large fish. She squirmed under his unabashed examina-tion of her—she who ran the gauntlet of the red carpet, surrounded by a gawking public and merciless re-porters, without flinching! It was ridiculous. She was let-ting one man's rude stare reduce her to a basket of nerves? What was wrong with her?

"What?" she asked again. This time her defensiveness was laced with anxiety. It was like being locked in a star-ing contest with a big cat intent on hypnotizing its prey before it struck. Her hand came up in an awkward bid to shield her mouth.

He recovered himself, and the penetrating look was replaced by a carefully guarded one, like shutters clos-ing tight over an open window, blocking out the light. "Sorry." He reached for his drink and finished it in one gulp, replaced the empty glass carefully on the tray in front of him, and then stretched out as best he could given the space and the length of his legs. He folded his arms across his chest and willed his body to relax.

Kenya watched him—waiting for what, she did not know—but experiencing a vague sense of abandon-ment now that she had been released from the skewers on which he had held her. That sense of abandonment grew when he closed his eyes and let his head fall onto his chin.

"Take a nap, Kenya," he said softly, without looking

her way again. "We've still got a long way to go. You'll need the rest."

He said nothing more.

Obediently, Kenya reached up and dimmed the overhead lights, put away her book, and closed her eyes, but long after the imposing body of the man next to her went limp, her own body remained taut and restless.

Sleep never came to rescue her.

Chapter 5

"Where's the rest of it?" Damon asked Kenya.

"Rest of what?"

He hoisted her small suitcase with little effort before setting it down on the curb just outside of the main entrance to Trinidad's Piarco International Airport. He was lucky to have enough space to allow him to do even that. Although years of traveling throughout the world had taught him not to be surprised at anything, Damon was a little taken aback by how busy the airport was, even though it was tiny by most standards. Though it was well past midnight, it was teeming with people, both inside and out.

Passengers poured from the doors, some, winter-pale, gleefully stripping off their coats as they greeted the warm night air. Others were returning nationals coming home from working abroad in order to enjoy Carnival. These passengers lugged suitcases and dragged cardboard boxes bloated with presents for family members they had left behind: electronics, clothes, shoes, and American foodstuff. Some had arrived intent on taking part in the masquerade that was to come, bringing with them their own sequined and spangled costumes weighed down with colorful ostrich plumes and peacock feathers.

Behind them, in the arched atrium of the main hall, a small steel-band ensemble, its members dressed in wide-brimmed straw hats and brilliantly colored print shirts, beat out a calypso melody on large chrome-plated steel drums. Its pulsing, outrageously sensual beat cranked up the pervading sense of anticipation yet another notch. A handful of performers danced on frighteningly tall stilts, dressed in a variety of costumes—from gorilla suits made of jute and canvas to tuxedos, spats, top hats, and white painted faces. They all looked exhausted but struggled gamely in their efforts to welcome visitors to their island at the height of the tourist season.

Damon, curious animal that he was, would have thought nothing of hanging around for a while simply to enjoy the spectacle, but he had business to attend to. "Your bags," he said briskly. He pointed at the single suitcase he had helped her collect. "Don't you have others?" When he'd met her at the airport, she'd been holding just her carry-on bag, so he assumed that she had checked her larger suitcases at the curb. In his experience, women travelled with nearly every article of clothing they owned, just in case they needed it. Surely, this woman, whose life was predicated on style and appearance, would be no different. "Don't you have more stuff? More clothes, shoes, jewelry cases?"

She arched her eyebrows in surprise. "Why would I?"

"I don't know. Most women travel with loads of bags, I guess."

The arched eyebrows rose even higher. "I'm not most women."

That, you aren't, he thought to himself, but aloud, he said, "I'm sorry. I just thought . . . I hope I haven't offended you." What was it with him? It seemed like everything he'd said and done since he'd met her served to tick her off. That was not the ideal way to start a working relationship!

She grunted but did not answer, making him feel decidedly worse than he would have if she had said something. Her tired eyes drooped, and he felt a pang of sympathy. Even though he'd tried his best to doze away a few hours during the flight, some part of his subconscious had been vaguely aware of her next to him, squirming in her discomfort, trying to settle down but unable to sleep. He could sympathize with her. His own insomnia was a curse he had borne for years; he had almost grown used to operating on empty. But Kenya looked so worn and weary that his heart went out to her.

The best he could do for her now would be to get her to their hotel pronto. He slung the broad strap of his duffel over his shoulder and then picked up her suitcase with one hand, cupping her elbow with the other in an effort to guide her through the fray. In his palm, her elbow felt small, almost knobby. She was such a tiny little thing, and that made him feel protective. "Come, Kenya. Let's get you to bed." He began moving forward, urging her along with him.

She glanced upward sharply, and he was sure that she was about to protest, but then he felt the fight slip away from her, like a departing ghost. Her small body slumped slightly against his. He repeated himself, "Come, let's go. I'll have you at the hotel in no time."

She nodded, saying nothing until their rental car, which Leshawn had so thoughtfully arranged to have waiting for them, had been collected. Among the sea of Japanese vehicles all around them, of which the Trinidadians seemed particularly enamored, he had chosen a solid American model. Although Damon could pretty much drive anything on wheels, he was happy for the sense of reliability and familiarity that American cars gave him. When their bags were securely packed away in the trunk, he opened the passenger side and stood courteously, waiting for her to crawl in.

She balked. "*You're* driving?"

He gave her a bemused stare. "It's a rental. That's what it's for. Weren't you paying attention?"

She touched her brow lightly as though it hurt, as though her thoughts swam around in there, colliding with each other. "I know. I know. It's just that I thought—"

"Thought what?" It took all of his patience to keep his tone level.

"It's a strange country, and it's the middle of the night, and we don't know where we're going."

"*I* know where we're going," he reassured her. "I've got a map."

She peered at his hands, both of which were empty. "Where?"

He tapped his temple. "Here."

"You're kidding, right?"

"No. I've got a photographic memory—"

She cut him off with a rude sound. "Nobody really has any such thing!"

He didn't take offence. "People do, and I'm one of them. I studied it this morning, and it's a very straightforward route. We take the highway all the way into the city. The Bird of Paradise Hotel is on the northern side, at the foot of the hills. It's a forty-minute drive, tops. No problem."

She didn't look convinced. "I was planning on taking a taxi."

"We've got a car."

"We could hire a driver."

"*I'm* your driver."

"They drive on the left here," she persisted.

"I know. So does half the world." He fielded her protest as effortlessly as he would a weak forehand lob. "I've done it many times before. It's not that difficult. You just need to concentrate."

She glanced from him to the car and then back again. If he wasn't becoming weary himself, her indecision would have been comical. But he had to take control, or they would be there all night. He stepped closer, until he was looking down at her uptilted face, and took her hand. But before he could say whatever it was he was planning to say, there was that buzz again, the one he'd felt on the plane that had thrown him for a loop. He was swamped with all kinds of startling emotions. A sense of protectiveness, the kind a father felt for a child—or a man for a woman. Curiosity, an itch to know why she was so prickly and defensive. A sense of being too big and too clumsy in the face of her tininess. And, most of all, an overwhelming awareness of the softness of the hand that lay still and unresisting in his palm.

For a moment, the airport, the people and their ruckus, the steel band, the dancers, the security personnel, the taxis and cars all melted away, and he was standing there alone . . . with her.

Finding his tongue took effort. It was stuck to the roof of his dry mouth. What had he been about to say again? He knew what he wanted to *do:* run the back of his fingers along her lips and take that pout away. Lift his fingertips to the lids of those deep brown eyes and rid them of their doubt. Touch her chestnut hair, all mussed up from that awful wig and the discomfort of the plane, in part to straighten it out, in part to see if it was as soft as it looked.

All of this, and more, was what he wanted to do right at that very minute. But what the heck was it that he had meant to *say?* Moments passed before he remembered, saving him from the embarrassment of blustering. "Kenya, Kenya," he managed, "promise me you'll do one thing."

"What's that?" She spoke in a whisper, but he heard her over the hum of the crowd, the music, the cars, and the blood in his ears.

"Trust me."

"What?"

"Rely on me. Lean on me."

The doubting light never flickered in her eyes for a moment, and that made him sad. "Why?" she wanted to know.

"Because that's what I'm here for. That's what I'm paid to do." Without letting go of her hand, he yanked at the top of his shirt until his collarbone and shoulder were bare to her sight. A coarse, uneven scar was visible under the harsh overhead lights. "Arrowhead," he explained shortly. "Suriname, deep in the Interior, four years ago. A client I had, a land developer, made a blunder, got a whole lot of tribal people angry, and they picked up every weapon within reach and came after us. We had to run for our lives. I saw the arrow coming and couldn't get him out of the way fast enough, so I took it for him." He pulled his shirt closed again, mildly embarrassed by her horrified stare. "And d'you know why?"

Her mouth formed the word "no," even though no sound came from it.

"Because that's my job. I go down before my client does. Hard to do, sometimes, but it's one of the demands of my profession." His face softened a little, and he smiled. "So, if I can throw myself in front of a hunk of sharp flint traveling at near bullet speed, don't you think I'd make sure you made it safely to your hotel?"

Her gaze flew back to his shoulder, even though it was

once again covered by the material of his shirt, and she looked abashed. She was the one to break their tenuous contact by withdrawing her hand. He almost resisted but let her go without a struggle.

"Sorry," she told him. "I didn't mean to offend you. I just never had an . . . um . . . a bodyguard before. I don't know what to expect."

"Whatever you need," he answered softly. "Whatever you want." Before he could be overwhelmed by the urge to kick himself for that statement, he saw a flush rise in her face, and then he knew for sure that she had been thinking what he had been thinking.

That was good.

No, he corrected himself. That was risky. This wasn't some pretty young thing he'd accidentally met on a flight. This was his client, and if that wasn't bad enough, this was a client who happened to be Kenya Reese, and if those clippings he'd read last night were anything to go by, Kenya Reese was a man-eater. A woman who was dangerous to know—and even more dangerous to work for.

A mask of neutrality slid into place, giving him time to collect himself, and he gestured toward the passenger seat with all the cool politeness he could muster. "Now, please, we should get going."

Kenya shivered briefly, as though the air around them had suddenly cooled. The look of bewilderment that flickered across her features was chased away by an equally neutral expression, as though she'd perceived his effort to bring his emotions in check. She decided that it would be wise to do the same. She sat, and before Damon could close her car door, she pulled it sharply in after herself, leaving him standing outside, with his hand still outstretched toward the door handle. Silently, he took his own seat, started the engine, and pulled onto the roadway.

East onto the highway, he repeated the directions to himself silently. *Make a beeline for the city.* He hadn't been kidding about his memory. He did, in fact, remember every detail of the route to the hotel, although he wasn't stupid enough to travel in a foreign land without a map, which was safely tucked away inside his bag. He supposed he could have mentioned that fact to Kenya back at the airport, but the incredulity on her face had been just too funny not to enjoy.

The road was busy, but the traffic flowed smoothly, and soon the city lights sparkled ahead. But the route only occupied the tiniest portion of his thoughts. The rest of his mind was filled with the echoes of his own words to her. The ones where he promised to protect her. The ones where he entreated her to trust him.

Trust him.

Why should she?

Because she didn't know. She had no idea that she was his first female client in several years, and a client he'd taken against his better judgment, to boot. He'd sworn off women, promising that having failed once, he would never give himself a chance to fail again.

Trust me, he'd begged her. *You're safe with me.* He squeezed his eyes shut briefly, before opening them again and forcing himself to focus on the road ahead. *What a liar you are, Saint Rose,* he chided himself. *What a fraud.* How could he protect one woman when he'd failed to protect another?

A familiar sensation ran through him, an uncomfortable flush that began in the center of his aching heart and rolled outward in waves, like seasickness. It didn't happen often, but when it did, it was a warning signal for what would happen next. He stifled a groan. He knew from experience that there was no use fighting. In his fatigue, he was no match for the rampaging demons of the darkest corners of his mind. He glanced at his side again, with a sense of trepidation, knowing who he would see seated there, in Kenya's place. Jewel. Poor, sweet, wonderful Jewel. Once as precious to him as her name. God, he missed her.

She was silent, as she always was when his frenzied imagination brought her forth. Silent, but even more beautiful than she had been in life, embellished in his memory by the ache of her leaving. Her hair was a halo, spilling down around her shoulders like sunlight upon the horizon at the dying of the day. She turned her head to him, lifting eyes that were as clear as corn syrup. The smile on her lips made her whole face glow.

The hand on the steering wheel itched to reach out and touch the shimmering, pearl-bright ghost seated next to him, but he knew from painful experience that to move was to chase her away. So instead, he remained motionless, reaching out to her only with his mind. He didn't even dare to look directly at her, as that, too, would make her skittishly leap out of sight. Sometimes when his aching heart conjured her up, she was wearing his ring, and sometimes, again, it was missing from her finger. Every time, though, it was one of the first things that came to his mind: was she wearing it, or wasn't she? To someone who was not in the know, that question might have seemed petty, but to him, it made all the sense in the world.

It was the ring for which she had been killed.

Chapter 6

If he had wanted to be easy on himself, he would have admitted that his failure toward Jewel had not taken place during his tenure as her security detail. The eight months that he'd worked for her in Brazil—while she carefully documented and studied the fading languages of several of the tribes that struggled on the banks of the Amazon against the encroachment of modernity—she had been perfectly safe. He'd taken her into the jungle unharmed and brought her out without a scratch.

By then, he'd become so mired in his feelings for her that he'd followed her to her native San Francisco to pledge his love, and to his joy and surprise, it had been readily returned. Two months was all it had taken for him to know that she was everything he had ever wanted in a woman. After weeks of searching and consulting with Leshawn, he found the perfect engagement ring. This one bore no diamonds; Jewel found them cold and hard. Instead, it was adorned with opals, full of fire and light to rival her own, and river pearls, to forever remind her of the mysterious, living, enchanting river where they had met. It was a ring for all eternity.

And although he was no longer in her employ, he'd

watched over her, as protective as a duck with its lone duckling, even when she'd laughed at him and reminded him that she was a grown woman and could take care of herself, thank you. He ignored her assertions and kept her close to his heart. When she was away from him, he worried and ached until she was near again. It took a supreme effort not to become protective to the point of being overbearing, but in any case, Jewel had been too smart, too stubborn, and too independent to let him.

So he'd let his guard down.

A week before their wedding, on a day that would forever remain burned in his memory with the agony that only hindsight can inflict, they'd lain among mussed-up sheets, limbs entangled, drifting in and out of sleep as the sun rose. Then she'd slipped from him, easing herself out of the enclosure of his embrace, lifting his heavy arm from her breasts and sliding a pillow into the space where she'd lain, so that if he stirred from sleep, he wouldn't miss her presence. Lethargic from long hours of lovemaking, he had been only vaguely aware of her departure. No alarm bells had gone off in his head.

An hour later, even before he'd had time to fully wake and discover that she had failed to return, he had been jarred from sleep by a knock on the door. It was an apologetic police officer, with a look on his face that had struck cold fear into Damon's heart before the man opened his mouth to speak.

They'd found Jewel lying on the sidewalk just two blocks from his apartment, the life already drained from her body through the tiniest of knife wounds, just below her breast. A torn grocery bag lay at her feet, and around her, the spilled results of her shopping. Ripe nectarines, mushy from their fall; sweet rolls and cheese; thin strips of prosciutto wrapped in waxed paper; and heavy, crunchy flatbread, which he loved so much. His favorite brand of orange marmalade, made from Naples oranges, in a jar covered with red checked cotton and tied up with a ribbon. And butter.

Her purse had been missing, and with it, thirty dollars, if that much. The fourth finger on her left hand had been bare. . . .

The dark interior of the car was a cinema with a private showing just for him, and on the screen, the same clip played over and over again. Anguish and regret. Then, the ghost Jewel, the one who usually darted out of sight the moment he dared to stare too hard, did something she had never done before. She touched him.

Damon almost leaped out of his skin. The shock of the contact caused him to swerve, and he struggled to regain control of the car, managing eventually to bring it to a stop on the emergency shoulder in the dim, orange light of streetlamps overhead. His heart pounded in his chest as he turned to the woman at his side, the skin on his arm burning where she made contact. She'd touched him! He'd felt it!

Only Jewel was gone, like a moonbeam dashing for cover under harsh light, and in her place, Kenya sat, eyes wide, focused on him.

"Are you okay?"

He struggled to ground himself in reality once more, feeling both foolish and exposed. "What's that?"

"Are you okay?" she repeated, more anxiously than before. She hadn't removed her hand from his forearm, and against his bare skin, her palm was hot. "You're as cold as ice. Your skin. And you . . ." She paused.

What had he done? Had she been speaking to him and not received a response? Or had he let that precious name past his lips without knowing? "What did I do?" he asked warily. He was ashamed, uncomfortable. These fugues were all well and good when he was alone, but when he had company, that was something entirely different.

"You . . . sighed." She released his arm, leaving him adrift again. Cold again. "You sighed as if . . ." She brought her hand to her lips, as though gauging the temperature of his cold arm through their sensitive skin. "As if something was breaking."

Only my heart, he could have told her, *but that broke a long, long time ago.* He wondered what lie he could come up with that would deflect any further inquiry. His own private grief was not something he wanted to share, not with anyone.

She let him off the hook with a shrug. "I suppose you must be tired," she reasoned, supplying her own response to her unasked question, but her eyes still searched his face.

"That I am," he agreed.

She nodded understandingly. "Do you need some air? We could get out for a few minutes, if you like."

"I'm fine," he answered quickly. It wouldn't do to acknowledge that she had scared him out of his skin, or rather, that he had scared himself. If he were honest, he would admit that he could do with a few moments, but that would be weak, wouldn't it? *Focus,* he reminded himself. *You're on duty. Focus, focus, focus.*

Ignoring him, she unbuckled her seat belt and popped the lock on the door. "Come on; get out. Let's just stand here for a few minutes. Breathe deeply, and you'll feel better."

As soon as he realized that she really did intend to get out, he did a hasty visual assessment of their surroundings. Standing around at this hour of the morning in a strange city wasn't the brightest of ideas. You didn't have to be a professional to know that.

The gaping darkness of the water to his right and the

pungent odor of ship oil and salt let him know that they
had reached the outskirts of Port of Spain, near the
harbor where the highway ended. Ahead, a huge white
cruise ship loomed at the dock like an iceberg appearing
out of the mist. In spite of the time, there was a steady
stream of traffic along the main thoroughfare, and the
stone-paved promenade nearby was packed with people.
He supposed they were either going to or coming from
Carnival parties. Couples lingered under tall trees lit
brightly with strings of fairy lights. A jumble of music
splashed out from half a dozen bars lining the promenade on both sides, joined by metallic squawking from
radios perched on hotdog vendors' bikes and the open
wooden carts of coconut sellers. The city was alive and
humming with excitement.

It seemed safe enough, he conceded. He eased himself reluctantly out of the car and walked around the
front to join her. He automatically patted his jacket to
make sure that the weapon he had retrieved from the
airline upon landing was still there, even though he
could feel the hardness of it against his skin. Touching
it always made him feel better. Ruefully, he likened himself to an old woman who kept some sort of religious
charm close to her simply because it was reassuring.

Kenya spotted the gesture. "I see the airline gave you your
toy back," she remarked, but not as sharply as she could
have. "You don't need it here, you know." She waved
around. "See? These are happy people. It's Carnival.
Everybody just wants to have a good time. Nobody's even
paying us any mind. Why don't you just leave it in the car?"

She was leaning against her car door, so he came to
stand next to her, his back pressed against the hard
metal of the vehicle, and folded his arms across his chest.
He wasn't in the mood for arguing, but her remark
begged to be set straight. "First off, a gun is not a toy. It's

a weapon. Don't ever forget that. Second, the thing about guns is, you never can tell just by looking around when you're going to need one, but when you do, you need it fast. You leave it in the car, it might as well be on the moon. And third, it's late, and we're both tired. Let's not fight anymore. Okay?"

To his surprise, she smiled, tilting her head back to look at him. "Sorry. You're right. I didn't make you get out just so I could jump on your case. I made you get out so you could take a breather." Her gaze took on an element of concern. "For a moment there, you looked really out of it. As though something . . . scared you."

The implied question hung in the air between them, thick and heavy. He remembered again the warmth of her hand on his arm and the alarm on her face after she had startled him. But even that was not enough to make him admit that he'd let his imagination run away with him, and that she had been part of the reason. He shook his head. "Nothing. Nothing scared me."

She was persistent. "Startled, then."

He unfolded his arms and shoved his hands in his pockets, looking down at his feet and nudging small pebbles along the bitumen paving with his toe. *No can do,* he wanted to tell her. He was keeping Jewel all to himself.

When it became clear that he wasn't talking, she made a gesture of surrender. "Keep your secrets, then." She sounded compassionate rather than petulant. "I won't force you." Then she, too, fell silent, turning her head from side to side, taking in the sights unfolding around them. She was right. Everyone was happy. Their excitement and anticipation rose up off them and commingled with the scent of the harbor nearby to fill the night air with an invigorating power. Damon watched, intrigued, as Kenya tilted her head back, closed her eyes, and inhaled deeply, sticking out the tip of her tongue to enhance the scent of the air with its intoxicating taste. The gesture drew his full attention to her lipstick-free, curved mouth, and again he had the dizzying sensation that he had felt at the airport: that in spite of the crowd, they were the only two people standing there.

At this point, wisdom would have dictated that he shift away from her, putting at least a foot or two of space between them just to help him clear his head. But he was in no mood to be wise, not with the warm skin of her shoulder brushing his elbow. He watched her face as it worked, reading the contentment there, and shared her enjoyment.

She let her arms rise in an embrace, as though she wanted to gather the entire city to her breast. Damon knew that her invitation was to the life bustling around them, and not to him, but it took an effort not to be drawn to her. In her enchantment, she was beautiful.

She opened her eyes, and delight danced within them. "I never thought I'd get here," she murmured, more to herself than to him. "I've waited all my life to see this for myself."

"The Caribbean?"

She shook her head. "Not just the Caribbean. Trinidad. Port of Spain. I've always wanted to stand at the gates to the city and drink it all in. Feel as though I'm a part of it."

"Why?" It surprised him how much he wanted to know. What was it about a small island, and its tiny capital city, that could make such a light come on inside this woman?

She let her arms fall to her sides, but her breathing was still deep, as though she wanted to suck in as much of the city's scent as she could in order to save it for later. "Because it's a part of me. My father . . ." She stopped, and then folded her arms jerkily around her bosom, mimicking his own self-protective gesture of a few moments ago. A frown dimmed the light within her.

Damon leaped in, anxious for it not to be completely extinguished. He'd been enjoying its glow far too much to watch it peter out. "Yes?"

"Nothing." The lips that had been sipping the air drew tight, like stable doors slamming shut against horses that clamored for escape.

He wasn't letting himself be cheated like this. He eased his weight off the car and came to stand before her, noticing once again the great disparity in their sizes. The top of her head barely reached his breastbone. She had to lean way back just to look him in the eye, and when she did, her look was defensive. He knew that if he pushed too hard, she would retreat, but his hunger for information got the better of him. "What about your father?"

A battle of indecision was going on inside her—caution versus trust—and then caution lost. "He was from here. Born here, raised here. In a very poor neighborhood in the hills, just outside the city." She lifted her arm and pointed. In the distance, twinkling lights denoted the shape of an otherwise dark mountain, which stood above the city like a tidal wave frozen in time seconds before it was about to come crashing down. "He always talked about what a struggle it was, growing up poor. He talked about rows and rows of little houses, like boxes packed one upon the next, along steep, narrow, twisting streets. He talked about living cramped inside one of them, elbow to elbow with the neighbors. How education was free, and in spite of everything, he did the best that he could. But after that, jobs didn't come easy, especially not for people who had his address. He struggled for a long time and could have settled, but he wanted more. He knew he could *be* more. He left for the States when he was a grown man. Looking for a better life."

"Did he find it?" he asked gently.

She nodded. "Yes. He was smart. He worked hard. Got into college when he was thirty-five. He met my mother there and married her. And, well, then there was me."

"And he never came back here?"

"No, never. He talked about it all the time but never came back. When I was a child, he was full of stories and promises. He used to tell me about his boyhood, about sneaking into Queen's Park Savannah—a huge park in the city—to watch horse racing. He used to talk about how dry the hills got at Easter time, and how the brush fires used to race down the mountains, and in spite of that, the forest trees still bore beautiful flowers. Flame-red and pink. Yellow. He used to promise me that one day he'd bring me back to see Carnival, make me a costume with lots of spangles and plumes, and buy me a coconut from a roadside vendor and let me drink the water from the shell."

She sounded bereft, as though she were grieving, as though that visit was never to be, so he asked delicately, "Is your father . . . still alive?"

"Yes. Yes, he is, but . . ."

He waited patiently on what would come after that painful "but." It was as heavy as a groan.

She didn't let him down. "But he's very sick. Multiple sclerosis. My mother looks after him. He'll probably never travel again. He doesn't have much longer, and what time he does have is filled with agony."

"And so you came to take your own stories back to him?" It sounded reasonable to him, even though he knew that she had walked away from the biggest opportunity of her career, if only for a little while. If her father was dying, and longed even for a secondhand adventure in his motherland, this visit would indeed be more important. He would have done it for his own father without a moment's hesitation.

She shook her head vigorously. "No. Not that."

She didn't clarify, so he tried again. "Did you come to notify his family?"

She flinched, and he knew that he had touched a nerve. Family, that was it. He could have driven that advantage home by peppering her with more questions but refrained for fear of scaring her into silence. It was like waiting in a photographer's hiding place for a shy deer to appear within range of the camera.

"Not really," she conceded finally. "My father never, never talked about his family. I know his mother's name but little else. He was very secretive."

I can see he passed that on, Damon thought, but said nothing.

Her front teeth worried her lip, and then she confessed. "But I *am* here about a family matter. Sort of."

For the first time he touched her, letting his hand fall lightly upon her shoulder, hoping that it would be reassuring rather than intimidating. "Tell me. I'm here to help."

"It's awkward," she protested weakly, even though there was little fight left in her. "Embarrassing."

"Whatever it is, I'll understand."

"It's private."

"I'm as discreet as the grave."

"It's none of your business."

"I was paid to make it my business."

There was no argument against that. She caved in. "You have to promise me, Damon, that this will never get out. I'm here to *make sure* it never gets out. Never goes public. There are newspaper reporters out there who don't seem to care that what makes for a few column inches of gossip for them could hurt a lot of people. Like my father. And my mother, if she ever finds out."

He kept his hand right where it was and increased the pressure lightly. "I'll be secrecy itself. You have my word."

She was too tired to resist. "Very well. I'll tell you." She glanced over her shoulder into the dim interior of the car, at her handbag, which sat on the front seat. "I got these letters. They're in the bag."

He didn't want to risk her being distracted by a bid to recover her bag, so he said, "You can show them to me when we get to the hotel."

"They're from someone here. This man. His name's Eric. Eric Reese, he says." She glanced around them nervously, as though expecting the person to step out of the shadows at the mention of his name.

"Family?"

"Sort of. I don't know. He claims . . . he says he's my half brother. He says my father was married to this woman before he left for the States. He sent me a copy of a marriage certificate. I don't know anything about these things, but there's a seal on it, and stamps. . . . It looks official. He sent me copies of his birth certificate, too. My father's name is on it."

"So your father was married before, here, to a Trinidadian woman. And they had a son."

"Looks like it."

"Does your mother know?"

"No!" Anguish made her eyes fever bright. "And she can't. That's why I'm here. I have to find out if it's true and stop him from telling her. It would kill my mother. It would break her heart."

"Why?"

The light glistening in her eyes turned to liquid and spilled down her cheeks. "Because this man, this Eric Reese, says my father and his mother were never divorced."

Chapter 7

Kenya had no idea whether she had tilted forward into his arms, or whether he had reached out and pulled her into them. All she knew was that he was warm, hard, and comforting. He said nothing and did not try to press her against him or let his hands stray over her body. He just remained still, providing her with something firm against which to lean now that her tired legs could barely keep her up. He was so big that he had to stoop to hold her, making her feel like a ten-year-old being comforted by a big brother after falling off a swing.

And, God help her, she blubbered. The hot rivulets coursing down her cheeks irritated her to no end. This was ridiculous! She never cried, not when she was alone and certainly not in front of strangers, in full view of the public, and she would have told him so, had it not been for the fact that by her actions she was negating that very assertion right now. The taste of humiliation coated the back of her throat. She hated having to expose her father's personal business, her family's business, to this man, but he was right. She needed help, and he was the only person around able to provide it. She had willed herself to clam up against him, shut him out until it was time to send him packing, but there was something about him that invited confidence. Maybe it was the patient way in which he had waited her out, giving her ample time to decide of her own accord to tell him her story. Maybe it was the gentle concern with which he was now patting at her tears with a clean cotton handkerchief fished out of God-knew-where.

She could have resisted, pulled away, but something in her welcomed his touch. She'd been trying to fight this battle alone, and that had sucked all the energy from her bones. Now she wasn't alone anymore. She had help. Her gratitude for such a small mercy made those bitter tears sting all the more. She put her hands up over her face to cover her shame.

"It's all right," he comforted her softly, trying to nudge aside her hands so that he could get at the fresh flood with his handkerchief. "Relax. Just let me—"

"It's *not* all right," she responded irritably, squirming to get away, but his bulk did not provide much room for escape. "I hate crying. And I hate crying in front of people even more."

"No crime in it." He must have known she wanted to get away from him, but he made no move to step aside. He didn't abandon his mop-up operation, either.

"Stop it, Damon!" she protested. "I'm all messy and snotty and red in the face. You shouldn't have to be cleaning me up."

"I don't mind," he answered with equanimity, but a glare from her made him immediately hand over the square of cloth so she could do it herself. Even then, though, he did not release her. He waited until she had dried her face and composed herself before saying, "Talk to me. Tell me about it."

"It hurts," she whispered.

"I know. I can only imagine just how much it hurts, but

I can't help you if you don't talk to me. Did you ask your father about it? What did he say?"

She shook her head vigorously. "No, I haven't. He's too sick. I don't want to cause him any more pain. And besides, what if I ask him? 'Daddy, is it true you left behind a wife and child in the islands? Is it true you've lied to my mother these past thirty years? Is it true that you're a bigamist, and I'm a—'"

His fingertips across her lips cut off the next word before she could even say it. "Don't. Don't even think it. Even if it's true, it doesn't change who you are, or who your father is. Or what he and your mother have meant to each other all these years. If it's true, then maybe he's made a huge mistake. That's not the kind of thing people do with the intent of hurting anyone. Maybe there were circumstances beyond his control. Whatever the reason, we'll get to the bottom of it. I promise you."

"But this man, Eric . . ." A man who might or might not be a brother she never knew she had. Who was now threatening her privacy, her piece of mind, and that of her parents.

"Yes?"

"He's blackmailing me!"

Some of the soft, gentle lines into which Damon's face had fallen grew hard again, and his dark eyes took on a dangerous glint. "Blackmail's a very serious word."

"He *sounds* serious! He said if I didn't come over here and meet him, he'd send all those documents to my mother. And the studio. And the press."

"What does he want?"

Even in the warmth of his comforting arms on this mild Caribbean night, a chill tripped down her spine. That was the problem. She had no idea what he wanted. In all those missives, which had grown more and more demanding, he had never stated, not in so many words, exactly what the price of his silence would be. "I don't know." She could feel the tears threatening to reappear, and she was determined to halt them by any means necessary. She squeezed her eyes shut. It didn't help the tears much, but at least she didn't have to look at the sympathy in his concerned stare. "He never told me. He just said he wanted me to fly down here. Right now. He said he'd tell me once I got here. He gave me a week. I tried to tell him I'd started a new job. I begged for time, more to clear my head than for anything else. But he wouldn't budge. He told me to fly here, or else. So . . ." Her voice quieted to a cracked whisper. "So here I am."

This time he did pull her closer, pulling her head against his shoulder. She could feel the point of his chin against the crown of her head and the fingers of his right hand lightly ruffle her hair. "Well, here I am, too, so you don't have to worry. We'll sort this out. I won't leave here until you do. You have my word."

Fighting him off was the last thing she wanted to do right now. That heady scent had a new high note: the smell of him. The sound of calypso and steel bands wafting over to them from across the promenade was joined by the sound of his breathing. The shivering stopped, and a warmth took its place. She let her senses drink him in.

It was not until her tears called off their assault that he let her go, setting her gently back so that she could support herself on her own two feet once more, and pulled away. He looked at his watch—a now familiar gesture—and his brows shot up. "We'd better get going. It's way past both our bedtimes. At this rate, that hotel should be ashamed to bill us for a whole night."

He reached out and opened the front door of the car, standing aside to make sure she was seated comfortably. "To-morrow we'll talk more. You'll show me those letters and tell me everything. We'll come up with a plan of attack. Then we'll meet this *Eric*." The way he said the name almost made her feel sorry for the guy, but another part of her felt like a maiden whose champion was going into battle with her scarf wrapped around his lance. The sense that everything was going to be okay was sublime.

"Thank you," she managed.

"My pleasure," he answered softly and shut the door carefully behind her. He walked around the car and got in next to her, frowning into space as he pulled up his mental map. With just a few seconds' hesitation, he put on his turn signal and drew onto the road again. "Ten minutes," he promised her. "No more."

She nodded and stretched. Even her bones were tired. "Good." Then she pressed her face against the window again, absorbed by the sights beyond the protective shell of their vehicle. She clutched the damp handkerchief in the palm of her hand like a talisman.

The Bird of Paradise Hotel was one of those delightful old-fashioned buildings that just invited one to relax. It was actually a refurbished Victorian-era mansion, and its new owners had maintained the look and feel of an old plantation great house. A happy shade of lemon was trimmed with white along the wooden jalousies and the elaborate carved trim that adorned the doorways and entrances. Brightly patterned cushions were piled upon the wicker furniture, which was strewn everywhere. Matching curtains were tied up out of the way with strips of cotton. Small fountains chattered to each other from across the lawn, cooling a garden already shaded by meticulously kept topiaries.

The hotel snuggled against the hills of St. Ann's, high up enough to offer a dazzling view of the huge Queen's Park Savannah, and beyond that, the harbor and the glittering blue of the Gulf of Paria. Wraparound terraces allowed guests to take full advantage of the view while they enjoyed their meals. Even though the sun was already high in the sky by the time Kenya sat down to breakfast, the dazzling light was uplifting rather than uncomfortable.

The hotel was bursting at the seams with Carnival tourists, but it was late in the morning, and most of the guests had already finished their West Indian breakfasts and wandered off on their chosen adventures. A few, who had probably been out as late as she, had lingered. Cutlery rattled against china, providing an almost musical accompaniment to the laughter and muted conversations. By the voices, she could tell that many of them were Americans, and she could safely assume that the occasional quizzical looks directed at her belonged to her own countrymen. Kenya could feel their eyes focused on the back of her head. It was a gift, or a curse, depending on how she looked at it, to be able to tell, *to know,* when she was being stared at.

She could almost hear them whisper: *There behind you, sitting at that table. It's that girl. The actress. You know the one. That lawsuit, remember . . . ?*

The warmth on the back of her neck spread around to her face and travelled unrelentingly down her throat to her breasts. "No place to run," she murmured to herself. Even in this tiny corner of the world, a speck on a map, her ruined reputation had followed, clinging to her as her shadow did to her heels.

Not that she was running. At least, that was what she kept telling herself. She was stronger than that. But it hurt to have so many ugly stories swirling around one's head. Even though they were lies, it hurt to have people believe them.

If she were to look at her predicament with the dispassionate eye of a casual observer, she would acknowledge that Tobias had done a pretty good job of wrecking her good name. His retaliation for their breakup was simple but effective, consisting of leaked stories to the papers that suggested she fed on her male employees as a spider would feed on fat, fresh moths that wandered into its web. That she was a woman who disliked being scorned.

Then, he sued her for sexual harassment. The gossip rags had had a field day. It was an old story, the kind that played out over and over again, every day, in America and the world over: someone made a pass, exerted sexual pressure, made demands, and when those demands were rebuffed, someone lost their job. This time, though, the story had a twist. It was the man who had done the accusing, and the woman who stood accused.

Things had developed thereafter with the lightning speed that only occurred in the entertainment business. A young man, a gardener who once tended the lawn of her parents' house part time, had stepped forward, claiming that he, too, had lost his job after refusing her advances. Then, within days, another young man spoke up. Kenya could only wonder how much Tobias had paid them to fabricate their stories, or what other leverage he had used to convince them that perjury, and the damage it could do her, were worth their while.

She found comfort in reminding herself that eventually justice would be done, and this whole lawsuit, and the sand dunes of lies on which it was built, would collapse, and her good name would be restored. It had to. For things to turn out otherwise would be unthinkable.

Until then . . .

The prickle at the back of her neck died away as her fellow diners shifted to something else, tossing her off their conversational hook like a fish that was too small to reel in. But before Kenya could enjoy the luxury of relief, a shadow fell over her table, and in the glare of the early morning sun, that shadow had the shape of a man. She knew who it was without having to look up.

Damon.

"Good morning," he rumbled.

Kenya looked up at him, simultaneously feeling dwarfed by his immenseness looming over her and startled by the stealth with which someone as large as he could move. Memories of her embarrassment at the way she had fallen apart last night flooded back. Weeping on his shoulder like a schoolgirl! What was she thinking? She hastened to apologize.

"Mr. Saint Rose," she began, before he could even pull up a chair.

"Damon," he interrupted. "We agreed on that last night, remember?"

She rubbed a tired forehand across her eyes. "Yes, yes, I know. We agreed on a lot last night, but I was tired. . . ."

"So was I," he responded affably. "But I hardly think that agreeing to use my first name needs to be a source of morning-after regret."

Morning-after regret. Now there was a phrase that certainly applied to how she felt about last night, albeit not in its more . . . intimate context. The sparkle of mischief in his eyes told her the rat was teasing her. It was almost as if . . .

A rush of blood filled her face and neck. It was almost as if he was not just referring to her humiliating loss of control on the side of the road, but to that earlier incident, back at the airport. To that brief moment—no more than half a minute, although God knew it had felt longer—when he'd pleaded for her trust. When he'd pulled open the neck of his shirt and showed her that ugly scar, which had held her attention for mere moments before it was snatched away by an awareness of the dark, hard expanse of shoulder upon which it lay. For some stupid, unknown reason, that glimpse of male flesh had elicited a response within her that she had been unable to hide, even with her acting skills. She was quite sure that if she had not been securely clutching at the strap of her handbag, her hand would have reached forward of its own volition and touched that rough, jagged flesh, as though she needed to convince herself that what she was seeing was real.

But that was ridiculous. She hardly knew this man. Now that she had let him in on her secret, and now that he had promised to help, she was able to squelch her determination to call up Ryan, have their little arrangement cancelled, and send Damon back home. She was smart enough to know that she needed him as an ally, albeit a paid one, to complete her quest—but that was all. She didn't need him to be leading her mind down tracks along which it had no business going. Men, even very good-looking ones, now held all the attraction for her of a train wreck. Tobias had seen to that.

Damon shifted slightly, moving the bulk of his weight from one foot to the other, and it was only then that it occurred to her that he was still standing there, waiting for something. Waiting for her to invite him to have a seat. She flushed again. She had her faults, but rudeness was not one of them. She gestured at the chair opposite her own. "Please, sit. I'm sorry."

He sat, sighing with gratitude as he took the weight off his feet. With a pang, she remembered the slight limp which he had walked with the night before and felt sorry for him. He must have been bushed if he'd slept the whole night, or what was left of it by the time they had checked in, and still awoken in pain. "How are you?"

He shrugged the question off. "I've been better, and I've been worse." His eyes were fixed upon her face. "More to the point, how are *you*?"

She cleared her throat. "I'm fine. And I want to tell

you how sorry I am for falling apart on you last night. I feel so stupid."

"Don't. I told you last night, it's okay. You've done nothing to feel bad about." He reached across the table, and his hand came down upon hers. Against the stark white linen of the tablecloth, their skin tones looked like contrasting pieces of wood, burnished mahogany and a lighter teak, worked into a single piece. She could have pulled her hand away but made no effort to do so.

"I sent your handkerchief to the laundry," she said almost irrelevantly.

He laughed out loud. "Thanks. But you didn't have to. I did bring a couple of others, you know."

What was it about him that made her say the most idiotic things? She was almost tongue-tied. Of course, he would have more: men who packed handkerchiefs on trips didn't take just one. She was ashamed to admit that she was, in fact, a little surprised to find that he carried such accessories. She wasn't too sure what kind of impression she had of men who dodged arrowheads for a living, but fine squares of hand-stitched linen handkerchiefs certainly wasn't part of it. It made her wonder if there was more depth to him than she had been willing to see last night. Maybe he wasn't the blackguard and vagabond that she had branded him.

"I'm having it washed for you, anyway," she said firmly. "It's the least I could do. Besides, I won't be needing it again."

There was not a hint of sarcasm when he said, "That's good. I promise I'll do my best to ensure that you don't shed another tear while you're here. I'll do everything in my power to make certain of that."

She tried to answer lightly but failed. "That's quite an undertaking."

He didn't bat an eyelid. "I'm up for the task."

Enough about her crying jag, she thought. She pulled her hand away from under the light pressure of his. He didn't fight her for it. She changed the conversation. "Hungry?"

"Very."

"Would you like something—"

"I ordered on my way in. It should be over here any minute."

Silence fell once again, a slightly uncomfortable one for Kenya, as she could feel him watching her gravely with attentive black eyes. She tried to fill the gap that yawned between them. "Did you sleep well?"

"Not very."

"Why not?" she asked and then immediately wished she hadn't, because the subject of him sleeping made her wonder whether he had found the night as warm as she had, in spite of the rattan fan that had whirred above her bed in her old-fashioned room. During the night, she had been forced to strip down to just her panties in order to enjoy the maximum benefit that the wind stirred up by the spinning fan blades brought her. This, in turn, led her to wonder if he had done the same, and that impertinent question once again brought unbidden to her mind the vision of those few square inches of exposed skin that had set her own skin zinging last night.

This time he almost smiled. "Bed was too small," he said. "It's a common problem for me. If I scrunch down to the bottom to make room for my head, my feet hang off the edge. If I wriggle higher up to the top, I butt my head against the headboard. I gave up pretty quickly and bunked down on the floor."

"That must have been uncomfortable."

"Not really. This was luxury. I'm usually just grateful for a roof over my head and a dry floor. Once you've

bedded down on a wet jungle floor or in a desert sand-
storm, you can pretty much do it anywhere."

"A regular Indiana Jones, huh?"

"If you like." He shrugged. "I never sleep well, anyway,
even in my own bed. It's an old problem I have."

Not just an adventurer, but an insomniac adventurer.
That was enough to give her curiosity a nudge. "Why?"

A veil descended across his eyes, and for a brief moment
he had that same haunted look that he had had last night,
when he'd swerved to the side of the road. Then it was gone.
He shook his head. "Nothing. A cross I have to bear." He
didn't invite further questions. She didn't ask any.

He looked around taking in his surroundings while
searching for something else to talk about. "Hot," he finally
said.

"Yeah," she agreed. "You hear about what it's like in
the Caribbean, but until you get to experience it. . . ."
She trailed off.

"Last night, too."

She could have sworn that the seemingly innocent comment held a note of mischief. *He can read my thoughts. He knows
that I was thinking about him, wondering how he dealt with the
heat last night in bed. Wondering if he stripped down to his . . .* She
made an inarticulate sound and covered up her discomfort
by taking a large swallow from her now-cold coffee. Fortunately for her, the need for a response was preempted by
the timely arrival of Damon's breakfast, which brought
with it its own distraction.

What a breakfast it was! Kenya watched in awe as the
chubby, pleasant-faced young waitress, whose white, ruffled blouse stood out against the splash of color in her
Madras plaid apron and simply wrapped headdress, un-
loaded dish after dish onto the table before him. First
came a basket of assorted breads: whole wheat and white,
small breakfast loaves studded with grain, round fried

pastries with steam rising off their surface, and evenly shaped cookie-cutter biscuits. Then, a plate of scrambled eggs, sliced ham arrayed with glazed pineapple, and thin slices of cheddar rolled into cigar shapes and spiked together with toothpicks topped with olives.

"Nothing like a little cholesterol to kick-start a body on a fine day like this," he joked.

Before Kenya could think of what to answer, another dish appeared, filled with several small fish fried crisp with their heads on, surrounded by chunks of tomatoes and rings of onions.

"Flying fish," he explained, and held the dish out to her. "Freshly caught, I'm told. Have some."

She looked down at her own plate of toast and jam, feeling almost embarrassed at her own tiny appetite. "I . . . don't think so," she stammered.

"They really do fly, you know." He poked at the elongated fins with the tip of a fork. "Look, wings."

"I think I'd be content enough to just sit here and see where you put all that," she joked.

He didn't force the issue but instead set the plate down and tucked in his napkin. It was a full five minutes before he said anything more. When he did, he went smoothly back to their conversation as though it had never been interrupted. "Don't worry about me and the bed, though. I've already spoken to management. They're having an oversized one put in my room before tonight. Usually Leshawn makes sure I get one from the get-go, but maybe this time he forgot. . . ." He halted in his verbal tracks and then put his cutlery down. "I'm sorry. I'm prattling on about beds and nonsense, and I know you're anxious to attend to your business."

She was, actually, but it would have been selfish to interrupt his breakfast over that. She waved it away. "No, eat first. We can talk about it afterward."

"We can do both." He withdrew the envelope she had given him the night before and set it down on the table between them. "I've taken a good, hard look at those documents you gave me."

"And?" she asked eagerly. She hoped that with his greater experience in these matters, he would have a better sense of their legitimacy than she did.

He shook his head regretfully. "And there's little I can do with them. They're all faxes and photocopies. Pretty poor ones, at that." He pointed to a blotchy signature on the marriage certificate. "Can you tell if that's your father's signature or not?"

She'd pored over those same two words so many times, wondering that very thing. Yet still, she took the paper from him and peered at it again, hoping for some new insight. Isaac Reese. A collection of hard, straight lines scratched out more than thirty years ago, apparently joining her father to some unknown woman named Camilla for all of eternity. "Hard to tell. Looks like it could be, but even so, it's an old signature. People's handwriting changes over time."

"That's a problem, too. The only way to confirm if these are genuine is to see the originals."

Crestfallen, she looked down at her lap. That was as far as she had gotten herself. She had half expected him to turn out to be some kind of Dick Tracy supersleuth. But so far, he wasn't proving very helpful.

He saw the look of disappointment and hastened to add, "But it's not a problem. We can check them out. I did a little asking around. Originals of all of these documents will be easy to trace with the relevant authorities, but not until Ash Wednesday, as the government offices are closed for Carnival."

He was right. It was Carnival Saturday, and the fever that would soon claim the entire country was only just beginning. Carnival Sunday activities were still to come, and then the festival would be unleashed in full force in the early hours of Monday morning and not cease until midnight on Tuesday, after the frenzy of Mardi Gras peaked. Until then, practically everything not related to the festival was put on hold, and that included government business.

She twisted her lips wryly. "Eric Reese knows how to pick his moments."

"He probably has a good reason."

"Like what?"

"I've got a couple of guesses." He retrieved the document from her and toyed with it idly. "Obfuscation, for one. He knew when he told you to come here this week that the country would be effectively shut down and that checking on his story would be difficult. Maybe he hopes to be able to convince you of whatever he wants, and get out of you whatever it is he's after, before you have the opportunity to prove him right or wrong. What better time than this? Chaos makes for great cover."

"Nice." If that were the case, this man who purported to be her brother was a fine piece of work.

"Then again, he may have another reason entirely. Impossible to guess, at this stage." Damon took a few moments to attack his meal once more, leaving Kenya wondering what would happen next. Eric had insisted that she fly in right away, and she'd done so. What next?

It wasn't until he was done eating that Damon spoke again. "In any case, it won't remain a mystery much longer. All we have to do is ask him."

"Ask him? How? When?"

He looked both satisfied and determined. "We're going to see him today."

Chapter 8

The mix of emotions that crossed Kenya's face—foreboding, anxiety, and doubt—made Damon even more hostile toward this Eric fellow, sight unseen. It was hard to gauge what type of person he was from the repeated demands for her attention and the vague threats that his letters contained. But if they were enough to cause Kenya such pain, well, that made him dangerously close to becoming an enemy.

Damon wanted to reach out and touch the back of her hand once more, anything to reduce the anxiety that his words had caused, but he was afraid to touch her again so soon. He didn't like what it did to him. It made him feel more protective than he should, as though he shouldn't just be accompanying her as she fought her battles, but that he should, in fact, be fighting them for her. The urge to nurture, which had led him as a young boy to harbor all manner of stray and homeless creatures, now led him as a man to want to make himself a shield between the hunter and the hunted.

Where women were concerned, that was dangerous.

He tried to make it sound as though this idea were no big deal. "It's the obvious thing to do. I know he's expecting you to just sit here and wait for him to contact you, but that puts you at a psychological disadvantage. It makes him the predator, and you the prey. If we take the first step and seek him out, it gives us the upper hand. Until we find out exactly what is at stake, that's the best way to play this. Now, Eric hasn't bothered to put his phone number on any of these letters, most likely to make sure that you came rather than called from the States." His finger stabbed at the small pile of documents that lay midway between them. "The fax number on this belongs to one of those business centers, so that's pretty much a dead end. We have neither the time nor the authority to try to track him down that way. I've looked in the phone book, and there's no listing under his name or his mother's. Assuming he has a phone, it's unlisted. So, the way I see it, we go find him."

Kenya threw up her hands. "How? There's no street address on any of these!" She grabbed a handful of the pages and shook them at him almost accusingly.

This time he did touch her, gently extricating the sheets of paper from her grasp before, in her agitation, she did them damage. "You really ought to trust me, you know. I know that there's no address, but we don't need it. He let his whereabouts slip. Look at this." He pulled out one of Eric's earlier letters from the pile and pointed at a line written in firm, careful black handwriting. "He says something about him being 'still here, in this old house, waiting for your father to come back,' just like his mother did."

"And?"

"He says 'still here.' Meaning in the marital home, where your father and his mother—"

"There's no proof of that!" Kenya said at once.

Clumsy of me, Damon thought. She was so sensitive on the subject. He had to remind himself that because it was her life they were delving into, she couldn't be as objective as he could when on the job. He hastily said, "Sorry, Kenya. I didn't mean to offend you. But if we're looking for the truth, we have to accept that it might not be what you want to hear. All right?" He waited for an answer, but it was slow in coming.

Eventually, as though it hurt her to do so, she conceded. "All right."

"Okay." He tried to be careful this time. "It seems that Eric is still living in the house where he *claims* your father lived. His old neighborhood. We just have to start there. I've found it on the map and plotted the best route—"

She surprised him by smiling. "You mean, there actually is a map? I thought you had it all stored in your head."

He grinned. "I had the route from the airport to the hotel stored in my head, but I'm not dumb enough to come here without a map on paper. Even a memory as good as mine has its limits!" He cleared away the remnants of his meal, creating a space on the table between them, produced the map, and unfolded it. The creases smoothed out easily under his big hands.

"Show me where we're going, then." She cocked her head to one side to look at the map.

He was pleased that she seemed willing to go along with his plan, but he decided not to comment on it, in case it made her back down or change her mind. She was still skittish, and he was in no mood to upset the applecart. So, with as even a tone as he could muster, he spoke, running his finger along the crisscrossed lines on the paper as he did so. "This is where we are, see? That's the Savannah, and here's the route we take. Eric's neighborhood, your father's neighborhood, is right here, east of the city, in these hills. The way I figure it, it's a ten-minute drive. Fifteen minutes, maybe, since I'm not too familiar with the road."

Kenya stared at the map for a long moment, trying to absorb every detail, and then lifted her eyes to his. "And then what?"

"Then we start asking questions."

In the clear light of day, the scenery was even more stunning than Kenya had thought last night. As they descended the narrow, serpentine road leading out of the picturesque St. Ann's valley, they joined a swirl of traffic at the foot of the hill. The majestic Queen's Park Savannah spread before them in all its glory. Over breakfast Kenya had admired it from the hotel, where she could gaze down upon the vast green expanse of it and the backdrop of the city, in which stood everything from houses that harkened back to architectural styles of yesteryear to skyscrapers whose plate glass windows reflected the busy port beyond. Close up, it was even more lovely.

Tall, ancient trees ringed the Savannah, dropping petals of pink and gold at their bases. The grass was transformed into a carpet so dense that Kenya longed to sink her bare feet into it. Within the embrace of the trees, children rode their bikes around a jogging track, and deeper still into the park. Athletes in crisp white uniforms played cricket, swinging their large, flat bats at the red ball while onlookers shrieked in encouragement and excitement. It was a gorgeous day. What a pity there was no time to stop and savor it!

Then the Savannah was to their backs, and movement slowed to a trickle, like the last drops of molasses through the mouth of a bottle. Time itself slowed, and the sun took advantage of their immobility to amuse itself at their expense. Even with the air-conditioning on full blast, Kenya could feel beads of sweat trickling down her neck and pooling briefly between her breasts before seeping down her belly and soaking into the waistband of her jeans. Maybe it was the fact that less than twenty-four hours ago, she'd been standing ankle deep in snow in New York City and had not yet become accustomed to the blazing heat of the Caribbean dry season. Maybe it was the tight ball of anxiety that had formed in the pit of her stomach—anxiety mixed with anticipation, dread, and excitement. The promise of finally seeing where her father had grown up was more than she had dared to hope for for many years, but the circumstances made that promise bittersweet.

Maybe, the flush of heat, which was not mitigated by even the blast of cold air from the car's air-conditioning system, had everything to do with Damon. The car was quite large, spacious by any standards, and would have provided adequate room for any normal-size man, but Damon was far from normal. He seemed to fill the cabin with his presence, and as small as she was, it only took a jolt or a bump in the road for her body to be rocked against his shoulders. Even when the traffic had slowed to a halt, and there was no movement to bring about that contact, his presence was so significant that he seemed to be touching her, anyway.

His scent, too, was still prevalent, a woodsy aftershave that smelled of rainwater on cut grass. What was wrong with her? It was as though the heat that he had infused her with the night before, when he had cradled her during her humiliating loss of control, was still there. Some little candle lit last night had endured until morning.

She dismissed the image of that single, glowing orange light and tried to focus on what he was saying. He'd been talking nonstop since they had left the hotel. He didn't seem to be the garrulous type, so she assumed that he was trying to put her at ease. Thoughtful of him, but it wasn't working. If anything, his deep, sonorous bass was disturbing her in a way that it shouldn't have.

"We should be moving again soon," he said reassuring her, although she had no idea what he had based that assessment on, since they hadn't moved much for almost half an hour.

"You think?" she answered, but without sarcasm. He was just trying to make her feel better again. Another unexpected kindness. She peered out the window at the snarl of traffic around them and at what was causing it. On either side of the car, crowds of people lined the roads, three or four deep along the sidewalk. Pedestrians and spectators jostled each other. Snow cone and peanut vendors sat astride bikes while pushing their carts ahead of them, and young men toted large wooden frames from which dangled every imaginable trinket: cheap sunglasses, baseball caps, windmills, balloons, whistles, cotton candy, beaded necklaces, and paper kites. Music blasted at them from both sides, the thumping beat of one calypso tune rivaling the other for its catchy, seductive beat. Gray-uniformed policemen contented themselves with maintaining a reasonable level of order but did little to keep the traffic flowing.

Never in her life had she seen so many children in one place. There were tens of thousands of them dancing up the main avenue, separated by police barricades from the press of the crowd and the cars that crept past like snails. They were dressed in costumes that caught both her imagination and her eye. Children's fantasies for a children's parade. There were soldiers, sailors and pirates, ladybugs and clowns, butterflies, bats, wood sprites, angels, and Spanish dancers and matadors. They danced and twirled, oblivious to the merciless sun. In fact, they welcomed the brilliant light, which bounced off their sequins and spangles, glitter and diamanté. The parade stretched out before them like a living river of brightly colored satin, lamé, tinfoil, and spray paint. The drumming of thousands of small feet as the children danced along the street kept time with the music blaring from the speakers like an accompanying bass line.

She was surprised to find that she was tapping her toes, half wishing she could abandon the car, leap out into the road, and join the revellers, who all seemed to be enjoying themselves immensely.

"At this rate, we might get there faster if we get out and walk," Damon said.

Kenya turned to stare at him. "I was thinking pretty much the same thing! Everyone seems to be having so much fun!"

"Too much fun to get out of our way," he answered dryly. "If you want, we could find a parking lot or something, and we could stop for a while. Look around. We've got plenty of time. There's no deadline." He cocked an inquiring brow at her.

She glanced out at the crowd again, half tempted, but then shook her head. "No, no. It's kind of you, Damon, and everything is so beautiful that I wish I were here for pleasure." The prickle at the back of her neck made her hastily change the term. The warmth engendered by his proximity once again made itself felt. "I mean, for relaxation, but . . ."

He nodded, giving no sign of having caught her verbal fumble—except for the slightest curve of his lips. The prickle at the back of her neck got a little warmer. "I got you," he said. "Eric first."

"Eric first," she echoed.

Damon lapsed into silence, politely leaving her to her thoughts. She returned to her window gazing.

It was quite some time before the traffic allowed them to ease past the parade, and by then, the neighborhood had taken on an entirely different personality. The regal old buildings that rimmed the Savannah, and the imposing new structures of glass and steel that followed thereafter, gave way to rows of smaller, more run-down buildings, and as they drove farther away from the city center, the streets grew narrower, the storefronts more shabby, and the dwellings visibly poorer. Kenya's spirits sank with them. The dancing feet of the children were soon forgotten.

This was the area from which her father hailed. Heat and dust had rendered the color of most of the houses a uniformly dingy shade. Stray dogs lazed in the middle of the road, revelling in the warmth of the softening pitch. Half-dressed children played in open doorways, oblivious to the arrival of strangers in their midst. Not so with the adults. Suspicion was written on the faces of the scores of young men who huddled on street corners, smoking or playing cards on folding tables on the sidewalk. Women braided each other's hair and shelled peas into large plastic bowls, but caution at the arrival of a strange vehicle was evident in their frowns. Tinny music rose from half a dozen radios. Somewhere a car alarm sounded.

Kenya could feel her heart beating faster with a mixture of excitement and fear. Her father had talked so often of these streets and of these people, but his stories had been colored by nostalgia and softened by time. He'd talked much about community unity and the strength of character it took to live under such circumstances. He talked about neighbor helping neighbor, brother looking out for brother. He'd forgotten about the stagnant drains and the curtain of dust that hung in the air. He'd neglected to mention the whiff of despair that now filled her nostrils.

She felt Damon lightly touch her arm. "We're here." He drew smoothly up to the curb and pulled on the emergency brake, but did not turn off the engine. He was looking at her, searching her face. "How do you feel?"

"I don't know," she said honestly, and then admitted, "Glad you're here with me."

"I'm glad I'm with you, too," he murmured.

That proves it, she thought. *We're stuck in The Incredible Shrinking Car.* It had suddenly begun to feel even smaller and warmer than it had before. He looked about to say something more, but the sting of dozens of pairs of frankly curious eyes interrupted him. He popped the buckle on his seat belt and made a move to get out. "You don't have to get out if you don't want to, you know. You can stay in the car. I'll ask the questions."

As intimidated as she was by the strangeness of this new place, and the eerie sensation of treading on the ghost of her father's past, Kenya was not a coward. "Stay in the car? Not likely. I didn't put my career on the line and come all the way over here to stay in the car." She undid her own seat belt. The click echoed like the popping of a clasp on a lifeline between her and the only safe place she knew. "I'm coming with you."

Damon struggled with his indecision for a moment and then nodded. "I expected you to say that." He sounded disapproving but resigned. Almost absently, like a forgetful professor looking for his glasses, he patted his chest on the side where she knew he kept his gun, more for reassurance than anything else, she supposed, as she could sense no immediate threat. She was becoming used to the gesture. It was at the same time both disturbing and reassuring. He was out of the car in a single fluid moment, again surprising her with his speed, in spite of his size and his injury. Before she herself could exit, he was around at her side, holding open the door for her. She didn't need the proffered hand but took it, anyway, more out of good manners than anything else.

Damon squared his shoulders and looked around

them. She could see his dark eyes darting from side to side as he assessed their situation.

"Where to start?" she whispered.

He answered without hesitation. "Here." He motioned to a small two-story building with his chin. The building had once been cream in color but had faded and flaked to an off-white. Curtains billowed from every open window on the upper floor, as though the occupants, in a bid to beat the oppressive heat, were determined to catch every breath of air that stirred. Even the wooden doors of the balcony were thrown open, revealing a glimpse of startlingly blue walls bedecked with prints, calendars and photos. The effect was almost tranquil.

The lower floor was another scene altogether. It was obviously a converted apartment, an architectural echo of the upper floor in almost every detail, but the wooden front doors were supported by solid burglar-proofing. A makeshift counter had been nailed into place a few feet beyond the doorway, and posters for local and foreign beers, rums, and colas were thumbtacked or taped up in every available space of wall. Men and women sat around in the bar as well as on chairs strewn around the yard, on earth that was packed so hard that little grass grew.

As they approached, all eyes were upon them, with a frankness that was not hostile, but wary. Kenya made an effort to smile. Beside her, Damon kept his demeanor relaxed, his body language nonthreatening. "Good day," he drawled pleasantly. "How's everyone?"

For a second Kenya thought that nobody would respond, but then one dreadlocked man, his playing cards clutched to his bare chest with one hand and his cigarette held almost gracefully in the other, answered. His Caribbean accent was melodious. "Afternoon, brother. What I could do to help you? You and the lady lost?"

Damon shook his head. "Not lost. Thanks for asking."

He continued his approach but stopped just within a few feet of the building. Kenya could feel the warmth of his hand on her upper arm, and the pressure of it was at the same time a reassurance and a cue to her to be silent.

"You looking for something, then?" asked the man, who seemed to have appointed himself spokesman for the group.

"Not something, exactly," Damon responded pleasantly. "Someone. The lady and I were wondering if you could help us."

Carefully, the man set down his cigarette in a heavy ashtray and placed his cards face down in a small, neat stack before speaking again. "You looking for someone? Someone in particular, or you looking for just any 'someone'? Because this whole hill full of plenty someones. You think you could be more specific?"

Damon smiled, moved a few paces closer, causing Kenya to keep step with him, and extended his big hand, palm up. "First, I'd better introduce myself. My name is Damon Saint Rose. I'm from New York—"

"You don't have to tell me you from New York," the man said. "I can hear it in the way you speak. I can see New York in that fancy shirt and them expensive jeans. I been there a few times, but not recently, though." He seemed briefly reflective, picked up his cigarette again, and took a long drag. "How's the weather up there? Cold these days, eh?"

Damon was still smiling. His hand did not fall. "Freezing. Bad weather all over. Blizzards these past few weeks. Glad to be here, I can tell you."

"Oh, I dunno. Couple of months of this kind of heat, you can find yourself wishing for a little snow. Even if it come in the form of a blizzard. If you ask me, snow easier to tolerate. If you need to warm up, you put something more on. But if you overheated, what you gonna do?

Take off your skin?" He laughed at his own little joke, looking around at his companions for their approval. The dozen or so other patrons of the bar rumbled in acknowledgement, their games of cards or dominoes forgotten, if only for the moment. It seemed that their arrival had suspended all other activities.

The man put his cigarette down again and then took Damon's hand in his own, slightly smaller grasp. "Austin," he volunteered but gave no indication as to whether that was his first name or last.

"Nice to meet you, Austin." Damon motioned to Kenya, who was silent at his side. "And this is my wife, Kenya."

Kenya was sure that her shock registered on her face. Before she could do anything about taming her look of incredulity, she felt Damon's arm come up around her shoulders, pulling her against his side. The pressure was firm but intimate, molding her body to his, and he looked down at her with an indulgent smile playing on his lips. "We're here on our honeymoon, aren't we, honey?"

Austin's face softened slightly. "Nice place for it," he conceded. The man's gaze flitted to the big hand that held her in that possessive embrace and then lifted to Kenya's face, which was flushing wildly. She hoped that he would attribute the sudden color in her cheeks to the midday heat and the stillness in the air, rather than to the disturbing sensation that Damon's touch had instilled in her. She felt a twinge of annoyance. It was bad enough that he had chosen to play out this little charade without warning her, but he didn't have to be this convincing! He didn't have to be gently stroking his thumb along her rib cage, just under the curve of her breasts. *He should be in Hollywood,* she thought to herself. *He's playing this ridiculous role to the hilt.*

Austin bought the story and gave Damon a knowing wink. "Trinidad good for that. Good for romance. The only thing you can do to take your mind off the heat is get a little loving, eh?"

"Got that right," Damon said and laughed good-naturedly, as though he felt completely at home. For a moment the two men were joined in fraternal amusement; they were just two guys having a laugh at the romantic frailties of women.

I'll kill him. She considered spinning out of Damon's over-familiar embrace and coming down good and hard on his instep with the heel of her shoe, just to get it through his thick skull that she certainly did not appreciate the idea of him and her doing anything more intimate to take their minds off of the heat than sharing an iced drink with a table keeping distance between them. But that would defeat the purpose of their being there. She grinned back and did her best to bear it. *I'll just kill him later.* The promise to herself lifted her spirits to no end.

When the two men were done sharing a male-bonding chuckle at Kenya's expense, Austin directed his next question directly at her. "You-all been here long?"

Flustered, she struggled to find her tongue, keeping her voice sweet and devoid of her murderous intentions toward the man at her side. "We just got in last night."

Austin rubbed his chin thoughtfully, as though that little tidbit of information took tremendous effort to digest, and then said, "And you looking for somebody . . . on your honeymoon?"

Damon's smile did not falter. "Yes, we thought that while we're here, we'd try to patch up a few broken connections. We're trying to track down a relative of ours. A whole family, actually. One we haven't been in touch with for ages. Name of Reese."

"Reese, eh?" Austin didn't miss a beat. "Never heard of

them." The slight softening of his features disappeared as though it had never been there. He was shrewd once again, still polite, but careful. "Sorry."

Oh, God, he's lying, Kenya thought. She could sense the careful attention of everyone else in the small yard to the conversation. Damon was undaunted. "They've lived around here a long time. One of them, Isaac Reese, was married to a lady named Camilla. They had a son, Eric."

Austin's recognition of the name was betrayed by a blink. Rapid glances passed between him and one or two of the other patrons, who had by now given up all pretence of ignoring them. *Gotcha*, Kenya thought, but her elation was tempered by the knowledge that that recognition could further cement the validity of Eric's claim against her father. But she had come to find the truth, and so, she waited.

Slowly, Austin shook his head, and Kenya listened incredulously as he said, "No, no, that name don't ring no bell, brother. You sure you got the right place?"

"Pretty much."

"Sure it's not farther down the road? You could try there. I bet you they'd know him there, farther down." A jut of the chin identified the direction he was suggesting, and then the cigarette found its place between his lips once again, signalling his reluctance to say much more.

That was ridiculous! The man was lying! She knew the man had recognized the name. She felt it in her bones. It was written all over his face! Why was he sending them away? "We've got the right street! You know we've got—"

The fingers that had been so gently stroking her side, as part of the little marital charade Damon had decided to play, hardened perceptibly, giving her a sharp warning jab and cutting her outrage off in midcourse. "Thank you, you've been very kind."

Austin dipped his head with almost old-world courte-
ousness. "You-all enjoy that honeymoon now." Then he
returned his concentration to the game, effectively dis-
missing them. There was an audible buzz as the scene
around them returned to the way it had been when they
had appeared: women laughed among themselves,
dominoes clacked loudly on tabletops, and ice clinked in
glasses. It was as though they had already left.

With a decisiveness that invited no opposition, Damon
steered her around and headed toward the road.

"What did you do that for?" she hissed. They'd been so
close!

"What would you have me do? Badger the man into
answering me? Pull out my weapon and wave it at him?"

"He was lying!"

"I know he was lying. But I pretty much expected it to
go that way, anyhow. He's on his home turf. Small communities like this have a code of secrecy. They may not
have much in material terms, but they stand up for each
other. Two strangers walk in out of nowhere and start
asking questions; well, that's suspicious." He couldn't
resist adding, "Even if we were only young newlyweds
looking up old friends."

"And that's another thing!" Frustration made her irritable.
"What's up with that? Why the whole newlywed routine?
Hanging on to me like you and I were in some"—she
waved her arms in a broad, expressive gesture—"some
thing! Was that really necessary?"

Damon released his hold on her so fast she almost stag-
gered. She held on to the car and regained her footing.

"Sorry," he told her, but he didn't look the least bit
sorry. "I know I caught you off guard. But it just popped
into my head right there. I thought it would be a good
way to cover the fact that we were wandering around, so
far off the beaten tourist track, looking for someone.

You have to admit that a newlywed couple is a darn sight more harmless than a woman and a bodyguard searching for a blackmailer."

He was right, damn him. He seemed always to be. "You're right," she conceded. "I know we don't belong here. We stick out like a pair of sore thumbs. Thank you for trying to make us less suspicious."

"You're welcome." There was mischief in his eyes when he added, "I rather enjoyed being married to you, even if it was only for about ten minutes or so. I bet they all thought I'd snagged myself a real feisty one, the way you were all ready to jump on old Austin there and scratch the truth out of him. Yessiree, I found myself one hot little pepper seed of a wife."

Kenya grinned sheepishly, letting him take just that one potshot at her. But the reason for their being there could not be denied, even for a moment of levity. She put her hands on her hips, looking worriedly up the street. "What now, Damon?"

He read the seriousness on her face and let the banter drop. "What now is we keep on trying. We go to the next corner and try there. And the next and the next. And we ask questions. And hope we get lucky."

Normally, Kenya was a person who believed in hope. Hope was what fuelled her world. But the dread in her bones, in the depth of her stomach, was still there, right where it had been, growing quietly stronger since this whole blackmail nightmare had begun. Her stockpile of hope was running low. "And what if we don't?" she asked pessimistically.

Damon drew his brows together, trying to think. His response was both encouraging and disheartening. "Then we find another way," he told her. He held out his hand and beckoned. "Come, Kenya. Let's find Eric."

She didn't take the proffered hand but fell into step next

to him as he walked along the hazy asphalt road. Once again, she thanked her lucky stars that because he was with her, she did not have to tread this difficult path alone.

"Here, let me."

Kenya let Damon pry the keys to her room from her tired hands, not even bothering to protest. Fatigue and despondency made her clumsy, and she had been struggling with the large, bulky, old-fashioned bunch of keys for several moments and still had not succeeded in getting her door open. She passed her hand over her eyes, glad at least that while the fatigue in them was evident, the tears that she had foresworn did not choose that moment to betray her.

It was early evening now, and yet the heat had not let up. She knew her feet would be swollen, even though she had been wise enough to wear light, comfortable sandals. Hours of dogged pursuit of her shadowy nemesis had brought them nothing but a series of deliberately blank stares, feigned puzzlement, and regretful denials. Resident after resident had been wary but polite. And not a soul, it seemed, who lived in the neighborhood that sprawled across the face of the hillside overlooking Port of Spain knew anything about any family by the name of Reese. Not now, and not in the past.

God, she was tired.

With an assured twist of his wrist, Damon worked the ancient lock, and the door opened under his hand. He stepped aside and motioned for her to enter. She did so gratefully, glad to be out of the hallway and even happier still to step into the relative coolness of the fans she had left on at high speed. She had selected the Bird of Paradise for its promised old-world appeal, but that, she was learning, had its drawbacks. Next time, she told herself, if there ever was a next time, she was checking into a more modern hotel, one that had air-conditioning in all its rooms. The quaint colonial style of the room, with its charming wooden jalousies and wide spaces between walls and ceiling, was delightful to look at, but it wasn't exactly designed to keep artificially cooled air in.

"What do you say, on our next visit, we blow off the cute old-world charm for an ugly, modern hotel, where we could at least crank the air-conditioning up to sixty degrees?" Damon joked.

Kenya looked at him sharply. Once again he'd voiced her exact thoughts. What was it with him? Was he that perceptive, or was she simply transparent?

Without even bothering to request an invitation, he followed her in and pulled the door firmly in behind himself, bending over once inside to pick up a folded newspaper that had been slipped under her door by hotel staff while they had been out. He stuck the paper under his arm, then took her bag from her and set it down on her bedside table.

"Now," he said briskly, "You're tired and despondent, I know. But if you go take a quick shower, I'll wait for you on the patio. When you come out, I'll have a cold drink waiting for you, and we can talk about our next step."

The prospect of cool, cool water cascading down over her from head to toe sounded so, so good. But she felt compelled to stay and express her anxiety. "Oh, but I—" she began, but he shushed her before she could get any further.

"Go on, Kenya. Take a shower. I'm not going anywhere. When you get back, I'll be right here waiting for you. We'll talk then. Believe me, things never look as bad as you think they are once you're clean and cool."

His logic was inescapable. She did feel hot, gritty, and miserable, and there was only one cure for that. Wearily, she bent over, freeing her sore, aching feet from the confines of the sandals that had transformed themselves in a matter of hours from cute accessories into instruments of torture. As the shoes came off, they revealed cruel bands of red, irritated skin beneath.

Damon spotted them right away. "Hurts?" he asked unnecessarily.

She nodded wordlessly and headed for the bathroom door.

"We'll do something about that, too, when you get out," he promised.

She didn't bother asking what he meant.

It was a full fifteen minutes before she was able to will herself to climb back out from under the cleansing splash of the water. Feeling bad about keeping him waiting that long, she dried quickly, rubbing a hurried towel through her hair, leaving it in damp spikes. A strapless, apple-green cotton dress was as much as she could stand against her skin, and shoes were out of the question.

She found him on the bandana-sized patio that was attached to her room. He was leaning against the wrought-iron railings, one hand holding on to the newspaper he'd collected from her floor, looking so enormous against the fine fleur-de-lis metalwork that if she had not reminded herself that as delicate as it looked, it was still iron, she would have been afraid that it would give way under his weight.

He was facing the open doorway, waiting patiently for her reappearance, and something inside her leaped at that thought. The feeling was almost comforting, like being guarded by a patient, unwavering Great Dane. When he spotted her, he smiled.

"Feel better now?"

She did. As she stepped onto the patio to join him, he immediately handed her one of the tall, dark blue antique glasses from the dumbwaiter in her room. It was filled with so much ice, there was little space for the fizzy lemonade. She immediately detected the zing of alcohol. "You spiked this!" she said in mock accusation.

"I certainly did." He lifted his own glass in salute and took a sip. "Good, twelve-year-old Trinidadian rum. It's wonderful. Couldn't beat it with a stick."

She finished her drink thirstily and let him fill her glass once again before she settled on one of the low wide woven rattan chairs, sinking back into the oversized, brightly patterned cushions. It was only then that she noticed that he had removed the light jacket that he had been wearing for the sole purpose of concealing his weapon. Patches of dampness marred the shirt he had on underneath, reminding her that if venturing out in the sun had been hard on her in just a blouse and jeans, it must have been murder on him dressed like that. Even the slim leather holster strapped around him left its damp imprint on his chest.

She was ashamed of her own self-centeredness. "Oh, Damon, I'm so sorry! You didn't have to hang around and wait on me. You could have gone and had a shower yourself." She gestured in the direction of his room. "Go on, you must be roasting!"

He dismissed her suggestion. "I'm fine. I didn't want to leave you."

"I don't need to be watched *all* the time! You don't have to—"

"I'm fine." The subject was closed. He tossed the newspaper on the matching rattan coffee table, finished his drink and put his glass down, not bothering to refill it as he had hers, and approached her.

"Now, let's see what we can do about those feet." To her surprise, he dropped to his knees before her and held his hands out, expectant. "Right foot first, I think."

He had to be kidding. He was offering to rub her feet? "You're joking, right?"

"Nope. They look awful."

"Thanks a lot!" she shot back. She didn't know whether to laugh or take umbrage.

"I didn't mean to offend you," he hastened to tell her. "I mean, they're beautiful feet. It's just that they look . . . tortured."

"They *feel* tortured!"

His hands were still open, palms up. "Come on," he insisted. "I give a great foot rub, and this is a onetime, limited offer. On the house."

"Then it's an offer I can't refuse," she chuckled. As she lifted one foot and placed it into his waiting hands, alarm bells that should have sounded, that should have warned her of the folly of her actions, were silent. Maybe it was the divine feeling of being cool and fresh all over for a change, or maybe it was that smooth-as-silk rum he'd fixed her—had he really said it was twelve years old? But his hands were huge, firm, and steady, and her foot disappeared between them. For several moments he said nothing, concentrating on the bands of redness that marred her flesh, using his thumbs to bring the circulation back and ease away the ache.

Kenya closed her eyes and let him work, following in her mind the ever widening circles he was making against her skin. Feet were a funny thing. Although, as a rule, she valued her weekly pedicure back in New York, the touch of her aesthetician was brisk, clinical. It was a job that needed doing, and so it was done well. But this, this was different. Although he touched nothing but her feet, her whole body felt at ease. She was barely aware of having sighed.

When he spoke, she had to shake herself to focus on his words. "Take heart, Kenya. We can do this."

"What?" His touch had drawn a curtain of fog across her mind. She had no idea what he meant.

"Eric. We'll find him."

He'd misinterpreted her sigh of contentment and relief for one of despair, and his reminder brought her out of the fog into which she had drifted. *My God,* she thought. *Eric!* When they'd entered the room, all she had had on her mind had been Eric and their miserable failure in tracking him down on his home turf. Now Damon's touch had chased him from her clouded mind as though he had never been there. She tried to take her foot away, sit up straight, and talk business, but his grip did not loosen.

"Don't," he said. "Relax. I'm not done yet. Don't let Eric rob you of this. Don't let him inhabit your mind. We didn't get far today, but that's okay. We'll try again to-morrow. I just brought him up because I know you're worried. I'm only saying this because I want you to know that tonight I'll think on this some more, and by tomor-row, I'll have a plan. But you've come all this way to this island, and there's so much for you to enjoy. Whatever the outcome, don't let it be a wasted trip. So put him out of your head, and relax, okay?"

A day ago she would have scoffed at that. Relaxing wasn't one of the things she did well, especially not now, when she was on a mission like this one. But Damon was right. Here she was, in this beautiful, beautiful place— her father's island. The fast setting sun had turned the sky bright red; and the mountains behind them, the shrubbery in the small garden onto which her porch opened, glowed in the reflected light. Crickets and small frogs, though prey and predator, sang in unison. The air was perfumed with strange, exotic flowers, and every-where there was the echo of calypso music.

And then there was this man, who was doing things to her entire body while only touching her feet.

"Will you?" he persisted.

And then something about the way he was touching her changed.

Chapter 9

The purpose of Damon's laying on of hands became less and less therapeutic and more and more something else. His knuckles took over from his thumbs, kneading the soles of Kenya's feet, sending waves radiating through her entire body. The soreness was long gone, and by rights she should have told him so and let him put an end to his kind gesture if he so desired. But his ministrations had brought, in the aftermath of banished pain, a pleasure that she had no right feeling. *Just a few minutes more,* she promised herself. *Then I'll stop him.* "I will," she choked. "I'll try to relax."

His voice was barely audible. "Good."

Even the attitude of his body changed: his back, ramrod straight before, curved as he leaned toward her, narrowing the space between them by a mere few inches in real terms. But to her it seemed that it had whittled down to nothing at all. Each of his hands encircled an ankle with the same ease with which she could encircle her own wrist, and then they stopped moving. He stared down at them. "You've got the smallest feet I've ever seen. Like a child's."

"I'm not a child," she reminded him.

"That, I know. It's just that . . ." He released her ankles, as though her tininess was too much for him to bear. Unable to draw away, he slid his hands halfway up her legs, cupping the fullest point of her calves. "Next to you I feel so huge. Clumsy. Like I could break you if I pressed too hard."

She struggled to force her words past an unexpected constriction in her throat. "You won't break me," she promised him. She leaned forward, reached down, and put her hands over his, pressing them against her flesh just in case he had decided to release her, but all the while her mind was frantically asking: *How did this happen? How did it get to this? He's touching me, and I . . . want him to.*

Madness.

Still on his knees, he bowed his head almost in an attitude of worship and then pressed his lips against her feet. First one, then the other, lightly, like a butterfly landing on her skin for a brief second.

The effect was galvanic. Rapid-fire shocks ripped through her, like sparklers bursting in the night sky. The sound of her sharply inhaled breath was muffled by her fingers pressed to her mouth. He stiffened at the sound, hesitating, and she was terrified that he would pull away, declare it a mistake, and rise to his feet.

Then where would that leave her?

Her fears were almost realized when he lifted his head, breaking that startling contact. "Kenya?" He looked as though he were struggling for words to excuse himself, to apologize, so she cut him off before he could find them.

"Don't stop," she pleaded, surprising them both. She was almost afraid that he would not heed her entreaty, as his piercing dark eyes, fixed on her face, searched for something, but then—to her relief—his head dipped again and that contact was reestablished.

Carefully, systematically, not wanting to miss an inch, he pressed a series of soft, light kisses from her toes, up along the rise of her insteps, to her ankles, and then higher still. Along her shins, slowly, inch by nerve-wracking inch, to each knee. As his lips made her every nerve go haywire, his hands soothed them down again, cupping her calves, giving them support as she held them out to him.

A glimpse of white broderie anglaise peeked out below the hem of her green cotton dress, flirting with him, erotically incongruous, like a saucy wink from an otherwise demure young maiden. He released her calves and carefully laid her feet on his thighs before gently holding that little slip of peekaboo lace between his fingers and thumb, examining it closely, as though admiring the fine stitching. Then, his examination complete, he eased the light garment up a little, barely an inch, revealing a band of thigh too narrow to be considered immodest by any standards but broad enough to make her feel as though she had laid her entire person bare to him.

While her skin cried out *Yes! Yes!* she waited for the kisses to continue up to that narrow strip of bare flesh, but he merely ran the tips of his fingers along it, back and forth, once, twice, and then again, until she thought she would scream. When she was sure she could bear it no more, she grasped both his hands, nails digging into his skin, because stopping him right now was preferable to losing her mind.

He did not resist when she pulled his hands away. He was panting like a runner. "I needed you to stop me," he rasped. "Your skin is so soft, I couldn't take my hands away. You smell like tea roses."

"I wasn't stopping you," she barely managed to reply.

"I was just . . . shifting . . . focus." It was ridiculous. His hands had burned trails along her bare flesh, and his lips had followed them like lost travellers—and yet he had not kissed her. Not on the mouth, at least, and that was creating jealousy among the ranks. Trust a man as unusual as him to go about this backwards!

She was rectifying the situation—right now. She half rose from her seat, and he recognized her intent. He supported her in his arms as she slipped from chair to floor, and then she was before him, her knees pressed against his.

Even when they were both kneeling, he was so much taller than she that she had to lift an arm, place her hand at the back of his head, and coax him down to her. He didn't need much persuasion. His eyes were so intense that she had to shut hers at the moment when their lips made contact to spare herself the complete invasion of her mind.

She had expected him to be forceful, almost domineering. But instead of conquering, his lips only explored, curiously asking questions that she felt compelled to answer. Apart from the pressure of his knees against hers, their only other point of contact was her hand at his nape. She could feel the short hair crinkle under her touch: it was crisp, supercharged. The muscles at the base of his neck were taut, and lower down, between his shoulder blades, they were as tense as those of a man struggling between the desire to go on and the prudence to put a stop to this, right now.

Uncertainty tinged her pleasure, contaminating it like a beetle falling into a pool of rainwater. She wanted this. How this lunatic desire had managed to take root in her, she couldn't tell, but she wanted this kiss to go on and on. But did he? She slipped her hand up between them, pressing her palm flat against his chest, feeling the thunder there. There were devils and angels doing battle within him.

That was wrong.

She twisted away from him, breaking their kiss and scooting back onto her bottom so that there was enough air between them for her to fill her lungs with several deep breaths. Damon's eyes were closed, his head lowered as though she were still pressed against him, and his sigh came from deep within. There was no way of telling whether that sigh was one of regret that she had stopped them or regret that they had started in the first place.

How humiliating! "Oh, my God, Damon, I'm so sorry!" Guilt was quick to replace desire. How could she have done that? She'd all but forced herself on him, even though his hesitation was there in the very tenor of his body. A hot flush of embarrassment ran through her. "I'm sorry, I don't know what—"

His eyes flew open, and he hastily tried to cut her apology off at the source. "Don't be. Don't be sorry. I should be the one to apologize. I got carried away. It's not like me. . . ."

He got carried away? She'd practically leaped onto his lap! Pushing herself up off the floor with her hands, she stood, looking down at him. She wondered what she could possibly say next to diminish either her embarrassment or his.

The sun had fallen out of sight with tropical suddenness, but it left its sticky heat behind. The delicious coolness in which her recent shower had wrapped her was gone. Even the air felt close and still. She wanted him gone, so she could be alone and think. She glanced involuntarily out toward the garden. It promised a means of escape. Either he left or she would, even though it was *her* room.

But what could she say to him? Did she dare open her

mouth and risk being betrayed by her own breathless blundering?

Fortunately, he beat her to it, rising to stand before her and rubbing his brow in bemusement, as puzzled as she was as to how things had gotten out of hand so fast. "I think," he began slowly and then pondered awhile before going on, "I think I'd better go. That would be best."

She nodded. What he was saying was the only sane thing he *could* say. It *would* be best for him to leave. They'd both made a mistake; they'd both been at fault. It was best they do the sensible thing and turn their backs against temptation before they made matters worse. But why, in spite of that implacable logic, was she half wishing that he would lack the strength to leave?

Strength, it seemed, was one thing Damon did have. He found his jacket and slung it over his arm. She followed him to the door. He looked about to go without saying anything further but then changed his mind and said to her, "We can put this behind us. We're both grown-ups. We both know it was a mistake. We can forget it ever happened. We have a job to do. Let's do it. Agreed?"

"Agreed," she said immediately, partly in an effort to convince herself.

The measured control of his words did not diminish his look of amusement at the rapidity of her response. "Attagirl. So, we press on. We'll have an early dinner and then get some rest. We haven't had anything to eat since breakfast. You must be starving."

"I think I'll just call room service and have something here," she said hastily. As raw as her nerves were, she wasn't sure whether she could handle the intimacy of a meal with him right now. "Maybe read the paper and go to, uh. . . ." The word "bed" balanced on the tip of her tongue, and she involuntarily glanced past him to the offending piece of furniture, which now seemed to fill the whole room. ". . . to sleep," she finished lamely.

To her relief, he neither protested her wish to be alone nor teased her for her coyness. "Very well. Early dinner, early night. And then, tomorrow we hit the streets again." He opened the door and stepped out into the hallway. His gaze dropped to her mouth, which was full and tingling with his kisses, and lingered there for a long moment. Then he chuckled to himself.

"What?" He was *laughing*? What about this situation could possibly be that funny?

He caught her quizzical look and explained. "I was just thinking—"

"Yes?"

"That shower you were suggesting I take earlier?"

"Uh-huh."

"If there was ever a time when I desperately needed a cold shower, this, my sweet, is that time." His low, rueful laughter echoed in her ears long after he had let himself into his own room and locked the door firmly behind him.

Chapter 10

Once the relentless pounding of cold water on his achingly aroused body had done its job—and even that had taken longer than he had expected—Damon did not find the situation all that funny. He'd slipped up. He'd lost it; he'd cast aside his usual iron clad self-control and kissed a woman. *A client.* No, kissing her had not been the point at which the battle had been lost. That had taken place the moment he'd held Kenya's delicate feet in his hands, felt the curve of her ankles, the softness of her skin, and the beating of a vein beneath its surface.

There was no irony in the fact that he had known this woman barely twenty-four hours. Attraction between a man and a woman was usually like that: instant, compelling, and undeniable. It had been piqued from the moment he had held that small glossy photograph of her in his hands, and her feisty response to his presence yesterday had only fed it. Last night, or, rather, in the early hours of this morning, he'd held her to offer her comfort in a moment of distress. He would have been fooling himself if he said that that contact—the feel of her, soft and pliant in his arms—had not gratified anything other than his sense of altruism. Even while dissolving in tears, she'd felt good, smelled good, and left him wanting to hold her again.

Touching her, that had been his mistake. Attraction without contact was no problem. In the four years since he'd lost Jewel, he'd met many attractive women and had been content to admire them from a distance. Stoically, he'd denied his own urges, finding other ways to distract himself: sport, books, anything, like a man trying to kick a nicotine habit. And though he'd always revelled in the look and scent and feel of a woman, and had a voracious appetite for sensual pleasure, he'd found that abstinence had been easy. The memory of Jewel had always sustained him.

And then he'd gone and touched Kenya, and like a handful of magic beans tossed carelessly onto fertile soil, that passing attraction had erupted overnight into a tangled, fairy-tale beanstalk of want and need that had ensnared him when he was not paying attention.

"Sorry," he murmured again. This second apology was not for Kenya, but for the woman whose absence from this world did not reduce his acute sense of having betrayed her. Since the day he'd met Jewel in the steaming Amazon, and in all the time thereafter that it had taken to win her, he'd not touched another woman. Fidelity meant something to him; it always had. Her death had not been a reason to change that.

And then, there was Kenya's reputation. Stories from the handful of newspaper clippings that he'd perused before meeting her came back to him in a rush. There were articles about her and her bitter breakup with her former manager, and the sexual harassment lawsuit that came after. And there had been other young men, hadn't there? Claiming the same thing? How much truth was there to that?

When he'd read them the day before yesterday—had

it only been two days ago?—he'd been prepared to believe it. Celebrities were different from everyone else. For a woman to force her attentions upon an employee was probably normal in the world that Kenya inhabited, that and a whole lot more.

But did that world inhabit Kenya? Damon stretched out on his bed, noting gratefully that hotel management had fulfilled their promise to supply him with a larger model, and laced his hands behind his head. What were the facts? True, he was technically working for her. True, she had been a most willing participant in their kiss; one could even argue that she had pursued it, pulling his head down to meet hers.

But that meant nothing. At least, nothing *bad*. Sexual aggression in a woman was a wonderful thing. He liked the idea of a woman knowing what she wanted and demanding it: shrinking violets had never been for him. She had reached out for and seized her pleasure, but there had been no force. His reluctance had not come about because of a lack of desire to be with her, but for other personal and professional reasons. And once she had sensed that reluctance, she'd brought the whole encounter to a close, even though he was not sure that he would have been able to.

To him, that did not sound like the actions of a sexual predator. *Nothing* about Kenya was such. And the types of publications that were obsessed with the private scandals of the stars were not exactly known for their truthfulness. So which was it? He shifted his gaze upward, staring at the regular pattern of furrows in the wooden ceiling above, almost subconsciously counting them off in a "she loves me/she loves me not" rhythm: *She's guilty/she's not. She's guilty/she's not.*

Whatever her private life was really like had no bearing on the matter. If anyone needed to take a stand, it was he.

Like any profession, his had ethical considerations. One simply did not get involved with someone you were hired to protect. Even with Jewel, he'd waited until their professional relationship had come to an end before seeking her out with the intention of starting an intimate one. With Kenya, the attraction was intense, compelling—and she lay in the room next door, on a bed, just a few feet away. Too accessible. He'd have to be more careful.

A discreet knock at the door signalled the arrival of room service. He got up and took the tray quickly. The sight and aroma of steaming red snapper adorned with wedges of lime, fat cornmeal dumplings, and an assortment of root vegetables with names he could barely pronounce—like *dasheen, tannia,* and *cassava*—reminded him of the hunger that he had sublimated throughout the day. He dug in with enthusiasm, glad for a distraction from his teeming thoughts.

He'd barely made it past the halfway mark when there was another knock on the door. This was not the muted, circumspect knocking of the waiter who had brought his meal. It was staccato, demanding, almost frantic. He leaped for the door. Only his cautiousness prevented him from opening it right away.

"Yes?" He pressed his ear to it, listening for identifying sounds.

"Damon!" Kenya's voice was an excited hiss. "Let me in!"

His skin prickled. *She* had come to *him*. His heart tripped into double time, but his brain fought to wrest it back under control. He was being foolish. Surely this visit could have nothing to do with what had taken place earlier! This had nothing to do with sex; no amount of self-flattery could convince him of that. Something had happened. Fear replaced excitement.

The moment he wrested open the door, she tumbled

in, an agitated blur waving a newspaper overhead. "Eric! Eric Reese! He's here!"

He stiffened. "Eric came to see you? Why didn't you call me? You spoke to him alone?"

She was breathless with excitement but managed to puff out, "No, no. He's here, in the paper. I mean, his name is here! I know where he is! Look!" She held the paper out, but her hand was shaking so much, he couldn't focus on anything. He pried it from her fingers and spread it out on the bed on the page to which she had opened it. Kenya hovered behind him.

"There! Look!" She jabbed an excited finger at a mid-sized black-and-white ad near the bottom of the page, nestled among a jumble of similar ads for Carnival shows and parties. Each looked so much like the other that it was a wonder she spotted it at all. He peered at it. It was for a calypso show being held at a nightclub called The Boom Box and listed the names of all the performers who were slated to appear. And there, fourth from the top, was the name Eric Reese. It was almost too crazy to be believed.

"Do you think it could be him? I mean, it has to be him, right? There couldn't be someone else on the island with exactly that same name, could there? It's a small country!" Her words tumbled over each other in their rush to get out.

"Could be someone else," he agreed rationally, "but the odds are against it. And right now, it's about the only lead we have, so it's worth following. But if you ask me, my gut instinct says that you've got your man."

She could barely contain her excitement and trepidation. "The show's on tonight. We've got to go. We have to!" Then she stopped suddenly, remembering her manners. "I mean, if you're not too tired—"

"Don't be ridiculous." He tore out the page with the

ad, took one more hard look at it to verify the address, and put it in his pocket. "This is the best thing that could have happened. We'd be foolish to let this chance slip through our fingers. Come on, let's go." He rose and began preparing himself to leave.

She seemed to have only then noticed the half-finished meal still on his table and looked sheepish. "You were eating."

"I was," he confirmed regretfully.

"We could . . ." She struggled to be generous, and in the face of her eagerness to leave, that effort warmed his heart. "We could wait until you're done, if you like."

The offer was tempting. This was the second meal that their ghost hunt had interrupted for the day. But he couldn't do that to Kenya. "Thanks, but no. From the looks of it, the show's already started. If we're going to catch him, we need to get cracking. Maybe when we get there, I can scrounge something more filling than a handful of peanuts at the bar."

Her relief was palpable. She reached out and grabbed his hand, making him glad he had chosen not to delay. "Thank you, Damon. I owe you one." Then she added hastily, "Dinner, I mean." Her flush showed him that she still had their truncated encounter at the forefront of her mind.

He could have teased her about it, but it was still very much at the forefront of *his*, so he refrained and instead said lightly, "When this is all over, I'll be sure to collect, because you seem determined to make a skinny man out of me. But in the meantime, we have your gene pool to dive into. Just give me a moment to clean up, and I'll be right with you. I'll be ready in five minutes."

He was ready in three.

* * *

The Boom Box was located in the heart of an old section of Port of Spain called Woodbrook. The small neighborhood's very architecture recalled the country's English colonial heritage. Old houses with high, sloping roofs snuggled up against one another, as though each relied on the other for companionship and support. Wooden patios were shaded by elaborate, white-painted overhanging woodwork that arced and rolled in loops and swirls, like antique lace. Most of the buildings, obviously designed as dwellings, now housed small businesses: designers' studios, hairdressing salons, coffeehouses, and nightclubs.

In some cases, old buildings had been torn down to make room for newer, fancier buildings, which although nicely appointed in their own right, looked odd and out of place next to their more sedate neighbors, like punk rockers at an old ladies' tea party. The Boom Box was one such building.

The club was packed with patrons, and their chatter and the sound of clinking glasses above the thumping, hip-swaying West Indian music made it almost seem like a social outing to Damon. Like—if he dared use that word—a date. It was a fairly small bar by any standards, but it seemed to be a popular watering hole in the neighborhood. Jovial patrons hailed each other above the din and lounged about with the easy familiarity of people who were accustomed to coming there to unwind.

The setup was straightforward: small tables and chairs filled the outer periphery of the establishment, and a well-stocked bar rimmed by a solid-looking wood-paneled counter dominated the farthest corner. A low stage was set aside in another corner for the live acts. Colored points of light—red, blue, green, and yellow— danced on the ceiling and walls and bounced off the glasses hanging in rows from the rafters above the bar in a display that seemed to keep time with the music.

Neon signs touted local Carib beer and a handful of foreign beers and whiskeys. At the bar, patrons were three deep, elbowing each other for a chance to make it to the front and win the bartender's attention.

There was little to eat besides finger foods, like chips and fried chicken wings, but Damon was reluctant to eat now because there was no telling when Eric would turn up and whether he would be called upon to act when he did. The distraction wasn't worth the risk. So, instead, he collected two bottles of Carib, eager to sample a beverage that seemed so hugely popular with the locals, and wove his way back to the minuscule table that they had managed to nab upon their arrival. Kenya was sitting, waiting for him.

Her head was turned toward the small, semicircular stage, intently watching the act that was taking place there. A youthful calypsonian dressed in a festive but slightly ridiculous gold lamé tracksuit, furry fedora, and gold-sprayed spats was cavorting with two barely dressed, nubile backup singers, who had obviously been chosen more for their ability to gyrate their hips with serpentine fluidity than for their singing voices. The ribald lyrics of the song, coupled with the antics of the threesome, brought raucous laughter from the audience at the end of every verse. Even Kenya was smiling.

He was glad that she seemed to be enjoying the show: at least, that would take her mind off of the moment when Eric Reese would put in an appearance. He'd done his best to find out exactly at which point in the lineup of the evening's entertainment that would be, but his queries at the door, the bar, and stageside were met with puzzled stares, a shake of the head, and the admonition to just let the show play out however it did. Nobody was a stickler for schedules and exact timing at Carnival, one of the stagehands informed him amiably. Eric Reese

would perform when he performed. "Just relax and
enjoy the show, man," the worker had said, "Eric Reese
singing just now." After only one day in this country,
though, Damon had learned that "just now" could mean
anything from within the next five minutes to sometime
tomorrow.

They'd just have to wait him out.

"Here you go." He had to bring his lips close to
Kenya's ear in order to be heard above the din.

She took the bottle from him with a smile and curiously inspected the deep blue and bright yellow label.
The beer was so cold that tiny chips of ice collected in
the neck of the bottle and a fine mist of cold air was visible as she put it to her lips. "Ah," she shivered slightly as
the coolness of the beverage rippled through her.
"Cold!"

"Just what we needed in this heat." He took a draught.
"This one'll penetrate down to our bones. Central cooling, you might call it."

She laughed and pressed the bottle to her throat. As
she did so, she tilted her head back, closed her eyes,
and pursed her lips. The moisture on the outside of the
bottle left a wet trail along her chin and neck, reminding
him vividly of the way that strip of skin had felt against
his lips just a few hours earlier. Involuntarily, his throat
spasmed, making it impossible to swallow another sip of
his own drink. He had to set it down on the little table
before he dropped it.

Immediately, she was concerned. She laid a hand
along his forearm. "You okay?"

"Fine," he fibbed. In an effort to deflect attention
from himself, he turned the question around and posed
it back to her. "You?"

She hesitated. "I don't know. This is all so confusing.
It's just so sudden. I wasn't prepared for it."

He hastened to be of comfort. "I told you before, don't worry about Eric. We've got it all under control."

She looked startled and then stammered, "That's . . . not what I meant. I was talking about . . . you know. Earlier. The way I behaved. It's not like me. I don't know what got into me. . . ." Even in the darkness he could see the heat of embarrassment infuse her face.

"Ah." That was different. That was something that was *not* all under control. He pondered what to say to her. The way he saw it, he had two choices. He could wave it off, tell her with a shrug that it was nothing, just one of those things that happened, and that as far as he was concerned, it was all water under the bridge. That would be the gentlemanly thing to do. It would also be a lie.

His second option would be to take advantage of her discomfiture and, while her guard was lowered, ask probing questions. Like, for example, what had prompted that impulsive kiss? Had it been spur-of-the-moment, or had she felt that same undeniable tug of attraction that he had since their meeting? And, if so, what did she want to do about it? A less gentlemanly option, indeed, but one that might bring real answers.

She wrenched the decision from his hands by speaking again, although more to herself than to him. "Ridiculous," she muttered.

"What?"

"It's ridiculous. I met you yesterday. And this evening I was all over you. I'm not like that. I'm not that kind of woman."

"I'm sure, you're not," he said promptly. He'd meant the words to make her feel better, but as he uttered them, some deeply buried intuition told him that they were true, and with that, every suspicion he had harbored about the rumors and controversy that swirled about her head died. This was no sexual predator, no manipulative young woman who used her feminine charms as a weapon. "I *know*, you're not," he added with deep sincerity.

She knew at once what he was referring to. "How could you know?" In the darkness, her eyes were bright, anxious, searching. "Back home everyone thinks they know who I am. What I am. They read two or three little articles about me in some gossip rag, and suddenly, they know me. A handful of lies and innuendos get scattered about, and everyone gobbles them up like hungry chickens after cracked corn. Even my own friends think they're true. So what makes you so different? I know I'm not that person, but how could *you*?"

It was the way you kissed me, he wanted to tell her. *The way you curled your fingers against the nape of my neck. No pressure. You wanted contact, not power. You wanted what I wanted. To be touched.* He could have said it, but the rock-solidity of his certainty scared him. It was as if that one intimate encounter had opened up some kind of gateway into her soul, and during that brief moment of contact, he had come to know her, just a little, and that knowledge left him wanting more. Instead, he simply said, "I can tell. I don't need anyone else to make up my mind for me about you. Especially not some bored hack sitting in a cubicle somewhere, staring out a dim little window into an alleyway, trying to cook up a story before press time. I make my own decisions about people."

"And you've made one about me?"

"Yes."

She stared off into space for a long while. He could see the multicolored strobes reflected in her eyes: dancing dots that chased each other. Then she said, "They didn't make it up. Those journalists. They didn't make those stories up."

He frowned, bemused. "What?"

She hastily sought to clarify her statement. "I mean, it's not true, what they said I am. But they didn't just make it up off the top of their heads. They were fed the story by . . . someone."

His frown deepened, becoming menacing. "You mean someone deliberately spread all those lies about you? Someone you *know?*"

She couldn't meet his eyes. Instead, she scratched at the label of the Carib beer with the pink-tipped nail of her forefinger, stripping away paper that was wet with condensate and rolling it into tiny balls. "You could say that," she finally said.

"Who?"

"The man himself. My old manager, Tobias."

Damon was shocked. "Your own manager spread fake stories that he's suing you?"

She hastened to correct him. "No, he really *is* suing me. It's just not true what he, uh, said I did. I fired him, yes, but not because of anything untoward."

"And those other young men? The claims they made?"

She shook her head vehemently. "Lies. I hardly know those guys. I can barely remember them. He must have paid them off. Or offered them . . . something. I don't know. I swear, I'd never do a thing like that. Honest."

He didn't have to ponder that for a moment. As it had before, the conviction just came to him. "I know that."

She gave him a look that was almost suspicious but didn't ask again how he could know.

He braved treacherous waters by asking, "So, why did you fire him? Your agent, Tobias."

Down went her head once more, and the attack on the beer bottle label became so vigorous that he had to gently take it away from her and scoop all the paper balls off the table and deposit them into the ashtray between them. When there was nothing left to distract her, she was obliged to confess, "Because it wasn't working out. Not just the business part, but the . . . personal thing between us. Our relationship had gotten to the point where it was more than I could take. He was more interested in controlling me than he was in managing my career. Tobias was very aggressive. Very demanding. Near the end, I couldn't breathe. I couldn't turn around without his say-so. I felt like I was dying." Now she actually did look at him, directly in the eye, and the hurt he saw filled him with empathy. "Understand?"

Damon hesitated before answering. The din made by the partygoers all around them was nothing like the noise going on in his head as he let this piece of information sink in. So Kenya and her manager had been lovers. At least that part of the rumor had been true. Happened all the time, he reasoned, but something inside him still rebelled at the thought. He had no idea what this man looked like, or what kind of man he was, or even how deep the relationship between him and Kenya had been. Maybe they'd been in love. Maybe they'd just enjoyed a casual relationship of mutual convenience. He had no way of knowing. But the fact that this creep Tobias had touched her, availed himself of her body, and then humiliated her before the world made his hackles rise. It was the kind of thing that made a man want to hunt down a total stranger and make him tell the truth, take back every single filthy lie he'd spread, even if it required the use of brute force.

"I understand," he said in answer to her plea, but in reality, he didn't. Or, perhaps, he understood but didn't like it. His curiosity, his need to know, went way beyond protectionism. Questions tumbled around in his mind, but his lips, firmly pressed together, gave them no opportunity to escape. Which had come first? Had manager and client become lovers, or had her lover offered to manage her career? How long had it been before one relationship was transformed into the other? Had she kissed this man, Tobias, with the same fervor that she had kissed him this evening? Had Tobias been as entranced by the softness and delicacy of her feet?

Had they been in love?

Before he could say much more, the act on stage was over, and the gilded young singer and his backup girls strutted off stage. The MC, dressed from head to toe in a bright red devil costume—complete with glittering red shorts, horns, red body paint, an oversized papier-mâché devil's head, and a tail—did a funny dance, rolling on the floor and kicking his legs in the air as though being tormented by brimstone and hellfire, writhing across the stage to delighted applause, before finally getting to his feet and taking the microphone. "Did you-all like that?" he screamed at the audience. A cheer rose up, but he was not content with their response. "I said, did you-all like that?" The cheer grew louder.

Damon glanced over at Kenya. Their discussion set aside for a while at least, she was enjoying the little interlude; her eyes refocused on the stage. He was glad that the antics of the clown in the red devil suit had managed to bring a little cheer to her evening. At least she was distracted from their uncomfortable, even painful discussion, even though he wasn't. To Damon's eye, the man looked ridiculous in his outfit, but if he could make Kenya smile, well, God bless him.

The devil onstage picked up his tail and began twirling it mischievously, grinning like someone with an exciting secret. "You-all want more?"

"Yes!" the audience screamed.

"Nah, it's getting really late. Maybe you should just go home," he taunted them, looking as though he was about to leave the stage with their demands unmet. He threw down his microphone, picked up his pitchfork, which looked like a black-painted broomstick with cardboard prongs stuck down with tape, and headed for the edge of the stage. Groans and cries of "Noooo!" rippled through the crowd but turned into a cheer when he spun around again and, with much pomp, threw open his red-painted arms and shouted, "Ladies and gentlemen, let me not keep you waiting any longer. It's time to introduce you to a man who's new to the calypso scene, but let me tell you, he's going places. Put your hands together for . . ."

The small band—comprising little more than a drummer, an electric guitarist, a trumpeter, a trombonist, a young man on keyboards, and a girl with a tambourine— gave an enthusiastic fanfare, and a handful of firecrackers went off before the announcer finished his introduction: "Mr. Eric . . . Reeeeese!"

The smile left Kenya's lips with the speed of whiplash. She sucked air in through her open mouth, and her body grew rigid. Damon laid his hand over hers, just to let her know that he was there for her. She didn't even seem to register his touch. He chalked it up to the turmoil that she was surely experiencing and tried not to give in to pique.

The strobe lights around them spun wildly, flashing in time with the prolonged fanfare, and then a single spotlight picked out a figure that was bounding toward the stage. Damon focused on him as he made his way up onto the little wooden platform, as interested in what he was about to see as Kenya was, if that were possible.

What he saw froze his blood. The young man was in his early thirties, small in stature, no more than five foot eight, Damon estimated. Slender, almost rake thin, with short hair braided in a fine cornrow pattern close to his skull, and a Van Dyke beard that covered a pointed chin.

He had seen that face before in its more feminine version: the same fine cheekbones, full lips, and high brows. The same thick-lashed eyes, the same skin tone.

Eric was Kenya's twin. If these were not siblings, there was no telling what they could be. He thought of the small pile of documents he'd left back in his hotel room, all purporting to support the allegation that Eric and Kenya shared a parent.

All those papers were worth nothing. At least, they didn't amount to a hill of beans in the face of the physical evidence before him. He heard Kenya cry out. She pulled her hand away from his grasp, slapped it over her mouth, and shut her eyes tight against the sight.

The band's fanfare segued into the opening vamp of Eric's piece, and the man began snapping his fingers and nodding in time to the music, biding his time until the point where he was to jump in. Then he began singing. It was a catchy tune, as upbeat as that of his predecessor, but the lyrics were nowhere near as naughty. The song was about the heady excitement of Carnival and the seductive lure of the dance. The deep baseline spoke to something deep inside Damon's belly. Had the circumstances been different, he would almost have enjoyed it.

But the circumstances were not different. Unaware of the devastating impact that this man's arrival onstage was having on one young woman's life, the audience tapped their feet and began clapping their hands in rhythm. Damon felt the table rock as Kenya leaped wildly to her feet. How she managed to squeeze past him, he had no idea. Anguish made her fast.

But his own size and ability made him faster, and before she could make it up the aisle and back into the foyer of the club, he was at her side.

Chapter 11

Kenya felt Damon trying to pull her close, but she fought him like a wet and angry wildcat. She felt as though her skin was at the same time both burning up and freezing cold; even in the warm foyer, she was trembling.

She had to get out of here.

"Kenya, please," Damon was doing his best to restrain her. She knew he was big enough to do so, and he could have used physical force if he chose to, but was trying to placate her rather than pin her down.

Good. Let that gentlemanly instinct be his weakness but her advantage. She bucked and twisted and freed herself. "Don't touch me again!"

Instantly, he let his hands fall to his sides. Her shout had been strong enough to draw stares from the handful of people scattered about the foyer. A bouncer clad in black, his massive gut overhanging a tightly drawn belt and straining against the restrictions of his cotton shirt, fidgeted ominously. Although his sagging bulk was certainly no match for Damon's solid muscle, he looked powerful enough to cause some trouble. His meticulously shaved head gleamed under the dim lights, and flesh bulged under his shirt with every drawn breath. A single diamond in his ear did nothing to soften his image. He didn't look like the kind of man one would want to upset.

The bouncer wasn't the only one looking. The curiosity of those around her brought prickles to her face. Public attention wasn't something she actually welcomed these days. The last thing she needed was another scandal attached to her name, especially something that had to do with a man.

Then, as if things weren't bad enough, the bouncer detached himself from his post and came over with the precise, deliberate steps of a man on a mission. His gait, ponderous due to his overweight body, was slow. It was like waiting for a great dinosaur to approach, all the while wondering whether, as he reached them, he would strike or merely roar. Kenya dipped her head slightly, trying not to be too conspicuous.

"Anything the matter here, man?" he asked Damon, but his eyes were fixed upon Kenya's face. His manner was conversational, but the note of menace was implicit nonetheless.

"No, everything's fine." Damon chose the path of diplomacy rather than matching, or even one-upping, the man's implied threat. There would be nothing gained by meeting aggression with aggression.

The bouncer, not yet satisfied, turned to Kenya. "Miss?"

Everything was *not* fine, but certainly not in the way that the man assumed. She couldn't bear to cause a scene, much less bring trouble raining down upon Damon's head—even though she was sure he was more than capable of handling it. "No problem, thank you," she told him. "I didn't mean to cause any disturbance." She failed to keep a tremor out of her voice.

The man examined her face shrewdly for several more moments, and then, seemingly chalking the ruckus up to a lovers' quarrel, returned to his post but continued to monitor them intently.

"I have to go," she panted. Somehow, she couldn't find the air to fill her lungs. "I can't breathe."

"Not yet," he urged her. "We've found him. You've found him. Stay the course. You came for answers. Let's speak with him and get them."

"But you don't understand," she protested. "You didn't see what I saw. Eric . . . he's my father reborn. The way he walked. The way he moved. His voice. His eyes. Everything . . ."

"I know. I mean, I guessed that. I don't know your father, but I saw Eric in you."

"So it's obvious, then. My mind isn't playing tricks on me." His confirmation made her even more despondent. Things were really bad, she realized, if you found yourself hoping that you were hallucinating.

He could have lied to her, tried to soften the blow, but he was too big a man to do so. "No, it's not."

Kenya leaned her back against the foyer wall and hugged herself in an effort to still her trembling. Damon saw the gesture, and for a moment she thought he would reach for her again, but he was adhering to her admonition not to touch her. She wondered if that was what she had wanted after all. She remembered the wall of comfort his chest had been for her last night and almost regretted her rash command.

He hovered over her, close, but making no contact, hands clasped patiently in front of him, waiting for her to say something. What could she say? She'd just run face to face into living proof that her father was a liar. He'd lied to her mother, and he'd lied to her. Everything she'd known about him, and therefore herself, was wrong. Obviously, she had a brother, and this marriage between her father and this man's mother, if it ever really existed, and if it had never been terminated, made the family she'd been born into and grown up in a sham. Her heart ached, filled with pain for her mother, anger toward her father, and the guilt and embarrassment that came with discovering a parent's disgraceful secret.

Why? If her father were here now, that would be the only thing she would ask him. Why lie? Why bury a marriage, and another family, so deep that they remained hidden for nearly thirty years? But even if he *were* here, her father was too sick to give her an answer. And her mother, bless her, had devoted herself to caring for her husband until his disease would finally claim him. She was worn down, fatigued from providing constant care to the man she loved, and too fragile to bear such a shock. Even asking a few probing questions, trying to feel around for information rather than coming out directly, would raise her mother's suspicions and open her up to a world of hurt. She couldn't afford to take that chance. There was nothing, but nothing, that Kenya wouldn't stop at to keep her father's dirty secret from her mother. So all that left was a pile of questions that no one was around to answer.

Except Eric.

Damon was right. She'd known when she left New York that there was more than a small chance that this was what she would find. She'd come to Trinidad in search of a brother, and she'd found him. She would stay the course. It was the only thing she could do. She lifted her head. A new determination filled her eyes.

Damon saw it and smiled at her. It was only then that he disobeyed her admonition and took her hand. "Good girl," he said. There was warmth and pride in his voice. "I knew you'd be strong." He gave her hand a gentle pull and began to lead her, not back toward the main doorway into the club, but toward a side door that was half hidden in shadows.

"Where are we going?"

"Backstage." That single word invited no opposition.

Backstage. To meet a brother she never knew she had. The strangeness of that thought was daunting, but if there was one thing Kenya was not, it was a coward. Determinedly, she fell into step with Damon.

The bouncer squared his shoulders as they approached, blocking off access to the shadowy doorway as he did so. He was still polite, but his body language let them know that they had a better chance of crossing the Great Wall of China than they did of getting past him without his permission. "Can I help?"

If he thought she was coming all the way here to have a roadblock thrown in her way, he was wrong. She held his flat gaze with admirable cool. "Yes, please. We'd like to get backstage. It's very important."

"Is it?" If the granite face could show any emotion, it would have been amusement.

She refused to let him intimidate her. "Yes, it is. We need . . . I need to speak with Eric Reese. He's one of the singers here."

Now there really was amusement evident on his face. "I know who Eric Reese is," he answered. "He's onstage right about now." He pointed in the general direction of the club's inner hall. "Why don't you go back in and enjoy the show? You still have time to catch the last verse of his song if you hurry. And a whole lot of other acts besides."

He didn't understand! She tried to clarify. "No, I mean we need to see Eric in person. *Tonight.* We have to!"

The man gave her an "I've heard it all before" look, and Kenya's hopes sank. He gave her a smile that didn't reach his eyes. "Babes," he began patiently, but the term of endearment had a slight edge to it.

Before he could say anything else, Damon butted in. He used the same congenial tone that he had with Austin back in her father's old neighborhood earlier that afternoon. "Excuse me." A glance from him flashed a single message to her: *Let me handle this*. With a magician's flourish, he produced a plain white business card practically out of nowhere and handed it over to the man. "My name is Damon Saint Rose. We've come all the way from the States for this meeting, so I'm hoping you'll hear me out. I know you're just doing your job, and believe me, I've been there myself, so I understand your position, but the lady and I have a matter of urgency to discuss with Mr. Reese."

The man peered at the card and then looked intently at Damon before returning to the card again. Then he placed it face down on the table before him, and miraculously, he was all ears. "Yes, Mr. Saint Rose?"

What could have been written on that card? Kenya would have killed to have seen it. Some macho nonsense, she was willing to bet. DAMON SAINT ROSE, SECURITY TO THE STARS, or something like that. In spite of herself, she was irritated. She'd tried to reason with the man and had come up against a brick wall. Damon hands over a piece of cardboard and commands the man's full attention.

Damon was still talking. "As I said, the lady needs to have a conversation with Mr. Reese on a matter of urgent business. Urgent *family* business."

Kenya was stunned. Surely, he couldn't be saying that! Here she was, doing her best to keep her family affairs private, and he was running the risk of exposing her! She gave him a warning glance, but he studiously ignored her.

She felt herself bearing the brunt of the same intense visual inspection that she had from the bouncer before, but this time he was looking for something else. His scrutiny was slow and deliberate, moving along her face, taking in the shape of her eyes, the length of her nose, and the curve of her jaw. Then the light of recognition went on. "Ah" was all he said. Slowly, he stepped aside and held open the door that he had been so carefully blocking. He waved them through. "You can go straight down to the end and wait for him in the little room on the left. The white one with the red chairs in it. He should be there any minute now."

"Thank you" was all Damon said. He held out his hand, and the man shook it briefly. Kenya could have sworn she saw another piece of paper change hands; this time that piece of paper was green.

Damon ushered her along with his palm flat against the small of her back. If it had not been so important, she would have resisted. Where there should have been relief at being allowed inside, there was only annoyance at how easily Damon had done what she had failed to do. "You bribed him!" she gasped.

He was unrepentant. "Yes, I did."

"How much?"

"Does it matter?"

It didn't, actually. "Not really. What matters is that you *did* it."

"Consider it a tip, if that makes you feel better."

"It doesn't. First, you give that man, Austin, and half of the city, some half-baked story about us being newly-weds. Then, you spill the beans about me and Eric, a man I have never met, being related. Then you give that person money to let us backstage. *And* you interrupt me while I'm asking him to let us through, as though I couldn't have done it by myself."

Damon hadn't slackened his pace along the dimly lit, narrow corridor. "Would you have been successful?"

She knew she wouldn't have, but that annoyed her even more. "Maybe not," honesty forced her to admit.

"Then let's just do what we came here to do." He couldn't resist adding, "You can thank me later."

In all fairness, he had gotten them past the bodyguard, and she knew she was being ungrateful. She should have felt ashamed at her outburst, but the ease with which he seemed to surmount obstacles otherwise impenetrable to her rankled. She was used to doing things her own way, to solving her own problems. His protectiveness made her feel like a child.

She would thank him later, she decided, when she calmed down a little. When she could say it and mean it. Right now her nerves were balanced on a razor's edge.

Unperturbed by her ungraciousness, Damon stopped in an open doorway. In sharp contrast to the foyer, the corridor, and the rest of the club, the little room to which they had been directed was brightly, even harshly lit. Brilliant fluorescent lights bounced off white walls, causing Kenya to hold her hand up before her eyes until they became adjusted. A red couch dominated the small room, and it was draped with articles of clothing and bits and pieces of gaily colored costumes.

"Not much space for you to sit," Damon said solicitously, "but I can clear a spot for you if you like."

Still irritated with him, she waved away his offer. "Thanks, no." Then she added, as an explanation, "Too nervous."

"I understand."

They waited, Damon with his arms folded, intently focused on Kenya's face, and she with her thumbnail grasped between her teeth, stripping away her manicure. The music emanating from the nearby stage was muffled but loud enough for them to hear it come to a final crescendo, and then a wave of applause swept the singer offstage.

Kenya braced herself and hissed a hurried prayer. A door opened.

Eric.

She could feel her heartbeat in her throat. Everything in her wanted to run, run, run rather than face this person who had so suddenly changed her life, and who threatened to change her parents' lives, but loyalty to them kept her put. She met the man's arrival with all the courage she could muster.

His step was light as he entered, still buoyed up by the elation of his enthusiastic reception onstage. He was loudly humming the last few bars of his song, and it was several seconds before he noticed he was not alone. When he did so, he stood stock-still.

She tried to put a name to every emotion that she was feeling but failed. All she knew was that they were whirling about within her, crashing around like silver balls in a pinball machine.

He didn't say anything right away but found a small towel and carefully dried the perspiration on his face before coming to stand just before her. He stared, searching her face with the intensity of a man examining a curious specimen. Looking for signs of their shared blood, no doubt, although they weren't that hard to find. To give him credit, she would have done the same, had she not been shaking uncontrollably.

"It's you," Eric said with a note of satisfaction. His breathing was still rough from his exertions.

"Yes."

"You found me."

"Yes."

Should they shake hands? Hug? Or, considering the manner in which he had drawn her there, should she brace herself for some manifestation of his hostile intent? Before she had a chance to find out, Damon cleared his throat, drawing attention to himself. Already on edge, she jumped slightly at the sound. Eric's arrival had all but shunted aside her awareness of Damon's presence. Eric looked almost startled to notice that Damon was in the room. He frowned suspiciously. "Who's he?"

Damon stepped forward, offering his hand as he had to the bouncer. "Damon Saint Rose."

Eric didn't take the hand. He directed his next question at Kenya. "Why's he here? Why did he come with you?"

She half expected Damon to concoct some sort of cover story to explain his presence, as he had done before, but he chose the more difficult path of total honesty. "I'm her security escort. I'm simply here to ensure her safety." His hand was still extended, but when it became evident that Eric had no intention of taking it, he let it fall gracefully to his side. He didn't look in the least bit put out by the snub.

Eric eyed him again, even more intently, like a male dog discovering another within the boundaries of his territory. Again, he addressed Kenya rather than Damon. "You came with a *bodyguard*?" His disbelieving laugh was a short, bitter bark. "I thought I told you to come alone? I thought I told you not to tell anyone?"

"But I didn't!" she protested. "At least, I didn't mean to. And I was coming alone—"

"You're not alone now," Eric pointed out accusingly. "You such a spoilt little movie star that you have to walk with your lackey? What, did you think I was going to hurt you? Did you expect to find a wilderness down here? What did our father teach you about us? That we're a bunch of barbarians?"

"No!" That wasn't what she'd expected at all! Far from it. Her father had never spoken of his island with anything other than love and nostalgia. "Daddy loved it here!"

Eric snorted. "Yeah? Not enough to come back, though. Not even once, to see his *family*."

Kenya cringed. Family. Here she was, meeting her unknown relative for the first time, and he was so full of bitterness that all she could feel was hurt.

Eric jerked his chin in Damon's direction. "You think you and I could do this alone? You don't need him; I promise I don't bite. We can just have a civil discussion in private, eh? Send your bodyguard away, and we'll talk."

Damon was not taking too kindly to being excluded like this. He spoke up. "First of all, Mr. Reese, Kenya did not hire me. She was provided with an escort by her manager, without her knowledge, so I don't think you would be right to see my presence as a slur upon your country. Secondly, now that I'm here, I stay here. I was hired to keep her company and protect her interests, so I'm sorry. I can't be 'sent away'."

Eric look displeased at Damon's interruption. He shook his head vigorously but directed his response at Kenya. "I told you to come on your own. I'm not talking to you unless we're alone."

"Your confidentiality is assured," Damon responded. "Whatever you have to say to her, you can say in front of me. I don't need to intervene; I just need to be here."

It was as though Damon had not even spoken. "Alone, or nothing, Kenya. Your choice." He pointed at the door in a gesture that spoke more loudly than his words.

Kenya's nervousness turned to dismay. Was he really planning on sending her away? After she had come so far? Surely not! She turned her pleading eyes on Damon. "Damon, please. Let me have just a few minutes."

He did not even hesitate. "I'm sorry, Kenya, but I can't do that."

What was he saying? Hadn't he heard Eric say that she

would receive no information unless they were alone? "You're not listening to me! I don't want you here!"

"You didn't want me around yesterday, either, or this morning, but I became useful."

She could have admitted that he had been a great source of support and solace to her since his arrival, but her frustration was mounting. He'd been helpful, but he was also a bully, and she'd been pushed around by a man once too often. If she needed his protection, she would darn well ask for it. "I'm telling you to leave us, Damon. I'm ordering you." She set her jaw, hoping to look tough.

If intimidation was her goal, she missed it by a mile. Damon was implacable. "No. And you can't order me to do anything. As I just explained to Eric, you are not my employer. And your employer's orders are not to let you out of my sight."

He couldn't be serious! Was he really planning on foisting his unwelcome presence on her like that? Despite her vociferous objections? "That's illegal!"

He lifted a brow. "In what way?"

She searched her buzzing brain. "Unlawful detainment!"

"I'm not keeping you here; I'm just staying wherever you are. If you leave, I'd leave with you."

That was true. She tried again, grasping at straws. "Stalking, then!"

Damon was unfazed. "Kenya, I am not leaving you alone with a stranger in his dressing room at this hour of the night in a strange country. Forget it."

"Ten minutes!" she pleaded desperately. "Five!"

Before Damon could answer, Eric, who had been following the conversation with a disapproving expression, cut in. "Look, tell you what. The two of you sort this out on your own. But my position remains the same. Either you speak to me alone, or we don't speak at all." He picked up a large black gym bag, quickly shoved a few items into it, and prepared to leave. "You know where to find me now. If you feel like leaving your guard dog home, let me know."

"No!" Kenya pleaded. She made a desperate grab at the sleeve of Eric's shirt, but he was already moving. "Do something!" she yelled at Damon. "Stop him!"

He shook his head regretfully. "I can't. I'm sorry."

The door to the little room was thrown open with such force that it slammed into the wall, and then all Kenya could see was Eric's stiff, receding back. When he was at the top of the hall, near the exit to the foyer, he turned slightly, just long enough to yell back at her, "Tell our father, I said hello!" With evident satisfaction at that last verbal salvo, he disappeared.

Kenya was so mad, she would have thrown something at Damon if there had been something nearby to throw. "See what you did! Do you see what you did? I found him! He was right here and willing to talk to me, and you ruined it! How could you?"

"I couldn't leave you," he tried to explain.

That old chestnut was beginning to get a little tired, as far as she was concerned. Who did he really think he was? "I *told* you to leave me! I didn't want you here!"

"It doesn't matter if you tell me to leave you or not; I can't do that. That would be dangerous, and wrong. Like I said, there's no way I'm leaving you alone in a place like this"—he waved his arm around the room—"in the back room of a nightclub after midnight, in a strange land, with someone you don't know. Forget it."

"But he's my . . . b . . . b—" She couldn't finish the word. Her anger had whipped up to gale force, and she could only bluster.

"Brother? There's no proof of that. Not until we can

do more checking come Ash Wednesday. And until then, we treat every situation with a healthy dose of caution."

Was he being obtuse? He already admitted that he had seen the resemblance between them. "But he looks just like me. Just like Dad! You said so yourself!"

At least, he agreed with that. "Yes, the similarities are there. And we'll find a way to prove it, yea or nay. But brother or not, this is a man who has been sending you threatening letters for months, full of innuendo. Threatening to hurt your parents' feelings. To embarrass you. Did you really want to be alone with him?"

"I'm not afraid of him. I'm not afraid of anyone!"

"That makes you reckless, not brave." For the first time, he moved from the position he had initially taken when they had entered the room and tried to lay his hand on her arm, but she danced away. Whereas he had shown no emotion at Eric's rejection, he looked hurt now. "Come," he pleaded. "Let me take you back to the hotel."

Was he kidding? Did he really think she was sitting in the close confines of a car with him after what he had done? That she was so dependent upon him that as mad as she was, she was going to climb into his car, meek as a lamb, and let him drive her home like an overbearing parent scooping up an errant teenager caught breaking curfew? If so, she had news for him.

She had to put some space between them, so she began hurrying up the hallway, almost tripping over her heels in her haste. He followed her, sticking closer than a shadow. As he did so, she noticed that his limp, absent for most of the day, had returned. He must be exhausted after a long flight, no sleep the night before, and an entire afternoon pounding the pavements and asking questions. She was too upset to feel sorry for him.

They passed the bouncer, who gave her a surprisingly warm smile and nodded at Damon as they left. Appar-

ently, whatever denomination Damon had slipped him
for granting them access to the back of the club was
enough to sweeten his mood as well. That knowledge
soured hers even more. It was as though he felt she
couldn't achieve anything on her own. Well, she was
showing him!

Without acknowledging the bouncer, she rushed
through the entrance doors and found herself on the
pavement outside. She was panting from emotion and
exertion, moving fast, scanning the still teeming streets
for a taxi. Damon might think he could boss her around,
but he was wrong. She was heading back to the hotel,
and she was going back alone.

Chapter 12

When well rested, Damon moved with amazing grace for a large man, but as exhausted as he was, he hobbled, betrayed by his unmerciful body. He almost fell out of step with Kenya; it took supreme effort to stick close to her. Outside, the streets were busy with partygoers and people who were still on their way to or from the plethora of Carnival shows that would continue at various hot spots in the capital city for most of the night. People who had spilled outside from the club lingered on the sidewalk, drinks in hand, chatting and laughing. They were a human obstacle course, and Kenya took full advantage of the fact by dodging between them, further slowing his pursuit.

Once she had put enough distance between them, she began hopping up and down on the strip of sidewalk directly in front of the club, straining her neck at passing cars, trying to spot a taxi. He could have warned her not to expect a checkered cab to appear out of the darkness to rescue her; this was not New York, and as far as he had read, taxis just did not operate that way. He did, in fact, recognize one or two of them, identifiable only by the letter *H* on their license plate, but said nothing that would make her any the wiser. Instead, he cut off her path, blocking her as he once had many an opposing football player intent on a pass. "What do you think you're doing?"

Her breath came in huffs and puffs, seasoned by a few soft curses. "Looking for a taxi, if you'd let me pass."

Did she really think he was allowing her to risk her neck like that? Not on his watch. He was tired and in no mood to soften his assertion. He informed her baldly, "You're going back with me. I brought you here; I take you back. It's real simple." Ignoring her gape of astonishment, and cutting off any protest before it could form on her lips, he removed the car keys from his pocket and clicked the remote in the direction of their rental. Oblivious to their tension, it chirped cheerily at them, blinking its lights and unlocking its doors with a soft click. He reached out, opened the passenger door, and said, "Get in, Kenya." His voice was low, but firm.

Rebellion blazed in her eyes. "You're *telling* me to get in?"

"Yes." He motioned toward the car seat once again.

"You're *ordering* me—"

"If you don't want to think of it as an order, think of it as a request. But this is neither the time nor the place for semantics. I'm tired, you're tired, and it's time to go home. *Please* get in."

"Like heck," she railed. "I do not appreciate what went on in there. You spoiled everything. Everything! Why'd you have to be so stubborn? Why'd you have to be so pigheaded? All you had to do was leave, just for a few minutes. All you had to do was cut me some slack."

"Cutting slack is not part of my job description," he responded dryly.

She dismissed his statement with an agitated gesture. "There you go! Hiding behind your job! Pretending that you're the way you are because of what you do for a living. Well, I have news for you. You're the way you are because of *what* you are!"

"And that would be . . . ?" At any other time, in another situation, he would have been almost amused by her outrage. But the edge in her voice, pitched high by agitation, reminded him that this was certainly no laughing matter.

Her response drove the last shred of amusement from him. "A bully! That's right, Damon; you're a bully. You're a control freak, and a mean one at that. You don't push me around and butt in on my business because you have to, you do it because you like to. Well, you know what? Whatever little power trip you get off on by imposing your presence on people, don't do it with me. I'm not a little girl, and I don't have to take this from you. I'm a grown woman! I can take care of myself!"

Her deafening words reverberated in his ears. *I can take care of myself.* Funny, he thought, once a woman says that to you, you never forget. *I'm a grown woman, and I can take care of myself.* The words rattled about in his skull like dried peas in a tin can. First, there was one voice, and then there were two. Kenya, enraged, bellowing for him to let her be. And Jewel, her voice clear to him, as though she were leaning over his shoulder and whispering in his ear. That had been her litany. Her plea for him to back off. Her declaration of independence. He'd always hated to hear her say it, partly because he had known that it was not true, and partly because he had feared that it just might be. He'd invested so much into guarding Jewel since the day he'd met her that stopping would have left him bewildered.

But she'd begged him, pleaded with him to back off, *to cut her some slack,* and he'd loved her, so he had. She'd paid the ultimate price for his negligence.

"You don't know what you're saying," he said raggedly, forcing his words past his pain. People were looking;

many of the laughing conversations that had been going on when they had exited the club had gone silent, but he was too blinded by pain to care.

"I know exactly what I'm saying," she countered. "I'm telling you to leave me alone."

He wasn't sure which was greater, his fury or his anguish. "I can't," he began. How could he explain to her how deep her words had cut, and how bound he was to protect her, without betraying Jewel? Without spilling his guts about his own guilt and shame? "I want to oblige you, but I can't."

"You don't have a choice," she snapped back. "I am not your prisoner. This is a free country, and I am an adult. I've committed no crime; you have no power over me. So I'm only going to say this one more time: go away. Leave me alone. Got it?"

Defeat. It burned in his throat and stank in his nostrils. And then he knew which emotion was greater. Fury had won. His anger expanded with the force of an exploding star, growing hotter by the second. "Very well, Kenya. I'll leave you alone. I take it, I'm dismissed." His teeth were so tightly clenched that it was a wonder he could speak intelligibly. He could barely see her face beyond the red veil that obscured his vision.

She hesitated and then confirmed his statement, "You take it right. Feel free to go back to New York any time it suits you. I'll talk to my manager and see if I can get him to let you keep your advance. Even if I have to reimburse—"

The humiliation of being sent home from a job for the first time in his career was bad enough, but for her to offer him money he had not earned, like some sort of consolation prize, was unbearable. "That won't be necessary," he said. "My cousin will have a check ready for Ryan Carey the day I get back."

She looked almost abashed, but her stubbornness won out. "Fine, if that's the way you want it." Then she seemed at a loss for anything more to say. They regarded each other in awkward silence across a fence of animosity.

He considered offering her a lift back to the hotel, since he was going there anyway, but feared yet another rebuff, so he turned toward his car. "Good night," he said, but his farewell was a whisper.

She heard him, anyway, and countered with, "Goodbye." She whirled on her heels, turned her back to him, and headed for the curb.

He shut the car door that he had held open for her and then opened his own. He was about to get in when something—and thereafter he would always wonder what that something was—made him turn and look toward her again. Then everything simultaneously sped up and slowed down. Time and space grew distorted. He had just enough time to register that she was about to cross the road, but he couldn't fathom why. To put more space between herself and him? Whatever the reason, he saw her turn her head to the left, looking for oncoming traffic, and then, seeing none, she stepped into the void.

Only, this was Trinidad, not back home, and here traffic came from the right.

The silver gray twin-cab pickup bearing down on her blended so well with its dark surroundings that it had all the visibility of a stalking panther. Damon heard it before he saw it—but Kenya did neither.

His mind went blank. There was no fear, no logic, no reason. Even the instinct for self-preservation was gone. All he could think of was her, and the fact that if someone did not intervene, she would be mowed down like a dandelion on a lawn. He lunged forward, a coiled bundle of power and speed, forgetting the limitations of his injured knee, the people around him, and his own safety. He could hear the screeching of brakes as the driver of the pickup spotted Kenya directly in his path, and he saw the horror frozen on the man's face in the yellow glow of the small houselight within the cab. He felt the impact of his body against Kenya's as he grabbed her, bringing to mind many a blow from his football days, as player collided with player. Even above the shrieks of the patrons and partygoers on the sidewalk, he heard Kenya's cry, which died on her lips as the breath whooshed out of her.

She was in his arms, and then both of them came down hard upon the roadway, and all he could do as he landed upon her was pray that he did not break any of her bones. There was a loud, crunching noise, which he knew would linger in his memory for some time to come, as the pickup, in a tailspin from which it failed to recover, slammed into their parked car, shoving it several feet until it was stopped by a light pole.

Agony. His knee felt as though it were caught in a tangle of barbed wire, which dug in deep, piercing his skin, shredding cartilage, ligaments, tendons, and flesh until it relentlessly caught hold of the bone beneath and held it in its grip. But his mind could not grasp the pain for long.

The only thing he could think of was Kenya.

There were shouts nearby as people converged on the scene of the accident, some to gawk, others to lend assistance. He could feel helping hands trying to lift him to his feet. He let himself be pulled up off of her but would not stand until he could see her face.

Her eyes were saucers rimmed with shock. Her face was so ashen that he feared for her. "You okay?" It was a plea, not a question.

She stammered an answer through dry lips. "What . . . what was that?"

"A truck. You were looking the wrong way. You didn't see it coming."

She rubbed her forehead in bewilderment as she sat up. "Did it hit me?"

"No," he answered sheepishly. "That was me. I tried to . . ." He reached out and began gingerly patting her down, checking for injuries. "Did I hurt you?"

"'I'll let you know when feeling returns to my legs," she answered, throwing him into further panic. But then she gave a smile that was half grimace, and he understood that she was simply indulging in her own brand of graveyard humor.

"Thank God," he breathed. "I thought I'd pretty much squashed you."

"I'll live," she answered dryly, and then the full import of her words struck her. "Thank you. *Thank you, Damon.*" She put her hand against his cheek, and it was trembling almost as much as he was. "You could have left me and gone on your way. I would have been—"

He couldn't bear for her to finish the thought, so he interrupted. "I wouldn't have left you." He was so relieved that she was all right that he wanted to lift her into his arms and hold her close, feel her heart beating against his to prove to himself that she really was alive and well, but, after all, an accident had taken place, and there were formalities to attend to.

By now the driver of the pickup had extricated himself from the vehicle, also unharmed, but as stunned by the turn of events as they were. After making one final check to assure himself that Kenya was all right and in good hands, Damon collected his thoughts, dusted himself down, and went over to him.

By the time the accident reports were taken, the visit to the nearest police station and the completion of the necessary forms and documents, several hours had passed. Damon was so tired, and his leg in such pain, that he felt twice his age. Once their taxi had dropped them off in the driveway of the Bird of Paradise, Kenya nagged him to lean on her, but he doggedly refused, even though each step up the hotel stairs was like walking barefoot on rusty nails. What kind of man would he be if he leaned on a tiny thing like her?

He unlocked the door to his room, expecting her to take her leave and go to her own, but she followed him in. The room was filled with a faint predawn glow, and that was all he needed. He chose not to turn on the lights and be forced to tolerate their harshness. All he needed was to crash and get some sleep, and if he didn't make it to his bed, the floor would do nicely.

But Kenya was fussing, pulling back his sheets and yanking at his clothes. "Get undressed," she ordered him.

"What?" His fuzzy brain couldn't process the information.

"Get your clothes off, and get into bed," she said again slowly, like a no-nonsense head nurse to a sick child. Her hands were working at the buttons on his shirt, but she was finding the job difficult. "You need to lie down before you fall down."

She was right about that. He didn't have the strength to argue, or to be modest, for that matter. He pushed her hands away. "I can do it," he told her. And then he added, just in case she took offence, "Thanks."

"I'll get the ice."

After carefully undoing his holster and placing his weapon in the drawer of the bedside table, he balled up his shirt in his hands and tossed it into a corner. Then came the painful task of sitting on the edge of the bed so that he could take off his shoes. He literally heard his bones creak, and then his body gave up the game. He could neither lie back nor get up again. The situation was so incongruous, he almost laughed. He felt like an old machine that didn't work so well anymore, with half its parts obsolete, and the other half out of order.

Kenya had been rooting around in his mini-fridge and returned with a tray's worth of ice cubes in a plastic bag wrapped in a face towel. She saw his predicament and came over to his bedside and set the ice down. Dropping easily to her knees, she then began to untie his shoe-laces. "Here, let me."

He didn't even bother to utter so much as a token protest but accepted her help meekly and thankfully. As she carefully removed his shoes, their encounter of the afternoon before immediately came to him. The last time their roles were reversed, and it had been he who knelt before her, taking her small, elegant foot in his hands, planting kisses along the instep.

What a long time ago that seemed! Since then, they'd had a fight to end all fights. He'd said things to her, and she to him. As she helped him, he examined her face for signs that the same sequence of events was going through her mind, but she was all business. Did this mean that a truce had been called? Or were her actions merely motivated by her gratitude for his having saved her life?

He shivered. How close they had been to disaster. How wrong things could have turned out tonight, if after they had finished shouting cruel things at each other, he had left her to her own devices. If that indefinable *something* had not made him look back. He would have lost a woman he was looking after . . . again.

He had to say something. "Kenya, I—"

"Shush." She was done with his shoes and socks and was now regarding him with her head tilted to one side, trying to figure out a delicate way to remove his belt and trousers.

He decided to spare her the discomfort. "I'll get that."

He popped the buckle on his belt and began working on his zipper.

Her professional, detached demeanor slipped a little. She lifted her hand to shield her eyes. "You'd better be wearing something under there!" she said hastily.

He'd have laughed if he hadn't been too tired. "Rest easy, my sweet. I'm modestly clothed under here. The last thing I'd do is offend you."

True to his word, he managed to wriggle out of his pants to reveal a perfectly acceptable pair of soft gray boxers, which, though close-fitting, did an adequate job of sparing them both any embarrassment. He couldn't help but notice, though, that her eyes strayed for a brief moment before rising to lock with his. Her confusion was visible, but brief.

Recovering fast, she placed her palm flat on his chest and pushed him back onto the bed. "Lie back," she advised him, unnecessarily, he thought, as that had already been achieved.

He felt the welcoming softness of the pillow beneath his head and closed his eyes. Whatever she was planning to do with him, she was free to do. He gave himself up to rest and her tender care.

The shock of the ice against his knee almost made him shoot out of the bed. In the flurry over the removal of his pants—and the sensation that buzzed through him at the precious look on her face when he did so— he had all but forgotten that her ministrations had been motivated by his injury, and not by him. His exhausted brain was thrown into such confusion by the contact that he was not sure if the sensation was one of extreme cold or extreme heat. He couldn't prevent a groan from escaping his lips.

"Take it easy." Kenya said softly. She was sitting at the edge of his bed, holding the ice pack in place, but still managed to stretch up and lay her other hand lightly on his brow. "Relax, Damon. I know it hurts. I can see that it hurts. But I'm trying to help."

"I know. It's just—"

"Don't you have painkillers?"

He shook his head slowly, so as not to dislodge her hand. That felt way too good. The last thing he wanted was to make her take it away. "No. Nothing. I never use them."

She frowned down at his knee and then back up at him. "Damon! You've got more stitches in your knee than a baseball! I've seen how much it hurts you. Why don't you take something for it? There are lots of powerful drugs on the market today that would put you out of your misery with almost no side effects."

He knew exactly what drugs there were on the market for his ailment, and powerful they were indeed. Too powerful. The problem with painkillers was that while they did ease the pain, they relaxed his mind as well as his body, and in so doing, they unleashed the monsters of his subconscious, which he could only keep at bay while he was in total mental control. The painkillers strong enough to end his physical pain brought sleep, too, and sleep brought dreams filled with the woman he'd allowed to be lost.

Call him a coward, but he'd rather suffer physical pain than drink the bitter cocktail of guilt, anguish, and loss.

Kenya was talking. "I've got a few tablets back in my room," she volunteered. "If you give me a second, I'll—"

"No!" He shouted louder than he had intended to, and she jumped, startled. He tried to soften his protest. "No, don't. Thank you, but I don't need any. I'll be fine. A little rest, and I'll be fine."

She looked doubtful, but she stayed. Then, curiosity got the better of her. "What happened?"

"What happened with what?" he asked, although he knew very well what she was referring to.

She took her hand away from his forehead and touched his leg lightly, just above his scars. "With this. What happened? Did you get it on the job?" Her last question was a whisper, as though she expected the perpetrators of the violence upon his person to come leaping out of the shadows, brandishing weapons.

This time he smiled outright. He vaguely remembered telling her something about it being an old war wound, back when they had first met, and letting her believe the worst. Now he was obliged to explain. "Football."

"Oh. College?"

"Pro." If his answer was a little curt, it was because it wasn't something he talked much about.

"Oh!" Her brows lifted in surprise, as though that little bit of information did not fit in too well with the thug image of him he had deliberately let her harbor. "You played pro ball?"

He nodded. "In another incarnation, yes."

"I don't remember you."

"You a football fan?"

"No."

"Well, then there's no good reason that you should. I was good, but I can't say I ever had the chance to become a star. I got this," he pointed down at his injury, "before I really reached my prime. Besides, you were probably too young to remember me at the time, anyway. You were probably in grade school."

"I'm twenty-seven!" she responded hotly. "I would not have been too young . . ." She trailed off when she became aware that he was only kidding.

"You look twenty," he said softly. *And, sometimes, act twelve,* he could have said, but her hands on his leg felt too good, and the last thing he needed right now was to send her storming from the room.

"Do you miss it?"

"Miss what?"

"Football. Playing."

Not as much as he had expected to, he thought. This job had brought with it more fulfilment than he had ever imagined, even though at the time that he'd begun playing, sport had been his first and only love. "A little. Not as much as I thought I would. When I was injured, I was young, and sports was the only thing I was interested in. I thought my life was over. But this job grew on me. I suits me, I think. I get to travel and meet people." His eyes lingered on her face. *Lord*, he thought, *she does look twenty.* His penchant for nurturing surfaced, and he added softly, "Take care of them, even if they don't want me to."

She took her chastisement meekly, gnawing on her lip to stop herself from saying something. Then, after a few moments, she said, "I'm sorry. I really, really am."

"What for?" he asked, equally subdued.

"For all those things I said to you last night at the club. I was mean. . . ."

They'd both been mean to each other. He let it pass. "Don't worry about it."

"No," she insisted, "I was horrible. I said some things that were unforgivable. My only excuse is that I was under stress, what with meeting Eric for the first time. And I was tired."

She looked tired. Strain showed on her face, pulling the corners of her lips down and bringing shadows to her eyes. Guilt overtook him. Here he was, prone, allowing himself to indulge in her tender care, when she looked about to drop. "I'm a pig," he began to apologize. "*I* should be seeing about *you.* I know you must be hurting, too."

She shook her head vehemently, her denial fuelled by pride. "Nope. I'm fine."

"I must have hurt you, falling down on you like that. We both hit the ground pretty hard, and I was right . . . on top of you. I'm not a small man."

The fatigue that was tugging at the corners of her mouth gave way to a glimmer of amusement. "That, you aren't. But I'm fine. Honest." To demonstrate, she stuck out an elbow. "Just a little graze here. It's a scratch, honestly. It didn't even bleed much." Then she turned her face to one side, so that he could get a clear view of a purplish blotch that ran along her jawline. "And this, but it hardly hurts at all."

Her stoicism made him feel even worse about having given in to his own pain. He felt a rush of affection for her. Always trying to be strong, even when she didn't need to. He reached down and stroked her cheek. He was about to tell her that he was feeling much better now, and that she should go to her room and try to get some sleep. But touching her proved to be a mistake. He could say nothing more. Instead, his hand spoke for him, moving slowly from her cheek to her jaw, his fingers gently outlining the shape of the bruise, seeking to soothe as well as to judge for himself the extent of her hurt, but she winced, and he relented. Instead, they followed their natural course to the curve of her full lips and then moved downward to her throat. He felt movement under his fingers as she swallowed hard.

All else was forgotten.

"Stay," he said quietly.

"What?"

"Stay. Here with me. The sun's coming up, and we're both exhausted. We both need sleep, lots of it. I'm not suggesting anything more. Just stay here with me. It's a big bed. All you have to do is lie next to me. Keep me company. Sleep here, Kenya."

He wasn't sure if what he saw in her eyes was fear, doubt, or longing. He was on the verge of hastily apologizing, taking back his request, and hurrying her from the room so he could bury his embarrassment deep in his pillow. But that spark that could have been longing stopped him. He watched her face intently, searching for more.

"Why?" was all she could ask.

Because I'm lonely, he could have told her. *Because the last time I had a woman's body close to mine was four years ago, and then I lost her. And it's a horrible, horrible feeling. And I almost lost you, too, tonight. If you stay here, next to me, if I keep you close, then I can keep it from happening again.* But there was no way that he could say all that. To admit as much would be frailty. Instead, he said heavily and truthfully, "Because I don't think I'd get to sleep if you left."

She was thinking. Her gaze ran the length of his body and then took in the bed on which he lay. It was a huge bed, indeed, and he almost rushed to reiterate that she didn't have to touch him if she didn't want to. She just had to be there. But before he could speak, a miracle happened.

Slowly, she rose from her seated position next to him and removed the ice pack that she was holding against his knee. She disappeared into the bathroom, but before he could become too anxious, she returned without it. Her eyes held his steadfastly, and he could see a glimmer of determination, of courage over doubt. Slowly, she pulled at the thin straps of her frosted lime cotton dress, which was by now grubby and ragged from her earlier fall in the road . . . and the dress fell in a puddle at her feet.

Underneath, she wore a plain, white cotton slip with a lacy hem, the same slip he had touched in awe as he had knelt at her feet the evening before. He found himself half hoping that she would keep it on, because he was quite sure that he would not able to bear the exquisite sight of her were she to take off anything else, but yet he was disappointed when she removed nothing more. Instead, she bent over and retrieved her dress, and then looked awkwardly around the room, seeking a place to drape it.

"Leave it anywhere, Kenya," he groaned. "Drop it on the floor. Throw it on a chair. I don't care. Just come over here."

She obeyed, letting it fall at her feet once again, and walked toward the bed. She seemed about to approach it from the side on which he lay, but that would have meant clambering over him to lie down. The mad flush on her face told him she was too shy to do that. Instead, she skirted the bed and climbed in from the other side. She stretched out, lying on her back with her hands folded across her chest like Juliet in repose in the family sepulchre. She stared up at the ceiling, seeming deeply entranced by the whirring of the rattan fan blades above them. Not once did she look his way.

He turned his head to her, taking in the shape of her profile, eyes moving down her throat to the curve of her breasts, which hid behind her barely there cotton slip like deer behind forest brambles. Beyond that, her belly rose and fell in a staccato rhythm, giving away her nervousness.

With great effort, he turned on his side to face her and reached across the expanse of bed that separated them. "Closer," he urged her. "Don't be afraid of me."

Always defiant, she denied his assertion. "I'm not," she insisted stoically. "I'm not afraid of you."

"Then come to me," he took the risk of asking. If she didn't, he decided, he wouldn't ask a second time. He would thank heaven above for small mercies and hope that his body would subside enough for him to get some much needed sleep.

For several agonizing seconds it seemed that she had not heard him. Then the tip of her tongue flicked out and moistened her lower lip . . . and she moved toward him. Next to him, pressed against his body, she seemed smaller than she did when they were both standing, and when they could benefit from the barrier that their clothing provided. He did not let that daunt him. She was small, yes, but she was no child. As she settled against his body, he could feel the full curve of her hip and the swell of her bottom and breasts. The feel of her was so entrancing, so giddying, that he immediately rued that rash promise he had made moments before about not asking for anything more than to sleep next to her. He ached to pull her hard against him and claim her mouth with his. That silly cotton slip was so thin that he could pop its spaghetti straps without effort and whip it off her with one hand. Then she would be bare to him. . . .

But a promise was a promise, and a gentleman's word was his bond. So he offered the crook of his arm as a pillow, and she laid her head against it, and with that, he was content.

"You okay?" he ventured to ask.

"Mmmm," was all she answered, signalling to him that words were not what she needed right now. He took the hint and shut up, closing his eyes and concentrating instead on the feel of her chest against his. He let his other arm rest upon her hip and willed his body to relax. He felt the pain slip away from his leg, as though drawn from him by a witch's poultice, simply because her own leg was pressed against it. As she drew the pain from him, she filled the void left behind with solace and a tremendous sense of peace. He closed his eyes.

It was amazing how long four years could feel. In that space of time, he had learned that eternity was relative. Four years was a little more than fourteen hundred nights, give or take. In the span of a man's life, it wasn't much. But when it was counted in terms of endless sleepless hours, in terms of the insomnia that had fallen upon him like a curse or a penance, it was plenty. He would not have bothered to waste his time to try to think back to a single night within that period in which he could honestly say he had fallen asleep content and awakened refreshed.

It was not just the loneliness. He'd become accustomed to sleeping alone, without the comfort of a woman's body next to him. It was the self-denial, the almost conscious imposition of this purgatory upon himself, as though the fog of restless exhaustion in which he spent his days somehow made up for his crime. Like Cerberus, the mythical three-headed guard dog, he'd lapsed into sleep while keeping watch upon a treasure of great value, and it had been stolen from him.

But this morning, for the first time in years, with Kenya's soft, warm body next to his, he fell into a sleep that weighed him down, entangling his arms and legs like overgrown seaweed, pulling him under the surface of the sea. It was a sleep of great peace, of tremendous consolation—until the anguished dreams began.

"Damon." Jewel's voice was muffled, but he knew it in an instant. He wanted to call out her name, but sleep made his tongue thick, and no sound could escape his throat. He felt her; he knew she was there, next to him, against him. He could smell her sweetness, hear her breathing.

"Damon!" Her voice was distant, panicked. A cry for help. This time he did wake, throwing sleep from himself like a heavy blanket that was threatening to smother him. The brightness of the orange strips of light visible along the edges of the windows, like window frames around the blinds, told him that he had been sleeping for a very long time. The sheets were tangled around him, clinging to skin damp with the sweat of nightmares.

The clouds of sleep billowed across his mind, and then it was clear again. He knew exactly where he was: he was in Trinidad, not New York. He was with Kenya, not Jewel. He turned his head to his side, expecting to see her as she had been hours before, lying curled on her side. But all he could see was the faintest impression of her body, a network of wrinkles in the sheets where she had lain. Once again, he'd fallen asleep with a woman in his arms . . . and woken up alone.

Chapter 13

Kenya splashed cool water on her face, welcoming its powers of revival. It was late, well into the day, and though she'd slept long and hard, fatigue was still heavy upon her. It was impossible to tell, though, whether that was due to the rigors of the night before or to the overwhelming presence of the man who had slept beside her.

What could have made her go to him? Last night she had been furious with him beyond all reason, screaming at him in the street, in full view of anyone curious enough to look on, and then this morning he'd stretched out his hand to her and asked her to join him, and without question she'd shucked off her dress and gone to him.

Was she mad?

Whatever could have possessed her? Gratitude, she tried to convince herself. It had to be that. *He saved my life, at the risk of his own, and I was grateful. I did a stupid thing, and if he hadn't been standing by—even after I'd told him to get lost—I'd have been done for.* What was more, the aftermath of a shock such as that one was enough to make anyone impulsive.

And sleeping with Damon, even though it had been in

the most literal sense, certainly was impulsive. If she wanted to be honest, it was flat-out foolhardy. There she was, still nursing fresh wounds from a relationship that had gone horribly wrong, with a man who had made it his purpose in life to publicly avenge himself, even to the detriment of her career and her image. A man who had sought to control her every move. After that nasty breakup, she'd sworn off men, and rightly so.

And then in walks Damon. A giant of a man, strong, smart, and protective. Overly protective. Controlling, even. Just the kind of man she could do without. Last night's scenario came back to her, vivid in all its details. He'd deliberately made himself an obstacle to the accomplishment of her mission, as though he thought he was some kind of superhero. But before residual ire could rise once again within her, she remembered the feel of him.

Oh, he had felt good. In spite of his injury and his size, he had maintained his body in top condition; he was all muscle. His solidness had made her feel like a squirrel curled up at the foot of an oak tree. After the last few horrible months that she had endured, the solace that he had provided had been welcome.

More than solace, though, there had been desire. On both sides. She had felt it in the way he had held his body, chivalrously trying neither to communicate it to her nor to succumb to it. But they were both grown-ups. They both knew it was there. She'd read this morning's situation well enough to understand that if she had turned her body toward his and murmured a single note of assent, neither one of them would have slept.

She finished her careful ablutions, which she had subconsciously extended so as to prolong her return to the bedroom from Damon's bathroom, rubbing her face vigorously with his hand towel. As she did so, she could not stop herself from inhaling the faint scent of him that still lingered on it. Her instinctive action only served to underline the enormity of her dilemma. How could she go back there? They'd managed to avoid the thorny issue of their now evident mutual attraction last night, but that had just been temporary. A few hours of stoic denial of desire did not make that desire go away. Suppose he was awake now and waiting for her? Suppose he could read her desire for him as easily as she could read his own for her?

She looked around the bathroom, half hoping to find an escape hatch, a portal of some kind that would allow her to flee to the sanctuary of her own room without having to face him again right now. Just to give her enough time to get her jagged thoughts in order, and to talk herself out of a folly that now seemed dangerously close.

How *could* she go back out there?

That decision was torn from her hands as the door to the bathroom exploded inward. In her confusion, she forgot that she had neglected to lock it and imagined briefly that Damon had torn it from its hinges, so powerful was the sound it made. She dropped the towel she had been holding to her face with a guilty start.

"Where the hell have you been?" he bellowed. His face was ashen, and his eyes held a wildness that truly frightened her.

"What?" The question was so ludicrous that it could elicit no more than a monosyllable in response. Where did he think she had been? There were only two places she could have gone to: the bathroom or her own room. And since he had found her here, standing barefoot on his rug with a damp face and a towel at her feet, she was sure that the answer to his question was self-evident.

Incredibly, he persisted, coming deeper into the

room, towering over her, his emotion making him seem even huger than he actually was. "Where were you?"

"H . . . here," she stammered. "I was right here." She bent over and picked up the towel from the floor and held it out, evidence to exonerate her from whatever wrongdoing he believed she had committed.

He brushed aside the obvious. "You left me. I woke up, and you were gone."

What madness was this? What could have incited him to come charging in on her like that, his eyes crazy with panic? Her voice wobbled as she answered. "I had to. I needed to use the bathroom." She added an apology, even though she still did not understand exactly what she had done to offend him. "I'm sorry. I . . ."

He passed his hand over his scalp, patting his head as though hammers were pounding away at it, and shook himself all over like a big dog. The effort to bring himself under control was obvious. He took a huge, steadying breath. The next time he spoke, he was almost like himself again. The glimpse of madness in his eyes was replaced with remorse. "I'm sorry. Kenya, I'm sorry." He held out his hand to her. "I lost it for a second there."

"You sure did," she said tightly.

He tried to explain. "I was deep in sleep, and I got up, and you were gone. I thought you were right next to me. I got up, and I felt for you, but you weren't there. You scared me." He took a step toward her.

She backed away warily. How could the man who had cradled her so gently this morning have transformed himself so suddenly into the crazed person who had burst in on her like that? And could she really believe that he could grasp whatever demon had possessed him, shove it back into its bottle, and be himself so fast? "*You,*" she threw back at him, "*scared me.*"

He was still approaching her, remorse turning to concern.

"Don't be afraid. I'm sorry. I have no excuse. I mean . . ." He paused. "I do have an explanation, but—"

"What is it?" she demanded. She moved even farther back, still cautious. The bathroom was pretty small, and with a few more steps, she would be up against the shower stall. She didn't like that feeling one bit. It was claustrophobic, to say the least.

He struggled with himself for a moment and then shook his head. "I can't. I would tell you if I could, but I can't."

"Why not? You barge in here, scare me half to death, and then claim you have an excuse, but you're not telling me what it is?"

"I can't," he insisted. To his credit, he recognized her discomfort with his approach and stopped moving toward her.

"Can't or won't?"

"Either. Both." His eyes were pleading. "Just believe that I do. It's just not something that I can share. If I could, I would. Take my word for it."

"Fine," she answered doubtfully, but the fire blazing from him was still fresh in her memory. It was time to take her leave. "I think I'd better go."

He looked pained. "Don't let me chase you away. You don't have to leave. I thought we could . . ." Involuntarily, he glanced over his shoulder to the tousled bed upon which they had lain.

"We could what?" she challenged, but it was all bravado. Inside, she was hot with embarrassment. *He knows,* she thought. *He knows what I was thinking and feeling about him.* How embarrassing! Had she really worn her desire on her sleeve like that? Then she looked down at herself and almost laughed. Sleeves. Ha. She was barely clothed as it was. All she had on was a pair of panties and a slip that covered little and bared much. It was as though her minimal clothing made her feel even more naked than she would have if she had been completely nude. Her nipples puckered at the thought, and she quickly brought her hands up to her chest to shield herself.

He saw the gesture at once. "Don't hide from me. Please, don't try to hide what you're feeling. You know you felt the same thing I felt this morning and yesterday. I know it's real. You do, too."

"I hardly know you," she countered, in an effort to deflect his attention from the truth.

"I know, but it's there all the same. This thing between us. And you can get to know me. I want to know you." He paused, trying to think of what to say next. "You have no way of comprehending how difficult it is for me to say this. You haven't got a *clue!*"

"So why ask?"

"Because I can't get you out of my mind. I can't get the feel of you out of my head. I want to touch you again. And yesterday, the way you kissed me, I know that you want it, too."

He was hitting many nails on many heads, and she wasn't sure she liked it. Behind him, the bed loomed large, and around them, the bathroom grew even smaller. He was still clad in nothing but his shorts, and his body was a dark landscape of well-toned ridges and hollows. She remembered herself the day before, abandoning both caution and decorum, and falling into his arms. This was a man that a woman could feast upon. But where would it end?

"Come. Come back to bed with me. We can take it as slow as you like. You're in charge; you call the shots. Just come to me." He didn't do anything other than wait.

To her immense shock, her feet propelled her forward. As she moved, he smiled in anticipation. But his

smile turned to a look of surprise as her last vestige of
self-preservation took over, and instead of going to him,
she squeezed past him—and began running.

"Kenya!" He whirled to follow her.

Because of the layout of the room, the sliding doors
that opened onto the patio and the garden beyond were
closer to her than the door that led to the hallway, so she
headed there. Damon didn't chase her, exactly. He
simply kept pace, apologies tumbling from his lips. The
doors opened easily, and soon she was past his porch and
standing in the garden. The dense, humid heat fell upon
them both. It was like stepping into a sauna.

"Kenya, I'm sorry. Please, don't be offended!"

Offended? He had it all wrong. He hadn't offended
her. He hadn't shocked her. She had shocked herself.
Oh, how much she wanted to go to him! Wasn't she the
one who had said she'd had enough of men? Hadn't she
been burnt badly enough? So what was she doing, allowing herself to once again be seduced by the flame?

The garden offered few places to hide. Each room
was bordered by a tiny, breast-high hedge of orange and
gold ixora bushes, which cut one off from the other.
Damon's little garden was also graced by a willowy,
spreading petria tree, which was in full bloom, its small
lilac flowers scattered below it like a patterned bed-
spread. She sought out the refuge that it offered, dip-
ping low to avoid its drooping branches. She plopped
onto the rich earth beneath the tree, surprised by its
coolness in the face of such oppressive heat.

He hunkered down beside her, anxious. "Are you okay?"

She was breathless, but not from her flight. "Fine,"
she puffed.

He looked abashed. "I'm sorry," he apologized once
again. "I misspoke. I thought . . . I was under the impression that you . . . wanted . . ." He paused, struggling

to find the right words. "Me," he ended lamely. "I was out of line. And presumptuous. Forgive me."

He was wrong. She did want him. Too much. This was all happening way too fast. If she gave in, what would he think of her? She didn't want him to feel that her reaction had been his fault, so she took pains to explain. "No, you weren't wrong." That admission alone was difficult to make. "It's just that I don't just . . . hop into bed with . . . anyone."

"Neither do I. As a matter of fact, it's been a very long time for me." His sigh came from the bottom of his soul. "Longer than you can even imagine." He put both hands upon her shoulders, partly in an effort to hold her steady and partly, she was certain, to ensure that she did not try to evade him a second time. "Kenya, listen to me very carefully. I'm not about to pass judgment on you. I hope you won't on me. We're adults; we should be beyond that. As a matter of fact . . ." He paused to let his thumb follow the line of her lips. "As a matter of fact, I'm not asking you to give me . . . everything. I'm not prepared for that, and neither are you. I don't do one-night stands. I'm only asking for as much as you're able to give. I can only give the same."

He paused to allow his words to sink in. She wanted so much to believe him! Unable to do anything more than nod, she let him go on. "If you come back with me, I promise you this. I will only go as far as you allow me, and no more. Your "no" will always mean "no," and your "stop" will always mean "stop." But until we get to that point, Kenya, sweetheart, I want you to relax and trust me. I want you to close those beautiful brown eyes and let go, and let me pleasure you. I want nothing in return." He stopped, slightly out of breath, waiting.

Her head was spinning. The heady scent of the earth and the flowery boughs that enveloped them, combined with the intensity of his words and the urgent desire in his eyes, left her giddy. *Let me pleasure you.* What a promise. What an invitation! Her own desire rose to meet his. Could she trust him? Should she?

She expected him to say more, hoping that this would buy her more time to think, but he had already stated his case, and now he waited. The ball was in her court. She knew that he was perfectly capable of fulfilling his promise: that if she gave in to him, she would be giving in to pleasure beyond all reason—even if, as he had said, they chose not to take their encounter to its culmination. Indeed, they couldn't: she had not come prepared with any contraceptive, and it was reasonable to assume that he had not, either. They were too wise and understood the way of the world too well to throw caution to the wind and act irresponsibly in that regard, but there were a hundred other ways in which they could please each other, each more delightful than the next.

Oh, temptation!

Then, without exerting any pressure, he leaned forward slightly, his body now excruciatingly close to hers, and brought his mouth near her ear. She could feel a puff of warm air against her cheek as he whispered a single word, which was heavy with a single question: "Kenya?"

Chapter 14

He tastes like salt was the first thought that entered her mind. *He smells just like the earth beneath me* was the second. A disturbing combination of courage and weakness possessed her, and she kissed him. For a moment he didn't kiss her back, and she wondered whether this was because he was afraid to scare her away again, or whether the inner demons of which he refused to speak were holding him back.

Don't make me do this alone, she wanted to tell him, but she didn't have to. Under the pressure of hers, his mouth came alive. His tongue darted out like a striking serpent to brush against her front teeth before retreating—once, twice, and then again, until she had to curl both arms up around his neck to reassure herself that he could not pull away.

Then Damon took over. He broke their kiss, and lifting her slightly, he tilted her backward, until she felt the soft cool earth at her back. He shifted from his squatting position to come to kneel over her, looming above like the Colossus of Rhodes. Overhead, the supple boughs of the petria tree swayed gently in the breeze, sending small purple flowers spinning down upon them both, whirling like miniature helicopters. He reached forward. She thought that he was going to touch her face, but instead he retrieved one of the delicate blooms from her hair and, pinching the short stem between finger and thumb, ran it lightly across her forehead, then drew a trail down the length of her nose. His touch was as light as butter-fly wings.

She closed her eyes, giving in to the moment, feeling the soft, rhythmic stroking along her brows and then along her fluttering eyelids. He drew the blossom along the outline of her lips and then moved it below to her chin and, after toying with her for several seconds, down to her neck. As the petals made contact with the hollow at the base of her throat, she swallowed reflexively. He was moving still lower.

The lightness of his touch against the upper curve of her breasts made her shudder. One spaghetti strap of her slip had fallen off during her hasty departure. He ran the little finger of the same hand that held the flower along the top edge of the garment, forcing the material down several inches until her breast came into view. He exhaled a loud hiss of awe at the sight of her. Then his flower resumed its journey, trailing along the mound of swollen flesh beneath it to stop at the tight knot of a nipple at the center.

It was a tiny flower, just an inch across, but it sent a mil-lion volts coursing through her everywhere it touched. She arched toward it, and playfully, he took it away until she protested.

He laughed, indulgently rather than mockingly. "You liked that."

There was no point in denying it. "Yes," she gasped.

He leaned forward, closer to her. "Would you like me to do it again?"

Her eyes flew open to take in his smiling face. He was

enjoying this torture! What was he waiting for? Was he really going to torture her like that? She grunted her assent.

He lifted the flower again and brought it near to her waiting breast. She sucked in a lungful of air, steeling herself so as not to cry out at the anticipated contact. But, instead of complying, he let it fall onto her bare breast and lowered his head. "Many more flowers where that came from," he told her. "And lots of time to pick them. But first, I need to do this."

She had no time to even feel disappointment at his abandonment of the tiny lilac instrument of torture, because he was kissing her again, and that blew every other thought out of her mind. His initial, gentle exploration grew into something more demanding and masterful. She gave in to the onslaught of teeth and tongue, not even caring that her body was starving for air, and that what little breath he allowed her only burned as fuel to her excitement.

The hand that had teased her with the flower now slid under her bottom, a warm interloper between herself and the cool earth beneath them. He slid his thumb under the elastic band of her low-cut panties, moving along inch by excruciating inch until he found what he was looking for: that flat diamond where the small of her back met the swell of her bottom. A zillion nerve endings were thrown into chaos.

Then the full weight of his body was upon hers, crushing the flower between them. She wondered how, given his size, she was not crushed, too, but God's engineering was a wonderful thing. Her feminine body was designed to support the weight of even a man his size—not just to bear it, but to revel in it. Even her ability to get her arms around his massive shoulders was a miracle in its own right.

The hand under her bottom lifted her up, pressing

her into him so that she could feel that he was as inflamed as she was. This knowledge scared her as much as
it excited her; it meant that his hold on his self-control
was as tenuous as hers. It was insane: the drooping
boughs of the tree gave them some sanctuary, but they
were still outdoors in a public place. Which of them had
the strength to stop, at least for as long as it would take
for them to rise and relocate? They should stop before
they were spotted . . . but ooh, how good he felt!

"We shouldn't be . . . doing this . . . here," she eventually managed to gasp out.

"Two minutes," he pleaded.

"One," she countered. They *really* must be going.

He stalled for time with a long, soul-searing kiss and
then insisted, "Starting now."

The opportunity for any further bargaining was
snatched from their hands by the sound of a child's
laugh somewhere in the distance. They both grew instantly rigid. The child sounded far off—but not far
enough. Her hands came up immediately to cover her
bare breast.

He was immediately apologetic. 'I'm sorry, honey. I
had no right to expose you like this." He moved her
hands out of the way and brought the straps of her slip
up into their rightful position, restoring her modesty
somewhat. He tried to get to his feet, but he was too tall
to stand under the low-sweeping branches, so he backed
out, bent over almost double, while holding out his hand
to assist her.

She hesitated. How close was this child, really, and was
anyone else about? They were, after all, in a hotel
garden. Of all the places to lose her sense of decorum!

He knew what her problem was. "The coast is clear,"
he let her know. Then he added, more to spur her on
than for any other reason, she suspected, "for now."

Giggling like a naughty schoolgirl, she followed him, emerging from their flowery hiding place and looking quickly around. She decided to play his game. "We'd better hurry, then. No telling when we could get caught in the act."

"That wouldn't look too good for you in the tabloids," he laughed back.

Tabloids. She shuddered, her face growing serious. She'd had more than her fair share of space in those. In her line of work, everything that you did made you fair game, but when a story was spiced up with sex . . . well, that just sold the papers all the faster, didn't it? And it would be bad enough being ratted out by an overzealous fellow guest, or even the hotel staff . . . but nothing stung more than having a lover lay you bare under the glare of media scrutiny.

She trusted Damon, to be sure . . . but was any of that trust misplaced?

Damon read the hodgepodge of emotions tumbling across her face and grimaced. "Oh, Lord, Kenya, I was kidding. In light of your experiences, I realize it was a stupid, insensitive joke to make. That was asinine. I apologize. Okay?"

She nodded slowly, but the frown still had not left her.

He hammered his forehead with the heel of his palm, an act of self-flagellation over his goof. "Kenya, sweetheart. Surely, you don't think that I'd . . . I would never do such a thing! Everything that takes place between us in private will always stay that way. Gossip was never my style and, I promise you, neither is kissing and telling. Please, you have to take me at my word." He put his hands on his hips and looked around them briefly before saying, "Come inside. We aren't alone, and we want to be. If you like, we can talk about this some more behind closed doors, but at least let's have that conversation in private." Without asking permission, he took her hand.

She let herself be led back into the room, her mind a jumble of thoughts and feelings. How far should trust go? Could you trust a man to guard you but not to share your secrets? Could you trust him with your secrets, but not with your body? Could you trust him with your body, but not your reputation? Or did all of these have to go together? Was trust a package deal?

It had to be. It just had to. This wasn't mix and match. Giving your body to a man already made you vulnerable. In fact, there was nothing more vulnerable than that— except for, of course, giving him your heart. And there was no question of that. Perish the thought. She had loved Tobias, and one soul-wrecking love was more than any heart could endure in one lifetime.

Damon, she liked, admired, wanted, desired—and, yes, trusted. But she didn't, couldn't, love him. For her, that Pandora's box was closed, wrapped with chains, and securely padlocked. If she had her way, she would heave it overboard into the sea, letting it sink to the bottom, where it would never be seen again. She didn't need it. She didn't want it.

She was sufficiently realistic to believe that if two people liked each other enough, and respected each other enough, they could make love without being *in* love. There was no law against that. And Damon would be kind. That, she knew. He would be warm and careful and generous, and he would bring her release for her body and solace for her spirit. There, she would draw the line.

Once inside his room again, he let go of her hand just long enough to lock the door and make sure that the screens over the glass doors were secure. She turned and watched him as he did so, noting the concentration on his face as he made sure that they would in no way be observed.

She knew he was more concerned for her modesty than for his own. Warmth for him rippled through her, followed by another wave, this one of desire.

When he was done with his security checks, he stood before her, his face sober. "Now," he began, "If you want to talk about it—"

She cut him off. "No. I don't want to talk about it."

He looked crestfallen, sure that she was backing out. "Why not?"

She was smiling. "No talk. We don't need it. I know all I need to know." As he struggled to understand the meaning of her words, she opened her arms, inviting him to step into them. His initial puzzlement gave way to a look of comprehension, and his smile was like the day's second sunrise.

He came forward with the hesitant steps of a desert wanderer who was half certain that the oasis spread out before him was a mirage. She moved toward him with the heart-thumping knowledge that what she was doing was totally out of character for her, but that she was willing to do it, anyway.

Somehow, they both met in the middle.

Damon's body ached through and through, but as far as he could remember, nothing ever hurt so good. Kenya was asleep, her head a dead weight on his bicep. The tips of his fingers tingled from the reduced blood flow through his arm, but he would let the entire limb fall off before he disturbed her. Asleep, she was beautiful.

What was he thinking? Awake, she was beautiful. Angry, she was beautiful. Even in her very ugly wig and hat disguise, she was beautiful. But asleep, she lost her grip on the rigid little self-protective shield she usually held up before herself. Looking into her face in full repose, he could see her for who she really was, sans her habitual prickly exterior.

And he was awed. She was capable of such a whirlwind of emotions, and having ridden that whirlwind with her, from irritation to sadness to hope to despair, from rage to fear, from coyness to full-blossomed passion, he was battered and worn. They had made love for hours—first hesitantly; then with greater and greater curiosity; then, their initial reservation overcome, with a hunger that he had thought long dead within him, and that he had barely suspected her capable of. And yet, he had not afforded himself the ultimate luxury of burying himself deep within her. This was something for which they were ill-prepared, and he was glad that they had both managed to retain some shred of sanity, even at the height of the intense, giddy pleasure, by not taking any stupid risks that could lead to unnecessary worry and regret.

But he had not missed that final, gratifying act, not in the least. It was amazing just how inventive two people could be in seeking alternate routes to pleasure. He was sated, completely and utterly satisfied. His heavy limbs and the mist of sweat that covered him were proof enough of that.

Sometime during those hours of heated loving, the rain had begun to fall. It had taken him by surprise, given the pervasive heat that had prevailed since their arrival. The sudden cloudburst had been audible long before it reached them, shushing down the hillsides, whispering to forest trees, before drumming on the roof above their heads like tiny pebbles cascading between the fingers of a giant hand. The sound of the rain, fed by relief and exhaustion, had lulled Kenya to sleep, but Damon had not followed. He had too much on his mind.

"So fast," he murmured to himself. "Way, way too fast." Measured against the yardstick of time, he barely knew this woman, but measured against his instinct, his body, and heart, he knew all there was to know. And, dammit, what he knew, he loved.

Loved. How? When? All she'd done since she'd met him was get on his nerves, frustrate him by building a hedge of prickles at every turn. She was beautiful and smart and sexy and wonderful, but surely, he didn't . . . *love* her.

That was ludicrous. That was impossible. Love didn't come for a person like that, sneaking up on them like a thief in the night. It took months, years, sometimes, for a man to know a woman, to become comfortable enough with her, to begin to explore his feelings for her. Love was a steady companion that grew over time. It didn't sucker punch you in the gut. Teenagers, perhaps, let themselves fall victim to giddy infatuation based on a wink or a smile, largely because they knew no better. As for him, he was well past his teenage years.

So he listened to the combined symphony of the rain pounding overhead and the breathing of the woman pressed against him and tried to unravel his dilemma. And, as he frequently had during the past few years, he asked himself, *What would Jewel think?*

Jewel. His body tensed, instantly becoming a much harder, lumpier bed to Kenya, and she stirred in discomfort, wrinkling her nose like a child having a bad dream. Immediately, Damon willed himself to relax. Just because he was in turmoil didn't mean that Kenya should be robbed of much needed sleep.

But the name of his lost love reverberated so clearly in his mind that he fully expected her familiar ghost to materialize in the room, either to offer advice or, more likely, to chide him for his infidelity. Because after four years of stoic abstinence, it felt very much like an infidelity to his still grief-torn conscience, even though his logical mind told him that that was nonsense. He had been faithful to a memory, to the sad remembrance of what had been and what could have been, had it not been for his carelessness. That had been his choice. And, this morning he had broken that vow. As a result, his languorous satisfaction after his and Kenya's delicious encounter was tainted by guilt.

But either his ragged emotions did not succeed in invoking Jewel or she was far too discreet to invade upon such an intimate moment. The room remained silent. But the thought of her had brought with it a solution to his dilemma.

This wasn't love. It couldn't be. It was an intoxicating cocktail of loneliness, need, and physical want. Fed by the presence of a beautiful woman and the disorientation brought about by unfamiliar surroundings, these hungers had exploded in him, leaving him confused. In short, he thought he was in love, because he wanted to be. He missed Jewel terribly; he had been on his own far too long. He'd let loneliness gnaw away at his mind like a fat worm at an apple, and that, he understood now, was the cause of his delusion.

In fact, he would go as far as to say that the memory of Jewel might itself have precipitated that final decision to cast aside his usual iron-clad reserve and make love to Kenya. He remembered those hideous, disoriented moments a few hours earlier, when he'd opened his eyes to find himself alone in bed. The shock of falling asleep next to a warm female form and waking up alone had thrust him back to the last awful time that had happened to him, when the mystery of his missing bedmate's whereabouts was solved by a visit from solemn-faced police officers.

So he'd panicked and gone rushing about like a fool looking for Kenya, scared out of his mind that something had happened to her, even though common sense had told him that she was sure to be completely safe. And even when he'd found her, innocently washing up in his bathroom, he had not been able to put his anxiety to rest. To his shame, he clearly remembered the shocked look on her face when he barged in on her, barking like a mad dog.

That was it. That had to be it. This thing he felt—this sudden, unexpected mixture of hunger and protectiveness—was not about Kenya at all. There had been three people in this bed this afternoon, and that was something he, and he alone, would have to deal with. As for Kenya, she was a wonderful woman, but he was not losing himself to her, as he had feared. He was *not*, not now and not ever again, falling into that dangerous, soul-smashing condition called love.

Comforted by this knowledge, he sighed as the crumbling pieces of his world fell back into place. When this was all over, when they left this sultry island for cooler climes, good sense would return, and the delusion would ebb away. For the time being, he enjoyed her company, as unpredictable as it was, and desired her physically. He knew without immodesty that she felt the same way about him. So why not enjoy each other? Why not taste of her, and let her taste of him? They were both old enough, and experienced enough, to take from each other what they needed, give to each other as much as they were prepared to give, and enjoy it for the while.

That was how it would be. That was the *only* way it could be. "Safe," he whispered to himself. He closed his eyes; a few hours' sleep would do him a world of good.

But just then, the warm shape beside him moved. Kenya stretched against him, slipping her arms over her head and arching like a cat shaking off its slumber. His newfound complacency was instantly dismissed.

He had found a place of peace in his mind and had

arrived at a decision he could live with, but how would *she* feel about what they had done? Would there be regret, guilt, anger?

He braced himself and watched intently as she opened her eyes and focused on him. Dammit, he was nervous. "Hello," was all he could say.

Chapter 15

I'm naked was the first thing that came to Kenya's sleep-drugged mind. *Naked, and in bed with an equally naked, utterly devastating giant of a man who's smiling shyly at me, as though he's half afraid that I'll run screaming from his bed.*

How'd that happen?

She knew exactly how it had happened. She'd been drawn to Damon since the moment she'd met him—even when she didn't want him around, even when she was mad at him. He'd emitted an aura that had sucked her in, in spite of her resistance, like a tiny meteorite being drawn into the magnetic field of an enormous planet that fate, destiny, or even pure chance had sent hurtling through her little corner of the galaxy. After a few feeble attempts to break his spell, and in the face of all evidence that what she was doing was folly, she had succumbed, given up, and given in.

And, by God, it had been good. So good, in fact, that she felt even more naked than was physically possible, as though, in allowing him access to her body, in letting him see her when pleasure had destroyed her every last defense, she had let him see her soul.

If ever there was a definition of ultra-naked, this had to

be it. Instinctively, she let her arms shoot up to cover her breasts from his view, even though those were the very same breasts whose rosy nipples had suffered greatly under the torture of his fingers and tongue not long before.

Damon's eyes took in her self-protective gesture, and, rather than look offended, he nodded and smiled. "Just a sec," he promised, "Let me get you something to cover up." With that, he hopped out of bed and walked—oh, dear, sweet Lord, he was splendid—all the way to the bathroom. She watched him as he went, riveted by the shape of his broad back, an inverted triangle that dipped inward to his waist, and the hard globes of muscle below. Her hands tingled as she remembered raking her nails along his firm rear, even when he had begged her to stop.

Oh, mercy.

She watched him as he walked, so entranced by the sight of him in all his unselfconscious glory that she forgot her own defensiveness and let her arms fall from in front of her. When he returned in a few seconds, his brows lifted slightly, and with a Cheshire cat grin playing about his lips, he handed over a pale blue terry cloth hotel bathrobe. Immediately, she covered her nakedness, sighing audibly with relief at her now reduced vulnerability.

"Better now?" he inquired solemnly.

"Much," she confirmed, nodding vigorously. Funny how a slip of cloth around one's body could alleviate a whole slew of insecurities.

"Good," he said politely, but there had been real regret in his eyes as her breasts disappeared from his view.

She did feel much better now, but there was a problem. *She* was now decorously covered . . . but *he* was still as naked as the day he was born, and he didn't seem to care two hoots about the fact. "I, uh, think you should do the same," she volunteered.

He flashed her a wicked grin. "I'm afraid most hotels

don't cater to men my size. Those robes don't fit me."
He shook his head in fake regret.

"Something must," she persisted. There was no way she
was sitting here having to look at him, looking like that, much
longer. She wasn't sure her heart could take it. "Come on,
Damon. Put something on! I did! Fair is fair!"

"All right, all right," he conceded with admirable
sportsmanship. "I'll play nice." He turned around once
again and proceeded—slowly—back to the bathroom,
giving her a first-rate show all the way.

She tried not to ogle, but it was like traveling all the
way to the Sistine Chapel and trying not to look up. "You
could hurry it up a little," she grunted.

"The knee. Slows me down." He pointed at the offending joint, but the smirk on his face betrayed him.

"I'll bet," she snorted.

In a few moments he was back, wearing a pair of
shorts, which took care of his bottom half but still left his
equally tantalizing upper half bare to her view.

"Better?" he asked. He made no effort to hide the
devilry in his face.

"It'll do," she answered. But there was no way she
could keep her scowl in place. Their eyes locked, and in
spite of themselves, they both broke out in smiles.

Then something seemed to worry him. "Your bruises.
From your fall last night. I didn't . . . hurt them, did I?"

Bruises? Oh, right. Bruises. She'd collected quite a
few when they'd hit the dust after he'd thrust her out of
the path of that oncoming pickup. In all the excitement
that had followed, she had all but forgotten. She ran
her fingers experimentally along her more tender spots.
If he had hurt them during their lovemaking, the sensation had only added to her pleasure. As that old song
went, if it had hurt, it had hurt so good. "Um, no," she
lied. "You didn't hurt me at all."

He seemed relieved to hear that. "Good. And apart from that, how are you feeling?" he asked, this time with genuine earnestness.

"Starving. Honestly, Damon, if I don't get something to eat right now, you're going to have a lot of explaining to do to the cops about how this dead woman wound up on your floor."

He looked at his watch. "Have mercy," he murmured.

"What?"

"No wonder you're hungry. According to this, we haven't had a meal in almost twenty-four hours."

She looked guilty. "And, if I recall, the last time you were eating, I interrupted you."

"You seem to have a habit of doing that," he agreed, but he didn't look as though he held it against her. "We're going to have to do something about that right away. As you said, I can't allow a woman to succumb to starvation right here on my hotel room floor. Especially one who has just . . ." He let his gaze drop to her mouth, and it was all she could do to keep her hand from shooting up to protect it from his visual caress. "Who has just expended so much energy," he finished meaningfully.

Kenya felt heat flood into her face. She *had* gotten pretty wild, hadn't she! Curse him for mentioning it.

"We'll see to the food problem," he said briskly but then, in softer tones, added, "but that wasn't what I meant when I asked you how you felt. I was talking about"—he jerked his head sideways, indicating the bed behind them—"I was talking about that. You and me. What we just did."

She knew that was what he'd meant. She'd just been trying to stall him. But there was no sense in continuing to be evasive. "How do I feel about that?" she repeated rhetorically, buying herself some time. "Awkward, I guess."

The devil that had prompted him to tease her and toy

with her earlier was gone now, and in its place was a sober spirit of empathy. "That's normal," he comforted her. "It's to be expected. First times are like that."

First times. Did that mean there would be more times? She tingled when she realized that she hoped so. She didn't know what to say.

When she didn't respond, he went on. "It takes a lot of courage for two people to let their veils, their public selves, fall away and reveal who they really are to each other. Admit what they want and need from each other. It's hard to give in to our sexual selves and to reveal those selves to other people, especially when we barely know each other."

A pained look crossed her face. *They barely knew each other.* And yet she'd abandoned herself so completely to her desire for him that she had become a woman she hardly recognized: lush, voracious, totally giving. It was scary. But what did that say about her? She hung her head.

He frowned. "Kenya? What is it?"

She wanted to speak, but her tongue was reluctant to comply. "I can't," she managed.

"Tell me," he coaxed gently.

She struggled with what she was thinking and then finally forced herself to begin, "I just don't want you to think—"

He cut her off before she could say another word. "Stop. Stop right there. Don't even *start* that, Kenya. I think no less of you than I did yesterday." He closed the gap between them, stooping down a little so that his face was level with hers and coaxing her to look at him, with gentle fingers under her chin. "Don't. Guilt has no place here, not in this bedroom. Not between us. And neither does shame. What you and I did here says as much about me as it does about you, and all it says is that we're alive and healthy, and that we have desires, and that we're

strong enough to own up to them. All it says about you
is that you wanted me as much as I wanted you." He
leaned forward to plant a light kiss on the tip of her
nose. "Still want you. And I hope you still want me." His
voice was husky with emotion.

Still want him? Was he kidding? Far from quelling her
desire for him, their hours of lovemaking had been like
dumping gasoline on a brush fire. If he touched her
again . . . A flood of warmth pooled between her legs at
the thought.

"Don't answer," he whispered, his lips close to her ear.
"You don't have to say anything. Just don't ever, every
worry about what I think of you. Because I think you're
wonderful, beautiful, delightfully sexy, and maddeningly
irritating, but I will never think any less of the delicious
sexual being that you are. Okay?"

She squeezed her eyes shut. Her thoughts were not of
Damon, but of Tobias, who for some reason had always
been deeply suspicious of her and had never passed up
any opportunity to question her morals or her motives.
How he had sought to reeducate her, and retool her,
into what he had wanted her to be, whether she liked it
or not. Her intimate knowledge of men had been largely
limited to these two, and it astounded her as to how
vastly different their attitudes could be.

Then it occurred to her that Damon was waiting for an
answer. She dredged her mind out of the past and managed to nod. "Okay." Then, after a few moments of
thought, she added, "Thank you."

"No, don't thank me," he responded, shaking his head
vigorously. "Respect is your entitlement. Your right. It's
not something I have to give to you."

There was little she could answer to that—and no time
to answer, even if she had chosen to, as his mouth fell
upon hers in a kiss that was a stranger to the deep, pas-

sionate ones they had traded before. This one was light, soothing, and yet said so much more than any that had come before. Her distressed soul quieted.

When he broke the kiss and straightened up, she was all smiles. "That's the spirit," he said approvingly. Then, more briskly, he added, "Now that we've got that sorted out, I think it's time we got some food into us, otherwise the police will be dealing with two corpses on my floor, not one. And that won't be pretty."

He was right. She was starving. But there were equally pressing needs to be dealt with. "We need to clean up first." They were drenched in the scent of each other, but as pleasant as that was, it would hardly go over well in a restaurant.

"That, we do," he agreed amiably. "Why don't we part company, go clean up, and rendezvous at the hotel restaurant in an hour? We could fuel up and then hit the town. It's Carnival Sunday evening; there's bound to be a million and one ways for us to get into trouble out there. I'll do a little reconnaissance work at the front desk, and then maybe we could take in a show or something."

That sounded good. The idea of spending time alone with Damon, just enjoying his company—almost as if they were on a date—excited her more than it had any right to, but she hesitated. They had come here for a purpose: to find her brother and learn the truth. Last night that purpose had been thwarted. Surely, it would be wrong to go out enjoying themselves while their work remained undone, and her father's mystery remained unsolved?

He spotted her hesitation and easily recognized the reason behind it. His hand came down lightly on her shoulder. "Not tonight, Kenya. Your brother, and the truth, will still be there tomorrow, and the day after. We've got more than enough time to find them. But

tonight I want to be with you. I want to take you somewhere and watch you smile. This is your father's island,
and we've landed smack upon it in its finest hour. You
told me yourself that all you have of Trinidad are your
father's memories. I want you to create new memories of
your own. And I want to be with you when you do. So
forget Eric. If he was motivated enough to contact you in
the first place, he's motivated enough to wait to see you
again. Let him go for tonight. Come out with me." After
that uncharacteristically long speech, he seemed
winded. He stopped and looked at her expectantly.

The ball was in her court. It was up to her to say yea or
nay. She was grudgingly forced to admit to herself that
Damon was right, even though he had, in fact, been the
reason for her failed attempt at drawing the truth out of
Eric last night, with his stubborn refusal to leave them
alone, if only for a few minutes. And in spite of what had
passed between them in this room this afternoon, that
still rankled.

She would have to find a way to achieve her own ends,
to get information out of Eric. But not tonight. She was
surprised by her excitement at Damon's suggestion that
they hit the town together. Seeing Trinidad was something she had yearned to do all her life. What better
time to see it than at its moment of glory? Strains and
snatches of calypsos that she had heard playing on the
radio and hanging in the air since her arrival began
swirling through her, and her pulse fell into time with
their seductive beat. She could see Port of Spain with its
many promised delights, hear the sounds, inhale the
scents, see the people, immerse herself in the festival, all
with this unbelievably awesome man at her side.

Did it get any better?

Damon's face reflected his relief as she gave in to a
smile of acceptance.

"Yes," she conceded. "Yes, please, that would be wonderful. I'd love for you to take me out tonight."

"Attagirl. Now, let's split up. Go take a long soak, wash your hair, do whatever girly things you have to do—"

"I don't do *girly things,*" she began to protest, before she realized he was teasing her. She struggled to keep an inane grin off her face as she headed for the door.

"Well, just do whatever it is you do, little darlin', to make yourself look as delightful as you usually look, because tonight we're doing the town. Meet you at dinner in an hour. And don't be late; I'm so hungry, I'm liable to forget the manners my mama taught me and start without you."

"You wouldn't dare," she laughed, and deftly avoiding a playful slap he aimed at her departing bottom, she made it to the door, forgetting even that she was still wearing his robe and pausing only to grab her bag and room keys from off his nightstand.

"I'll miss you while you're gone," he murmured at her retreating back just before she shut the door.

He had to be kidding, she decided, so she didn't bother to respond.

Chapter 16

"Look! Look!" Kenya clutched at Damon's arm for the tenth time that evening, as an enormous Carnival costume glided by them. The glittering edifice was bedecked with orange and black plumes arranged in a fan that was at least fifteen feet high and easily as wide. Ostrich feathers ruffled and bobbed in the mild breeze as it went, leaving behind the faintest scent of glue. What amazed her most was the fact that as enormous as it was, the costume was being borne on the shoulders of a single masquerader, and a slender woman at that, whose close-fitting black vinyl jumpsuit offered her camouflage against the rest of her costume, making it look as though the entire stunning creation was moving forward on its own.

"I'm looking, I'm looking," Damon answered, as amused by her excitement as a father taking a small child to the circus.

"It's a girl carrying that! On her shoulders! Did you see her?"

"I saw her."

"How'd she do that?"

He shrugged. "Beats me. Maybe that great big thing is lighter than it looks."

"Maybe she's stronger than she looks," Kenya countered.

He looked down at her and let the arm that he had placed around her shoulders tighten a little. "Women usually are."

The warmth in his voice suffused her body, making her tingle under the light denim jacket she had worn on the advice of the desk clerk. It was a beautiful night out. The rain had long stopped, but its legacy to them was a crisp, clear night sky spangled with bright stars, and a cool wind, which was welcome after the last few sizzling days. The breeze swept down from the hills above them, bringing with it a sweet night perfume, which inflamed her senses, adding to her barely controlled excitement.

The Queen's Park Savannah, that huge open park that spread out for acres in the middle of the city, was alive with thousands of people, who thronged at the touchstone of the nation's Carnival activities. It was the biggest night of the festival, Dimanche Gras, and Damon's inquiries had led them to this place, affectionately known as the Big Yard, the epicenter of it all, where most of the major competitions would be held. Here, tonight, champions of calypso would pit their musical skills against each other, vying for the title of Calypso Monarch, while masqueraders sporting enormous, sumptuously decorated costumes competed for the title of King and Queen of Carnival.

The contests would extend well into the early hours of the morning, after which patrons would file away to join the many huge parties that were taking place all over the city, or would mill about, eat, drink, and laugh with each other until Carnival was officially declared open. After that, the streets would be filled with hundreds of thousands of participants dancing to the beat of the music belted out by live bands and DJs from the backs of dozens of trucks that would roam the city.

The friendly hotel clerk had gone as far as to advise them to eschew the stands, where locals and tourists could view the festivities from on high, directing them instead to the grounds of the Savannah, where they could experience the action from close up. And what action it was! Even as a native New Yorker who was used to crowds, festivals, and parades of all kinds, Kenya was awed.

Everywhere there were people: young girls half naked in the shortest of shorts and skimpy tops, their hair dyed or sprayed wild colors and bedecked with shells and beads; young men sporting gleaming, bare chests and oversized jeans that would have hit the ground were it not for strips of cloth or red, gold, and green woven belts; couples embracing, gyrating against each other to the strains of almost deafening music being pumped out from overhead speakers; children laughing and playing under the trees that lined the perimeter of the Savannah; and overweight matrons in garish cotton blouses and shorts, toting picnic baskets full of goodies. It was bedlam, and Kenya loved it.

"Having a good time?" Damon asked, although he didn't need to. He was taking pleasure in her pleasure. She grinned. "I've never seen anything like this!"

"Neither have I," he agreed. "And I've travelled to places I can't even spell." He grasped her hand. "Come, let's see if we can get closer to the stage. Let's see what's on now."

Kenya let herself be led, holding on to his hand, afraid that if she lost him in a crowd of this magnitude, she would never be able to find him again. He snaked in and out of rows of vendors' booths from which emanated delightful smells: corn boiled with pickled pigs' tails or roasted on open coals; corn soup overflowing with hand-rolled cornmeal dumplings; fried blood pudding; hot balls of split peas, deep-fried and served with mango chutney; and smoked herring on coconut bread, as well as more common fare, such as popcorn, hamburgers, and fried chicken. Peanut vendors wheeled their bikes along on the grass, balancing strange-looking wooden warmers built right onto the backs of the bikes, with steam shrieking through attached metal whistles as it escaped the confines of the boxes, drawing the attention of any potential customer within earshot. She almost regretted having eaten so heartily back at the hotel. She would gladly have experimented with any one of these new tastes, just to boast of the experience.

Her eyes misted over. Here she was at last, living what her father had lived. Seeing—no, not just seeing, experiencing with every one of her senses—all that her father had described to her in such detail so many times. The people, the food, the music, it was just like he'd always said it would be. She wished she could have experienced this with him. She wished he were well enough to be here. She bit down hard on her lower lip, so overcome by the assault of her emotions that she was unable to keep walking.

Damon felt the tug of her hand and, aware that she had stopped following him, halted. "What? What is it?"

She couldn't speak, so she shook her head.

"You winded? Want to sit for a while?" Before waiting for an answer, he craned his neck, looking in vain for a place for her to sit.

"No," she began.

"Maybe we should go up into the stands after all?" His furrowed brow reflected his concern.

"No, no." She shook her head vigorously. How could she explain this? "It's just . . . my father used to . . . talk about this. I always wanted to see it with him. For him to bring me here, for me to experience my roots for myself. And now . . ."

"I understand. If this is too much for you . . ." He

made a gesture in the vague direction of the lot where they'd left their car.

"No!" Her hand shot up to stall him. "I'm not going back! Don't even think it!"

"I just don't want you to be uncomfortable."

"I'm fine," she insisted. "I'm good."

"Okay," he said doubtfully. He thought for a second and then, as though inspiration had struck, suddenly craned his neck once again, looking for something. "Come." He clutched her hand even tighter, leading her on with what purpose she did not know. But as the crowd parted for a brief moment, she understood.

A large, patient-looking gray donkey stood in a clearing, harnessed to a decrepit wooden cart that was loaded with bunches of coconuts. The yellow and green orbs were piled high, and beside them, a thin, wiry-armed coconut vendor with straggly hair and a long, drooping moustache deftly opened the tops of the coconuts with a wickedly sharp cutlass. He did so with the skill of a chef, tapping the tops of the coconuts with deceptively little force and sending them flying off.

As Kenya scratched the weary animal comfortingly between the ears, Damon dipped his hand into his wallet, paid for two coconuts, retrieved them easily with his big hands, and led her away to enjoy them. "One more thing," he said briskly before he handed one over. All she could do was watch, mystified, as he waylaid another vendor who was working the crowd with a huge wooden frame on his back. The frame was laden with trinkets: cheap plastic hats and shades, funny masks, necklaces, and glittery bits of nonsense. He bought a purple sequined domino mask and a thin glow stick hanging from a pink cord.

The mystery was too much for her. "What are you doing?"

Instead of answering, he held out the coconuts to her. "Here, hold these." She took them mutely and watched as he busied himself with breaking the fragile inner lining of the glow stick. As the two liquids within the tube blended together, a chemical reaction caused the stick to glow a brilliant neon pink. He hung the stick around her neck with a smile and immediately attempted to slip the domino mask over her face.

He's lost his mind, she decided. "What are you *doing*?" she asked again. She pressed her chin down against her chest in an effort to look at the new addition to her personal adornment, which was now glowing cheerily between her breasts.

He retrieved one of the coconuts and, putting the opening to his lips and tilting his head back, took a deep draught of it before saying, "Have a drink. I could have gotten you a straw, but it's much nicer if you drink it from the shell. Go ahead. Have a gulp."

He really was maddening. "Damon," she said warningly.

"Okay! Okay!" He lifted his hand and patted the mask lightly, and then let his fingers slip to her temple. She could feel the drumming of her pulse under his touch. "I remember that night we arrived, down on the promenade, when you were telling me about your father. About how he always used to talk about growing up here, in the city, and all the stories he used to tell you. And do you remember what you said?"

She shook her head. She had been distraught that night. She'd probably said a whole bunch of things. Whatever could she have told him to lead him to make these bizarre purchases?

He answered for her. "You told me that you've always wanted to come to Trinidad with him at Carnival time. You wanted to buy a costume and join the parade. You wanted him to buy you a coconut from a coconut vendor around the Savannah and drink water straight from the shell." He paused. "Well, you have no idea how sad I am that your father can't be here with you, so you could share this with him and see it all through his eyes. I know I'm a sorry replacement, but I thought that at least I could give you some sort of memory to take back with you. And I know it's not much, but"—he touched her mask again—"this is the best I could do on short notice as far as a costume is concerned." He added more cheerily, "Maybe we could come again another time, and we could get you a real one, with spandex and sequins and feathers all the way up to here." He stretched his hand on high.

Kenya felt her throat tighten. *Maybe we could come again another time.* Did he mean that? Did he really expect to be seeing her again after this trip was all over, or was he just using a turn of phrase?

Before she could ponder any longer, he went on. "And I thought you'd like the coconuts. We could drink to your Dad." He held his out, inviting her to toast with him, but to her shock, she couldn't move her hand to meet his. He remembered. She'd said something in the midst of her anguish—she'd made a passing comment, shared a private pain—and yet he'd remembered. He'd filed it away somewhere in his mind, and at the appropriate time he'd sought to do something about it. There was such tenderness in the gesture, so much kindness. How could he be so thoughtful?

There was so much more to this man than she had thought when she'd met him. A brute and a vagabond, she'd labelled him. A big, dim-witted gun for hire, dispatched to be a watch dog over her by a jittery manager. But with every encounter, he'd shown her more and more of him. As over-protective as he was, as overbearing as he could be, he was sharp-witted and compassionate. This afternoon she'd discovered that he was as generous a lover as he was demanding, and as strong as he was gentle, and as capable of dominance as he was of submission.

And now she was seeing something more. Something that went beyond compassion, to a point where he was feeling her hurt as though it were his own, and seeking to do something about it. He'd known, through some sixth sense, that although she was enjoying the festivities as any tourist would, she was also experiencing it through the eyes of someone whose roots were buried here, whose blood was answering the whispered call of the hills and the trees and the grass. Damon understood what she was feeling even before she could label it for herself, and he'd tried to put a bandage on her hurt. It was just a simple coconut, a silly, cheap plastic mask, and a glow stick that would peter into dullness in a matter of hours, but the hugeness of the heart behind it overwhelmed her. In that small, simple gesture, she lost the fight.

"Kenya?" His face was close to hers, his dark eyes anxious. "Did I do something wrong? If it was presumptuous of me, I apologize. I was only trying to—"

Her coconut fell to the ground with a thump, splashing water on her sandaled feet and the hem of her jeans. Her eyes stung, but she scrunched them hard, keeping the tears at bay through sheer force of will. Since she'd landed here, she'd been a complete wreck, spilling tears at the drop of a hat, and she hated herself for it. She was not, repeat, *not,* going to cry!

Damon must have set his own coconut down beside hers, because both his hands were on her hips, and she felt herself being hoisted into the air. She opened her eyes in surprise. "Damon!"

He held her aloft with ease, as though she weighed nothing. He was still apologizing profusely. "I'm sorry!

I'm sorry! I didn't mean to upset you. I was trying to make you feel better."

"You didn't upset me. You didn't. Not the way you think. That was sweet of you. It was just that . . ." She was in the unique position of being able to look down on him from above, and he was beautiful. She touched his face lightly, running her fingers along the shape of his brows, down his eyelids and the ridge of his nose, and tracing the curve of his lips, like a blind person reading Braille. "Oh, no," she gasped.

"What?" He was still frowning, still uncertain.

Undone. Something had crumbled. Something in her had broken—a wall, a barrier, a protective shield of some kind—and Damon had rushed in and taken possession of her soul. Not in the way Tobias had, like a Viking smashing his way through an unguarded castle, pillaging and plundering as he went, but with great stealth, slipping past the cracks in her defences while she was not looking.

And now, against her will, against her better judgment, she loved him. "Oh, God," she groaned.

Instead of inquiring again what was the matter, he merely looked up at her and let his eyes lock with hers, letting his powers of perception bore into her mind with the ease of a laser slicing through a wafer-thin sheet of metal. And he understood. "Oh, honey," he said softly.

"This isn't happening! It's not supposed to!"

"If it is, it's okay," he soothed. "It's okay. I wouldn't hurt you, not for anything. It's all right."

All right? That was easy for him to say. He wasn't the one whose world had just spun off its axis and been sent careening through an unknown universe. *This is just a passing thing,* her feverish brain tried to comfort her. *It's not forever. What's done can always be undone. There were ways. . . .*

But before she could explore those ways, or even come up with a few, he was lowering her a little, so that she was pressed against him, being held tightly with one arm around her waist and another supporting her under her bottom. "Come here," he whispered, and even with the din going on around them, she heard him. It was like being able to hear the snap of a single twig above the roar of a thunderstorm.

Still positioned above him, she lowered her head, and her mouth came in contact with his. Pandemonium! Earlier that afternoon, when she'd lain with her limbs entwined with his and her body coated with a heady mixture of his sweat and hers, she'd come to know the taste of his mouth, but tonight their kiss was seasoned with an emotion that had taken her unawares, and that made all the difference. Sweetness flowed from him to her and back again.

And whereas it had earlier taken long, purposeful coaxing on his part to elicit the desired response from her body, this newly discovered and unexpected love for him was a spark to a tinderbox, setting her body aflame. What he had achieved earlier with patience and concentration, fingers and tongue, he now drew from her with a single deep kiss. She gasped in shock, but the sound was barred from escaping by his lips against hers. Her fever-drenched body shuddered, and she pressed her hips against his, needing ever more contact. She had believed that after the hours she had spent in his arms, her thirst had been slaked after a long drought. She had been wrong.

The mask that covered her eyes became a barrier between them so she whipped it back, letting it dangle around her neck by the thin strip of elastic attached to it. The second it took to do that was far too long to break their kiss, so she tilted her head to kiss him again, but he resisted. She mewed in frustration. "What?"

"Kenya, all I want to do right now is to strip you down. . . ."

"Kiss me," she demanded.

". . . and lay you down right here on the grass under this huge, bright sky—"

"Kiss me *now*, Damon!"

"I don't know if I can again," he panted. "I don't know how much self-control I have left."

"You don't need it!" she blurted. "If you don't kiss me again right now, I swear . . ." She couldn't find an adequate ultimatum, so she trailed off, leaving her threat hanging in midair.

"I want to! I want to!" His voice was filled with equal urgency. "But there are so many people around. Sweetheart, we're in a very public place. Had you forgotten?"

In the heat of the moment, she *had* forgotten them. She looked around. If anything, the crowd around them had gotten larger. Most people seemed to be going somewhere, and those who weren't moving were settling in around them, some with beers and flasks of rum in hand, some with small children perched on their shoulders, some dancing and singing loudly. Nobody was paying them the slightest mind. "Nobody cares," she pointed out.

"I do," he replied. "I care. I want to kiss you over and over again, but I want you to myself . . . at least, as much to myself as I can get you in a place like this."

He still had not set her down, so she looked around, searching vainly in the midst of the chaos for a small oasis of privacy. "There!" she pointed over his head at a spreading Samaan tree near the border of the Savannah. "Under a tree!"

He didn't even bother to look around. "Ground's still wet from the rain. And I find it hard to imagine that there would be a tree anywhere on these grounds that hasn't already been claimed." He thought fast and then said, "I've got it. Let's go." He started moving off with her still in his arms.

Surely, he wasn't intending to drag her along like that! She tapped him on the shoulder. "Put me down. I can walk."

He laughed. "Sorry. I was in such a hurry." He bent forward, and she felt the ground under her feet once again. As she steadied herself, he had her hand and was already moving.

"Where are we going?" she wanted to know, but the question was moot, as she was already trotting along, trying her best to keep pace with him.

She didn't bother to ask a second time. He led her up the paved roadway that cut through the Savannah and into its very heart, the main stage. Even though large wooden barriers screened much of the stage from the view of the thousands without tickets who prowled its outskirts, Kenya was afforded a glimpse of the activity upon it. Brightly clad limbo dancers vied with drummers and performers on stilts for the attention of the audience. The main stands were chock-full with spectators, but stretching on both sides of the venue were several bleachers that would remain unoccupied until the next morning, when the daylight street parades would begin. These were protected from the roadway by flimsy wire fences. She had no doubt that this was his destination.

"We can't go in there!" She could barely stifle a giggle.

"Yes, we can. Look, there're a few holes in the fence. Go ahead; squeeze through, and I'll be right after you."

"We'll get caught," she protested, but she was already testing one of the gaps in the springy fence by yanking on it. It yawned open easily under her hand.

"No, we won't. Nobody's paying us any mind. Trust me. We'll be just fine."

Maybe it was the desire to be with him, and to take up once again where they had left off, that made her reckless. "Okay."

She had just squeezed easily past the fencing when he yelled, "Cops!"

"Damon!" She looked around frantically, expecting to see a handful of gray-uniformed officers descending upon them. There was no one there.

His grin told her he was pulling her leg. "Just kidding. But I had you going there for a moment, didn't I?"

She pursed her lips, unwilling to admit that she'd been had. "No, you didn't." Then she added a zinger of her own. "Although I must notify you that I'm not very . . . uh, *romantic* when I'm ticked off."

That put an end to his game right there. "Yes, ma'am. I read you loud and clear." He put on his best expression of sobriety and, with some effort, managed to squeeze his bulk through the same hole through which she had passed. "Now that," he panted, "was like trying to cram a whole month's worth of clearinghouse catalogues into a mailbox slot."

She patted him on the shoulder. "You did well."

"Thank you." He smiled down at her. "Well, we're inside. Where to next?"

She shivered with excitement. Pretty soon she would be in his arms again. That knowledge made her both excited and afraid. "You tell me."

He didn't need to think about it. He jerked his chin toward the top of the stands. "Up there. Hurry."

She hurried. At the top, he immediately began yanking off his denim jacket. He wasn't *undressing*, was he? To her relief, he merely spread the garment across the highest step and, with a gesture, invited her to sit. He settled down next to her and took her hand.

From where they now sat, they could look out along

the length of the main concourse that led to the stage,
as well as across much of the Savannah, until the farthest
reaches disappeared into the darkness. On the distant
hillsides twinkled lights from communities that were too
excited to sleep. One of them was her father's neighborhood. She could have given into sadness at that
thought, but she felt only contentment at being here
with Damon on such an enchanting night.

"It's beautiful out there," he murmured. "You can see
everything."

"Yes," she agreed.

A low laugh reverberated in his chest, and he shook
his head. "You know something?"

She looked up at him, smiling. "No, what?"

"I don't think I've made out with a girl in the bleachers since senior high."

"I don't think I've *ever* made out in the bleachers" was
her rejoinder. "My folks would have killed me."

"Strict, huh?"

"You said it. So, does it bring back lots of memories?"

"Well," he said modestly, "I wouldn't say *lots*. I hit six
feet by the time I was thirteen. By the time I was old
enough to be interested in girls, I'd scared off most of
them. But, yes, it does make me cast my mind back a bit."

"Does it make you feel old?"

He pondered for a minute. "No, no, it doesn't. If anything, it makes me feel young again. Thank you."

"What for?"

"Because when I'm with you, I don't feel like a burned-
out old wreck with a busted knee."

His fingers were laced with hers, and he ran his thumb
in circles in the palm of her hand. In the ocean of noise
and bustling activity that churned around them, they had,
indeed, found their quiet place. They were, effectively,

alone. She hung her head, overcome by uncharacteristic shyness.

"Am I scaring you now?"

"Like you did those girls, you mean?"

"Yes. Or in any other way. You tell me."

She was forced to be honest. "Maybe a little. But not in the way you imagine. Not because of how big you are. Although . . ." She glanced at him sideways. Even seated, he towered over her. "Although you're easily three times my size."

"Just about," he agreed, chuckling ruefully. "But there's little I can do about it. Maybe we should just fatten you up some, get you closer to my weight."

"Not a chance!"

"But you know I wouldn't hurt you," he added earnestly. "I'd handle you with the utmost care."

"I know." He'd showed her that already, proving even in the height of their loving that bulk did not translate into force. In fact, the sensation of being enfolded by him, engulfed by him, had brought her more pleasure than fear.

"What else, then?"

What else? How about, for starters, that she had just stumbled upon the shocking discovery that she was in love with him? And worse, even more devastating, that he had looked into her eyes and *known*. That knowledge gave him all power, lopsided power, because although he now knew without a doubt how she felt about him, she had no way of knowing what he felt for her, if anything, beyond sheer want.

But how could she explain this? *Should* she explain? She wet her lips nervously. Her courage failed her, and she waffled. "I don't know. It's just that I don't think . . ."

When she failed to go on, he grasped her chin in his hand and made her look at him. "That's just it: don't think. Feel. Feel, Kenya." He brushed his mouth against hers. "Feel this." He ran his fingers lightly down her throat to the opening of her blouse and stroked the valley between her breasts, like a pianist skimming over piano keys. "This."

She did feel him, and it was good. The embers that had cooled somewhat during their search for privacy whooshed into flame again. She clenched her teeth to prevent sound from betraying her.

"Does this scare you?"

Unable to speak, she shook her head.

He eased her jacket off her shoulders and let it fall onto the wooden step beside her, leaving her arms and shoulders bare. He bent forward and planted six light kisses in a straight line from her shoulder to the base of her neck. She closed her eyes and allowed her other senses to take over.

"This?" he asked.

"No," she managed to say, but so softly that she wasn't sure he'd heard her.

"Good," he whispered like a horse trainer soothing a skittish pony. "Then don't fight it. Give in. Come to me." Without asking her permission, he gathered her up in his lap and, instead of kissing her again, nestled her head against his chest and rocked her.

Chapter 17

Damon ruffled his hand through Kenya's hair, massaging her scalp and letting his fingers move from her hairline to her nape, over and over. By rights, his legs should have fallen asleep, since she had been perched in his lap for quite some time now. But to him, it was no more demanding than allowing a puppy to doze on him. He'd sought this sanctuary with her with every intention of trading more of the passionate kisses that had begun out there in the open, but that plan had fallen by the wayside, and they'd both been more than happy to sit quietly together in the shadows. And while he was quite sure that she had dozed off for a few moments from time to time, for the most part she keenly watched what little she could glimpse of the goings-on on the huge wooden Savannah stage and the endless stream of increasingly bizarre characters strolling past below.

They didn't say much to each other, and he was glad for that, as their mutual silence gave him time to think. How had all this happened? *What* had really happened? Hadn't he, mere hours ago, promised himself, consoled himself, that this thing between him and Kenya, as sweet as it was, was not love? Hadn't he decided that these feelings that tumbled over each other inside of him were the product of loneliness, sexual deprivation, and cultural displacement? He was supposed to have a handle on this. He was supposed to have this under control.

But he didn't. If this had been all about sex, would he have been happy to sit in the dark in this strange place, hold Kenya in his arms, and just watch people? Not likely. Any sexual hunger that had not already been slaked would long ago have motivated him to whisk her back to their car, and back to their hotel. That's what men in lust did. Sitting quietly, holding hands, enjoying the rise and fall of a woman's breathing, and feeling as though he'd stumbled into a state of bliss, well, that was the act of a man in love.

And what was better—or worse, depending on how one looked at it—was that Kenya loved him back. He knew it. He'd seen it with his own eyes, watched it happen just hours before. Their eyes had locked, and then something inside her visibly changed. It was as though a spirit of some kind had lit upon her like a bird upon a tree branch, and settled in, making her its home. She'd been poleaxed—and frightened. He didn't blame her. He was pretty scared himself.

Before he could ponder the subject some more, Kenya stirred.

"Uncomfortable?"

She laughed sheepishly. "Cramps."

"Get up, then." He let her get to her feet and then stood beside her, feeling the blood run back into his feet. Now that their little intimate bubble was popped, he felt awkward, not knowing what to say. She looked as though she was in the same predicament. "Show's finally over," he eventually commented as the last of the results of the various competitions were announced. "If that wasn't the longest show I've ever seen . . ."

She seemed glad for a neutral topic of discussion and agreed, waving her watch before his face. "Look at the time! It's almost two in the morning!"

"And the crowd keeps getting thicker and thicker. These people are amazing."

"And it's only just begun," she reminded him. "In a little while, the mayor's going to declare Carnival officially open, and then the J'Ouvert celebration starts."

"Jour what?"

"J'Ouvert. It's French Creole; it means the opening of the day. My father talked about it all the time. People get covered in clay and mud and go dancing in the streets until long after the sun comes up."

"Mud, huh?"

She was grinning excitedly. "And paint. And axle grease."

"Axle grease?" he echoed incredulously.

"That's what my Dad always said. He said when they were teens, he and his friends used to raid their mothers' closets for old nightgowns and slippers for the J'Ouvert parade. They used to wander about the streets with women's underwear on their heads."

"Whatever for?"

"Because they were young, and they thought it was funny. Because it's a rule of the game that you go out of the way to look as silly as you possibly can, and now, just for today, you can wear women's clothing, and nobody questions your masculinity. Because it's Carnival, and anything goes."

"This, I've got to see."

She held out her hand to him. "Then we have to get going. We'll see it best if we walk down to the promenade. Where we stopped that first night."

"I remember."

"Well, that's where most of it's going to happen. You game?"

"I'm game." He was glad for the opportunity to see more of Carnival, but even gladder for the fact that the activity would spare him having to think anymore about this situation in which he now found himself. All this merry madness would be the ideal diversion. When he was back in the quiet of his room again, he would let himself think. But not now.

Instead of taking her hand right away, he reached down and collected both their jackets from the bleacher step, handed hers over, and began to shrug on his own. As he did so, he saw her glaze flick to the holster that was strapped to him. He could hear her thoughts as easily as if she had spoken them aloud. "I have to wear it, Kenya."

"I know," she said, but she didn't sound happy about it.

"I still have a job to do. I'm here to watch over you."

"I know."

He was glad when his jacket was on, obscuring the offending weapon from her view. That done, he took her hand, which was still extended. It was small and warm in his. Side by side, they began to descend the steps.

Apart from the surprised look of a young woman who happened to be passing by their access hole as they popped back through the fence, nobody paid them any mind. Everyone seemed to be going somewhere. Everyone seemed to have plans. "Lead the way," he told her.

Her brows lifted in fake surprise. "Me? Don't you have your little city map etched into your brain?"

"Yes, and in my back pocket, too."

"You brought it with you?" She sounded genuinely surprised.

"Of course. I wouldn't want to lose you. Precious cargo." He watched her face flush and then added, "But this is your father's odyssey. It's up to you to retrace his steps."

They joined a flood of other people who all seemed to be headed in the same direction, drawn by the same purpose. As they left the Savannah behind them and followed the flow toward the port, the crowd grew even thicker, pressing in on them. The smell of bodies, cigarette smoke, and rum was heavy, mingling with that of discarded orange peels and coconut shells in the drains that ran along the sidewalks.

"Stick with me," he instructed, all business for a change. He had to yell above the din to be heard. "Whatever you do, don't let go of me."

She seemed amused by his protectiveness. "If we get separated, I'll stick my glow stick up in the air. You look around, and you'll find me."

He shook his head vigorously, not willing to take her teasing lightly. She was far too excited to spot the many potential dangers of being engulfed by such a large crowd. "Glow stick, nothing. First of all, half these people are wearing glow sticks of their own. Second, you're five foot zero. Even if you did hold your hand up in the air, I doubt it could be seen above a crowd this size. Stick with me. Don't let go." For emphasis, he squeezed her fingers in his.

"Yes, boss," she grumbled, but she didn't stay disgruntled for long. There was way too much to see. By the time they made it down to the Promenade, as hampered as their speed had been by the thickness of the crowd, Carnival had officially been declared open. Neither the activities that had gone before, nor Kenya's blithe description of the event, had been enough to prepare Damon for any of it.

It was chaos, pure and simple. As though a dam had broken, rivers of people poured out of nowhere. True to Kenya's word, whole bands of them were slicked in every imaginable wet substance. Men and women, old and young, had stripped themselves down to the barest essentials required for decency and then smeared themselves from head to toe in yellow clay, brown mud, or gruesome globs of red or blue body paint. Some sported cardboard devils' horns and rope tails; some wore haphazardly made African tribal headpieces and costumes, complete with grass skirts, handpainted tin shields, and broomstick spears. And, yes, here and there men wearing ladies' nightgowns and bathrobes stumbled around in women's slippers and high heels, with hideous wigs perched carelessly on their heads like hats, looking mighty pleased with themselves.

Music blasted so loudly from the backs of trucks that crawled slowly alongside the masqueraders that nearby shop windows vibrated with the beat. Steel bands and dozens, even hundreds, of musicians earnestly coaxing the sweetest of melodies out of what looked like upside down oil drums did their best to be heard above the superior volume of the electronic entertainment. They were balanced on huge silver floats and conveyed along the roadway by dozens of volunteers, who alternately pushed the floats and paused to gyrate to the beat of the music.

And the people celebrated, having been given permission by the very nature of Carnival to strip off the constraints of an otherwise conservative society and be whatever they wanted, and do whatever they wanted, if only for these two fantastic days out of every year. Couples kissed with abandon and danced and laughed; men passed along bottles of rum, drinking deeply, even pouring the liquid on each other's heads. The younger participants chased strangers with buckets of mud, threatening to smear them unless a small forfeit, like a dollar or a cigarette, was paid. Even small children, excited at being allowed out with their parents at such a late hour, darted in and out of the crowd, rubbing their hands along the backs and bellies of accommodating grown-ups and then stamping muddy or paint-smeared handprints along the walls of unfortunate business places along the route. It was as though Bacchus himself had descended upon the city and declared himself king.

"This is insane!" Damon shouted in Kenya's ear.

She grinned up at him. Her spirit had been seized by the beat, and she was dancing excitedly beside him, hopping up onto tiptoe every now and then to try to peer down the road to see what else was coming. "Isn't it great?"

Damon wasn't so sure. He loved to travel and to soak up every experience that came his way, and this was one that he would never forget. Even Carnival in Brazil was not like this. And had he been alone, he would have let his guard down—perhaps even stepped into the roadway and indulged in the revelry of party and paint—but he had Kenya's safety to think about, and she didn't seem to be very adept at thinking about it herself. "I guess it is," he answered doubtfully.

"You *guess* it is?" she repeated. "I've never seen anything like this! I've been waiting my whole life to experience this. It's wonderful!" She dragged her hand from his grip and threw her arms up and waved them in time to the music, like palm fronds waving in the wind. "Dance with me!"

Dance? With his knee being what it was? That would be a spectacle. "I wouldn't know how."

"You just move!"

"I couldn't," he apologized. "I'm sorry."

"Spoilsport," she grunted but didn't seem to take it personally. She returned to dancing on her own, a blissful smile on her face.

Damon tried to be glad for her. The enjoyment on her face made him happy that they had come. At least, when this was all over, she would have the memory of this eventful night to look back on. So he did the best that he could, watching her, sticking by her side even in the midst of all that excited shoving and pushing.

But, as it turned out, his best fell just short of good enough, because right then his worst fears were realized. He wasn't sure how exactly it began, but the tumultuous crowd parted like the Red Sea, people crying out in alarm. In the middle of the road, two men were fighting. One wore mock army fatigues, the other just blue jeans and little else. His bare chest glistened with sweat, and in one outstretched hand, Damon spied something small, metallic, and sharp.

He sprang into action, grabbing Kenya by the elbow. "Come on, let's go."

"What?"

"Let's go. This is getting too rough."

"Go where?"

"Away. I don't know. This is going to get nasty."

She wrenched away from him. "Are you serious? You're joking, right?" She waved her arms in the direction of the brawling men. "You're worried over that? That's just two men who've had too much to drink. They're yards away from us. It's just a little fight, Damon; that's all. Calm down!"

He was insistent. "Fights set off other fights. That's the way it goes. Come, now. Move away."

To his despair, she choose just that moment to be difficult. "I am not a little girl. I'm not—"

He never found out what she was going to say next, because at that moment a bottle arced skyward, shattering on the concrete sidewalk, and everyone scattered, shoving and screaming as they went. "That does it," he decided aloud. "We're going."

But she wasn't there. People scurrying from the brawl

darted between them, cutting her off from his view. Damon set his shoulder against the flow of the crowd, forcing his way through the revellers in the direction where Kenya had been standing, but he could not see her.

"Kenya!" He yelled her name, but in the din he could hear no response.

He was truly frightened now. He'd lost her. Just like that. She'd been standing right there, giving him lip as she always did, and then the river of people burst its banks, and she had been washed away. He'd done it again. Lost a woman. A client. A lover. He'd slipped up, and she was gone.

The brawling men rolled past him until they were separated by friends, who dragged them away in opposite directions, sparing them from doing harm to each other. Then the Red Sea closed again, leaving Damon standing alone.

Too many people. They were all around Kenya, pressing hard on her on all sides, and she couldn't see Damon anywhere. She tried to quell a momentary surge of panic. Where was he? All she remembered had been a rush, and hot, moving bodies had shoved her along. Her survival instinct told her that she had better move with them, or risk falling and being trampled. Now there was space between her and the spot where she'd last seen him. Not much, maybe thirty or forty yards, but in a crowd this thick, and with dawn still a long way off, it might just as well have been a mile.

She craned her neck, trying to get her bearings from nearby buildings. A bank, they'd been standing near a bank. She remembered that because its façade had been all boarded up, a small but vital defense against people who might choose to enhance their excitement by hurling objects through its plate glass frontage. If only she could get to higher ground, climb some steps, maybe, she'd be able to see better.

A strong, familiar scent carried on the wind distracted her briefly from her purpose. Incredulous, she sniffed the air. *Chocolate?* It couldn't be. She had to be imagining things. She turned to face the road again. A new band of revellers had taken center stage, and they, incredibly, were doused from head to toe in chocolate. They danced along the street, wave after wave of cocoa-covered bodies moving in rhythm, having the time of their lives. As nervous as she was at being separated from Damon, she had to choke back a laugh. These Trinidadians were endlessly innovative. However had they come up with that?

"Having fun?" The voice in her ear was friendly and loud. One of the dancers, a small, gawky man of indeterminate age, was standing next to her, clad in nothing but slippers, a pair of shorts, and several ounces of oily chocolate sauce. His bare knees and knobby elbows stuck out at odd angles, making him look like a strange little bird. Even his glasses were smeared with the stuff, making her wonder why he bothered to wear them in the first place. It coated his hair, leaving it standing straight up in stiff spikes. The only thing that was not chocolate covered, ironically, was his grinning mouth. "Having fun?" he asked again.

"I am," she admitted. "Or, I was, but I got separated from my friend."

He laughed. "I'll be your friend. That's what Carnival is all about. You lose friends, and you find new ones. I'm Fred." He grasped her hand and shook it hard, leaving a sticky brown smear in her palm.

Politeness caused her to respond in kind. "Um, Kenya." She looked around, still hoping to miraculously spot Damon in the crowd. "But, I—"

"Kenny?"

"Kenya!" she yelled even louder.

He seemed neither to hear nor care. He wasn't taking no for an answer. He held out a metal flask. "Here, have some chocolate."

"Uh," she stammered. "No, thanks. I'm not hungry."

He shook his head, delighted by her naive response. "No, no. Not to eat. To wear! Rub it on!"

Under any other circumstances, that might have been fun, but not right now. She didn't like being separated from Damon. She knew that it was in her interest to find him and stick a little closer to him from now on. "I think I'll just watch, if you don't mind!"

"Oh, no, no, no. No watching allowed. No spectators, only participants." To her horror, he squeezed out a handful of the glop onto his hand, rubbed a large smear on each of her cheeks, and ran a stripe down her nose with one finger. Then, like a crazed artist, he stepped back to admire his handiwork. "Great, Kenny. You look great. Now, come on! Dance!"

He's so silly, she thought. *So funny.* But she shouldn't. She opened her mouth to protest, but he preempted her. "Don't disappoint me! Don't waste all this wonderful music!" He slipped one chocolaty arm around her waist and whirled her around. "See, like this!"

She should have refused and extricated herself from his grasp, but the gesture was so endearing that she gave in and took a few steps. She wasn't even trying to imitate his awkward, jerky, comical movements, but he was delighted nonetheless. "That's it! There you go! Having fun now, right?"

She never got the chance to answer, because a bomb went off right there and then, and she and her strange new companion were at ground zero.

Chapter 18

Kenya watched the odd, chocolate-covered man go flying backward until he hit the pavement and skated to a stop. She looked around, nonplussed. What had happened?

The answer wasn't long in coming. Damon had happened. Before she could react, he was standing between her and the fallen man, towering over him, one fist still raised.

"You hit him!" she squawked and rushed to place herself between the two men. The poor fellow on the ground look dazed and could do nothing but stare bewilderedly up at his assailant. "What did you hit him for?"

"He was dragging you around!"

"He was not dragging me around! He was dancing with me!"

He gestured at her. "And you're covered in . . . What is that? Mud? Grease?"

Irate, Kenya raked her hand across her cheek and smeared the residue across Damon's lips. "Chocolate! It's only chocolate! Nothing sinister about it. See?"

Damon rubbed his lips and stared down at his fingers, perplexed. She turned her back to him and struggled to help the little man to his feet, but he seemed to be searching for something. From the flustered frown on his face and the way he was myopically sweeping his hands across the sidewalk, feeling rather than looking, she understood: his glasses. She found them with some effort, but to her dismay, they had either broken in their fall or been smashed under uncaring feet. She hesitated before handing them over to the man, who was glancing, bug-eyed, from Damon to her and back again. "They're broken," she apologized. "I'm so, so sorry."

She looked up at Damon, wondering if he was going to add to her apology, but although obviously unsure of himself, he had not relaxed his aggressive pose. "What are you going to do, Damon? Hit him again?" She helped the man to his feet and proffered the broken glasses again. He took them and turned them over and over in his chocolate-smeared hands, as though he was unsure whether they were indeed his.

Damon finally lowered his arm, mortified, and began apologizing profusely. "I'm sorry, I'm sorry. I misunderstood."

"Damn right, you did," she snapped before her new friend could say anything.

"Did I hurt you?" Damon asked, concerned now, but instead of answering, the little man shrank back.

Kenya was still livid. "What do you think? He's even smaller than I am, and you sent him flying. What's wrong with you? Don't you stop to think before you do something like this? Do you think what you did is okay? Well, it's not. You can't just go around hitting people, Damon!"

He defended his actions. "I thought you were in danger!" He turned to the man, reaching into his jacket pocket and pulling out his wallet. "I'm sorry. I was wrong. Let me pay for the glasses." He began extricating a number of high-value American bills, much more than the glasses could reasonably cost, and held them out. But Kenya's new friend had had enough. With one final, frantic glance at Kenya, he squeaked like a terrified rabbit and fled.

"Don't! Please, take this," Damon shouted after him, but the crowd had already swallowed him up, and he was gone.

Kenya put her hands on her hips. "Happy now? Are you happy, Damon?"

He put his money away, leaned his broad back against a building, and let his head fall into his hands. "No. No, I'm not happy."

"Ashamed, then?" she needled him.

He nodded wordlessly. He couldn't even look at her. He looked so devastated by his own actions that she would have felt sorry for him had she not been so mad.

"You can't just go around hitting people!" she said once again. "Can't you understand that?"

"I thought he was hurting you!" he protested.

"Did he look like he was hurting me? Did I look like I was being hurt? Did you even take the time to find out for sure?"

He thought about it for a while and then admitted, "No, I didn't. I saw him dragging you around, and something tripped."

"And you just came charging in."

"I came in and did my job. I was hired to protect you; don't ever forget that."

She snapped her fingers dismissively. There it was again: his job. The rock behind which he always sought refuge whenever she questioned his behaviour. "Don't give me that. Even if you thought you were doing your job, every job leaves room for discretion. You're supposed to think before you execute your mandate, not act like some sort of robot programmed to protect me at all costs. And as far as I recall," she added caustically, "I fired you two days ago."

He winced and then rubbed his brow slowly, as if nursing a headache. "You did."

"Yes, I did. And just so as there is no mistake about it, I'm doing it again right now. Get off my back, Damon. It doesn't need to be watched."

He didn't even try to talk her out of it this time. He nodded with weary acceptance. "Okay. But you should know that there's a reason for the way I reacted. Something that happened a long time ago. Not that it makes it right. But there is a reason."

"Spill it, then," she said impatiently.

A battle went on behind his face, but his will lost. He shook his head vehemently. "I can't. I can't talk about it."

"Oh, so I'm supposed to accept that there's a reason, but you won't tell me what it is?"

"*Can't* tell you what it is. I'm just asking you to trust me on this."

Trust him? Therein lay the problem. She thought she had. Just hours before, she had sat on his lap, revelling in the warm scent of him and the feel of his arms around her, and she had trusted him then more than she had ever trusted anyone. She'd even felt the first scary beginnings of love, but now that had been crushed. Love and trust, trust and love; they were a package deal. You couldn't have one without the other.

And trusting him was just plain impossible. How could she when he held this possessive, overwhelming anger down inside him, like a monster chained to a rock? So far, she had witnessed only the rattling of those chains, and that had been scary enough. What if one day those chains snapped under force, and that monster was set loose?

Tobias had been controlling; he had sought to dictate what she wore, whom she spoke to, and what direction her career should take. That was why she had left him. But Damon, he was different. He seemed propelled by an otherworldly force, something she couldn't even hope to fathom, and that made her powerless. How could you fight an enemy you neither knew nor understood?

Her hesitation made him anxious. "Answer me, please," he begged. "Can you trust me?"

She was too weary to answer, but her silence spoke for her.

He read her response, and a pained look crossed his face. "If you don't want me working for you, I understand that. I accept that. But there's more going on here than just this job. What about us? You and me? I know you feel something for me. You didn't even have to say anything; I saw it on your face. I felt it when you touched me. You couldn't hide it. That's more important than any stupid job. It's worth more, and I'm not prepared to give up on that so easily. We need to see where this goes."

That was true. She had felt something, and denying it would be pointless. But her chest was so tightly constricted that she couldn't tell if she was feeling anything right now, apart from the urgent need to get away. So she shook her head.

"Don't do this," he pleaded. "Not now. We were just . . . beginning."

"And now I'm ending it." She sounded more certain than she felt, and that was a good thing, because if Damon had any inkling of her lack of conviction, he could persist, press a little harder, and change her mind, so great was her weakness for him.

Even without that encouragement, he tried. He stepped in front of her and took both her unresisting hands in his, bringing them up to his mouth. He brushed his lips along the tips of her fingers and then turned her hands over, palms up, and pressed a kiss into each one. "Sweet, this isn't over. This is too good, too big, to be over. Come back to the hotel with me—"

She couldn't give in to him. She had to be firm. "No." She wrenched her hands away, because with that simple touch, her resolve had begun to erode.

"We're both very tired," he insisted. "We're too tired to make any rational decisions right now. Let me take you back to the hotel, and we can shower and sleep, and then, when we wake up fresh, we can talk this over. But don't do this here in this place. It's way too loud and too dirty. Let's take this somewhere private and talk—"

"*No!*" she repeated. "There's nothing to talk about."

He wasn't giving up. "There is, and you know it. Don't try to tell me you didn't feel—"

A desperate need for self-preservation made her lie, "Nothing. I don't feel anything."

He stared in stunned disbelief. "But I thought . . . I know what I saw—"

"You misunderstood." She had to bite her lip to keep it from trembling.

He looked about to say more, but then the fight went out of him, and his shoulders sagged. "Fine. That's it, then. You win, Kenya."

Win? Why didn't she feel victorious? Why was there nothing in her stomach but a burning sense of loss and grief?

He gestured uptown. "Let's go, then."

"Go where?"

"Back to the car, if it's still there. Just let me see you safely home, and then I'll let you be. I have never in my life forced my company—or my attentions—upon a woman, and I'm not about to start now. I'll fly back to New

York as soon as I can arrange a flight, and then I'll be out of your hair."

If she went with him, if she found herself alone in the confines of a vehicle with him, she was sure her resolve would weaken, so she refused. "I'm not going back. I like it here."

He was stunned. "You're staying? Here?"

"Of course!" she forced a laugh. "It's Carnival. Look around you. Everyone's having a good time. I've waited all my life to experience this. I didn't come all the way over here just to walk away in the middle of it all. I'm not going home now."

He looked doubtful. "It's still a little dark out."

She pointed toward the east, where a pink glow tinted the sky. "Sun's coming up. I'll be just fine. Besides, I'm an adult. I'm allowed out on my own, aren't I?"

There were a hundred things that he could have said, and she prepared herself for any one of them, but all he did was hold her in one final embrace and place a light kiss upon the top of her head. His sigh was almost a groan. "As you wish, sweet" was all he said. Then he left her.

Damon stood under the steaming water of the shower, letting it pound down upon him until his palms and fingers were wrinkled, but no amount of hot water could wash away the film of shame, self-disgust, and despair that clung to him. When he eventually shut the water off and stepped out of the stall, his entire bathroom was swathed in a cloud of mist, as at a hot spring in the middle of the jungle. He was glad that the mirror was fogged over; he had no desire to look himself in the face right now.

He didn't bother to towel himself dry. Instead, he clambered wearily onto his supersized bed and stretched out, oblivious to the damp marks he was leaving on the clean, crisp sheets. He'd never felt so alone in his life, not when he was off on an assignment, stuck in a remote corner of some far-off land, or back home at his New York apartment, holed up between jobs and decompressing from a long, arduous trip. Not when he'd first injured his knee and found himself spending days, weeks, flat on his back in bed, strapped into metal torture devices masquerading as medical equipment. Not even in the months right after Jewel died.

He closed his eyes, trying to relax both body and mind, hoping to create an atmosphere conducive to a visit from her. He had no power to conjure her up, but his unconscious mind, merciful as it was, often allowed him a glimpse of her whenever his life became dark. He was no fool: he knew she wasn't real. He didn't believe in ghosts or apparitions. He knew that the wraith that misted in and out of his life was merely a figment of his imagination, but yet, she always brought him solace. If he ever needed her, it was now.

"Jewel?" he called softly into the ether. There was no response. He called again, more softly yet.

He let out a broken sigh. Still nothing, but he hadn't expected an answer. Something inside him knew that it was over. There would be no more visits, no more imagined conversations. Without even knowing it, Kenya had swept Jewel away like cobwebs, packing her up and bundling her into his hope chest of memories, along with love letters and old bottles of her perfume.

It didn't mean that he loved Jewel less. He was sure that he would be eighty and still his love for her would be as fresh as it had been on the night that he had presented her with the ring that had brought about her destruction. But the human heart was a funny thing: it was infinitely expandable. No matter how much space this remembered love occupied, there was always more than enough room for Kenya.

There was no fooling himself anymore. What he felt for Kenya had nothing to do with what he had felt for Jewel. It was not transferred emotion, not an illusion that could be dismissed once he returned to New York. This was something geography could not change. It was something time could not change. It was enduring, and it was real.

And he'd gone and messed it up. He'd acted rashly, foolishly, without thinking. If only he had had the wisdom to give himself fifteen seconds, ten even, to analyze the situation in which he had finally found Kenya after frantically searching for her, he would have understood that she was not in harm's way. But he hadn't. Instead, he had acted on impulse and brought hurt and embarrassment to an innocent man, and worse, destroyed the fragile tissue of trust and emotion that had been growing between himself and Kenya.

He didn't expect her to forgive him; he was hardly prepared to forgive himself. But there was one thing he wished she would understand: he had acted not out of possessiveness, as she assumed, but out of overprotectiveness. His desire had never been to own her, to dictate where she should go and whom she should speak to. That, he knew, was the stumbling block upon which her previous relationship with her manager had fallen. All he had ever wanted to do was to save her, preserve her from a world that harbored far more ills than she would ever know. That had been his real crime. For that, he'd been tried, found guilty, and sentenced to being alone.

If he didn't hear another human voice, he was sure he would go mad. He considered going out to the hotel restaurant, but he balked at the merrymaking that would in all likelihood be taking place out there, with some guests coming in from the city all grimy and excited at what they had seen, and others filling up on a good meal before stepping out into the mayhem. These were times when even calling the speaking clock seemed like a viable way to hear a friendly voice.

He hesitated and then reached out and picked up the phone from the bedside table, dialing a number from memory. It rang several times before it was picked up on the other end. "Hello?"

Relief trickled into him, warm and comforting. "Cousin," he said. "What were you doing? The phone rang half a dozen times. Where were you? Aren't you supposed to be working?"

Leshawn laughed. "Nice to hear you, too. And sorry about that. Marilee's out shopping with her mother. Girl stuff, you know. Shoes or something. I took the easy way out: I stayed home with the baby."

"How's she doing?"

"Getting on my nerves, but they can do that to you. She already broke a lamp, ate some shoe polish, and scared away the cat. And she's only been up half an hour."

The image made him smile. His niece was still only at the crawling stage, but she ran on self-charging batteries. "Glad to hear fatherhood is agreeing with you," he said indulgently.

"Oh, it is. It is." There was a pause, and then Leshawn asked carefully, "So, how's it going out there?"

He briefly considered putting up a brave front and pretending that things were okay, but that was not what he had called to do. He answered honestly. "It's not going at all. We've been fired."

Leshawn was incredulous. "You what?"

"You heard me. Kenya Reese fired us. Fired me."

"She didn't hire you," Leshawn pointed out rationally.

"Doesn't matter. She told me in no uncertain terms

that she doesn't want me around, and I'm not about to split hairs on that subject. So I'm coming back as soon as I can."

"Want me to arrange a flight for you?"

He shook his head, even though Leshawn couldn't see him. "No, that's okay. I can handle this." He waited for Leshawn's questions.

They came. "What happened? Why'd she fire you? What was she there for in the first place? Did something . . . ," he hesitated, ". . . go wrong?"

So much had gone wrong, he didn't know where to start, but he knew just where Leshawn was coming from. He decided to put his fears to rest at once. "She's fine. She's not hurt in any way. At least I managed that much."

"What, then?"

He supposed he should start at the beginning, so he quickly filled his cousin in on Kenya's reasons for being there and the single disastrous encounter with Eric Reese at the nightclub.

When Damon was finished, Leshawn asked for clarification. "So she's upset because you refused to leave her alone with the man?"

"That, and a bit more." He thought once again about the chocolate-covered catastrophe that had taken place earlier that morning. That was one thing he was too ashamed to own up to, even to Leshawn.

"Well, you were perfectly correct. You'd have been delinquent to leave her alone under those circumstances."

"I know that. But she thinks I threw a monkey wrench into her works, as far as getting information from him is concerned. She hasn't forgiven me for it."

"Well, just because this man is her brother, or half brother, doesn't say he means her no harm."

"I'm not even sure he *is* her brother. There's something

about him, and this whole scenario, that doesn't sit right with me."

"But all the signs point to the probability that he is."

"Maybe, but I don't like him. I haven't been able to do any checking, because all the government offices are closed for Carnival. They should all open up on Ash Wednesday, but I'll probably be on my way back by then. I want to help, but my hands are tied. She doesn't want me."

"Doesn't want you, huh," Leshawn echoed. His tone spoke volumes.

Busted. Leshawn knew. His voice had somehow communicated what he felt inside for Kenya. No confession would be forthcoming, because none was necessary. He stayed on the line in hangdog silence.

"Damon, what have you gone and done?" Leshawn asked softly.

"I haven't done anything. It just happened. Do you think I would be nuts enough to plan something like this? Deliberately?"

Leshawn took the rational approach. "It's not real. This is an illusion. She's a beautiful woman, an actress. These people, they thrive on glamour and glitz. You're probably not even seeing the real her, just what she wants you to see. Whatever you think she is, it's probably all fantasy."

"I've never met anyone so down-to-earth in my life," he argued in Kenya's defense. "She may be in the business, but the business isn't in her. Understand?"

Leshawn counterattacked. "Well, then, it's all about Jewel. You're lonely, and you miss her. Then you're thrown into the same set of circumstances: you're alone in the tropics with a beautiful single woman. You're trying to recapture what you had before. Your mind is playing tricks on you."

That had been his own first guess, but he knew now

that he'd been wrong. "I thought that was it, but it's not true—"

"It's the island. It's the excitement. Come back to New York; once you get the cold wind in your face, you'll be able to think rationally again. You'll see. Once you put some distance between you two—"

"This is not about where I am and where she is, Leshawn!" He protested a little more vehemently than he had intended to. "This is not going to go away with a plane ride."

Leshawn was placid. "Okay, okay. I'm sorry." He seemed to be thinking for a while. When he spoke next, he'd decided to give Damon the benefit of the doubt. "What are you going to do, then?"

What *was* he going to do? What *could* he do? Kenya had shunned him, and he deserved it. "I don't know. She thinks I'm a monster. And she could be right."

Leshawn leaped at that statement. "Why? What happened?"

He couldn't bear to explain, so he answered vaguely. "I scared her. I lost it this morning, thinking I was doing the right thing, and I scared her."

"That doesn't make you a monster, Damon." Leshawn tried to soothe him, but it didn't work. When Damon looked at himself, he didn't like what he saw. In the last four years he'd let himself sink deeper and deeper into a prison of his own fears. That wasn't something you just shrugged off like an old coat. It would take time, and introspection, to make those demons go away. And he would have to start right now.

"I think I'd better go, Leshawn," he said abruptly. At least, if there was one advantage to his banishment, it gave him the solitude to work this thing out.

"You sure?" Leshawn sounded doubtful and was reluctant to let the conversation come to such a sudden end.

"I'm sure."

"You'll be all right?"

"I'll be fine." He was more sure of that than he had been since he came to this island. "I just need some time to think."

Leshawn hesitated but gave in gracefully. "Okay, but if you ever need to talk about it, I'm on the other end of this line, right?"

"I know that." It was comforting to know that if he ever needed a rock to lean on, his cousin would be there. "You go take care of my niece, okay? Before she brings the house down on you both."

"Roger that," Leshawn managed to laugh. "Take care."

"I will." The line went dead. He was alone again, but it didn't feel so bad. He remained on the bed, still naked, staring up at the fan overhead, allowing the whirring blades to lull him. But even though he appreciated the solitude, he listened for the slightest squeak next door, the sound of a footstep, that would let him know that Kenya had returned. He had no intention of intruding upon her when she did come back: she was still much too angry for any approach that he might have made, but he needed to know that she was safe. The problem was that his gut told him that he would be hearing no such sound anytime soon.

He knew Kenya. When she set her mind to something, there was no stopping her. Even in the midst of all the madness taking place outside, she had a goal to fulfill, and she was going to achieve it, no matter what it took. He knew where she was headed, and that both pained and scared him. Because he'd given his word that he would butt out and leave her alone. There was not a thing that he could do to help her. . . .

Or maybe there was. He frowned, thinking hard. Kenya didn't want his protection, but she hadn't said a thing about refusing his help. He had the training and knowledge to do a little snooping of his own, and although it was true that Carnival had shut down many avenues of information in Trinidad, there was more than one way to skin a cat. He hit the redial button on the phone, which he still held in his hand.

It picked up on the third ring. "Hello?"

"Me again."

Leshawn sounded immediately anxious. "Did something happen?"

"No."

"What then?"

"I need a favor."

"Shoot," Leshawn said.

Damon told him exactly what he wanted.

Chapter 19

The sun had long come up and was now relentlessly beating down from overhead. The mud and clay that once glistened on the happy faces all around Kenya were now dried and caked, flaking off in great chunks or crumbling from human skin like artifacts being blown to dust on hot Saharan sand. And still, the people danced. Never in her life had Kenya witnessed any party that had ever gone on so long and with such perpetual energy. Watching the endless pantomime playing out around her, she even became convinced that somehow, magically, the masqueraders had contrived to suck the energy directly out of her, like marrow from her bones.

Tired, she sat on a stoop in the doorway of an old, shuttered house and contemplated her position. It wasn't the happy people swarming around her who had robbed her of her energy; it was her own anger. Anger at Damon. He had gotten on her very last nerve back there. Angered her, disappointed her, and even scared her.

Now, why'd he have to go and do that? Things had been going so well. The thing that had sprung up between them had been so fragile, like a little flower struggling its way upward through a crack in the sidewalk, and then he'd gone and stomped on it. She put her hand to her mouth, feeling gingerly for traces of his kisses. Her lips felt as though something were missing. Her arms felt awkward, empty. They missed holding Damon.

Stop that, she chided herself irritably. *That was a mistake.* It was too crazy to have been real. It had to have been the atmosphere, the buzz of excitement that hung in the air all around. That was it. The festive air had gone to her head faster than a shot of overproof rum. Now that he was far from her, she could think sanely again—rationally. And her rational mind explained to her that the last thing she needed in her life right now was another man who just had to be in control, who watched every step she took. She'd already been to that place, and she'd hadn't liked it one bit.

The disturbing thing, however, was that unlike Tobias, Damon's compulsion for control wasn't born out of jealousy or insecurity: he was simply so terrified that something would happen to her if he wasn't around that he wasn't prepared to let her out of his sight even for a moment. She didn't need that. She couldn't stand to live like that. Getting rid of him was the right thing to do. Wasn't it?

But that mournful look of puzzlement that he had given her when she'd pushed him away still haunted her. He truly couldn't understand why she had been so mad. He was like a big, loyal dog who insisted on following his mistress to school every day, whether she wanted him to or not. But what was done was done, and that was the end of it. She shook off her guilt.

It was better like this. Damon had gotten in her way, and not just during a little innocent dance with a kindly stranger. He was a hindrance to her search for the truth about her father. Eric Reese had made it very clear: he was not prepared to speak to her if Damon was present. Well, Damon's presence was no longer a problem. The most she could do was take advantage of that.

She got to her feet slowly, her bones letting her know just how little they appreciated how badly she had been treating her body over the past few days. "Just a little longer," she promised herself with as much sincerity as she could summon. "Then we can put this all behind us and take a breather." The problem was, she didn't exactly believe her own attempt at reassuring herself. The mission she was about to undertake was folly itself, and she was lucky if all she came away with was a pair of very sore feet and a serious case of fatigue.

She strained to get her bearings. She was in the part of town where The Boom Box, the nightclub where Eric sang, was located. But, as far as she could ascertain, the neighborhood of Woodbrook spanned several city blocks, and she had no way of knowing whether the club lay to the east, west, north, or south of her.

She didn't let that stop her, and instead of wandering aimlessly in search of a familiar landmark, which, in this chaos, would have taken forever, she solved the problem the same way she would have back in New York: she asked the nearest police officer—who just happened to be riding a very large and intimidating-looking chestnut horse.

Even with the policeman's patient directions, it took her the better part of an hour to find the small club. She found herself wishing that Damon was still there with her, guiding her, solving pesky problems, like finding places in the quickest possible time. But what was she thinking? She didn't need him! She could handle this herself.

At the entrance to the club, she stopped. Like many of the other bars and party places she had passed, it was teeming with life, even in broad daylight. Tables had been set up at the entrance, and a handful of bartenders sold drinks right there on the sidewalk, fishing into open oil drums filled with icy water with their bare hands to pull out frosty bottles of beer and stout, or serving small flasks of potent rum to patrons who lingered nearby, watching the parade, or who were part of the parade themselves.

She hesitated, searching the faces of the busy workers, hoping for a sign that her questions would be welcome or, at least, tolerated. Hoping for a familiar face, even in the midst of this mayhem.

Then she found one. Incredibly, she spotted the heavy-set bouncer who had been itching to pit his strength against Damon's when he thought she had needed rescuing, and who had later been accommodating enough to allow her access to Eric once Damon had slipped something into his palm. He was patting his forehead with a small hand towel with the air of a man who had pushed the barriers of exhaustion and gone beyond.

He was the answer to her prayers. She hurried forward, stepping directly into his path. "Hello," she said loudly above the music. She tried to smile self-assuredly.

The man didn't seem to hear her at first, or was prepared to ignore her, but then he stopped. Recognition flickered. "Miss," he responded.

"Remember me?" she asked tentatively.

He nodded. "Saturday night. Almost got yourself killed in the road. Nobody ever teach you to look where you're going?"

She took the gentle chastisement with good grace. "I was stupid."

He shrugged. "Careless, maybe." He glanced behind her. "Where's your friend?"

Again, her heart constricted, and she again wished that she hadn't been so rash in sending Damon away. Why was it that even though her mind told her that she had done the right thing, her spirit was still heavy in his absence? She had to steel herself not to look back over her shoulder; logic said that he would not be there.

"Um," she stuttered, "he . . . he's not . . . with me." She left it at that, unwilling to delve deeper into the question. "I'm alone," she added unnecessarily.

He could have said more but didn't. Instead, he waited patiently for her to speak again.

"I came looking for Eric," she finally ventured.

His expression said, *no kidding*, but his tone was still courteous. "He's not here. He didn't come in last night."

She stifled a groan as her spirits dipped even lower. Would nothing good come of this day? She resisted the urge to abandon the attempt and slink away. "Could you tell me how to find him? It's very important. I'm his . . . He's my . . . brother." The last word almost choked her.

The bouncer's face registered no surprise. "That's a Reese face, all right." He didn't seem curious to know more. "Even if I told you where to find him, how would you get there?" He gestured at the mob all around them. "How would you get through this?"

"I don't know," she confessed, but her will, although severely wounded, was not yet dead. "But I'll find a way."

The man stared down at his towel, patted his face again, and sighed heavily. "Look, Miss, I'll tell you what. I just pulled a double shift, and it's time for me to go home. Eric's house is on my way. I'll take you, if you like."

Even as she found herself nodding gratefully, she shoved aside any misgivings that her more sensible self might have had about accepting a lift from a man she barely knew, in a place as strange and as chaotic as this. *Damon would have a fit.* But this was about family, she reminded herself. This was for her father. What Damon didn't know wouldn't hurt him. "Yes," she found herself eagerly saying. "Yes, please!"

He showed neither pleasure nor disappointment at her acceptance but jerked his chin in the direction of a dilapidated white car parked in the club driveway. It was smeared with paint and mud from passing bodies, and muddy handprints slicked the windows and windshield. "Wait there," he instructed. "I'm leaving in five."

"This is it?" Kenya asked, sticking her head out the car window, which had refused to go either up or down.

"That's it," her companion said dryly. He reached across her and opened the door on her side, waiting tiredly for her to get out.

Stunned into paralysis, she didn't move. Incredibly, he had stopped on the very same street on which she and Damon had parked on their first foray into her father's old neighborhood. Nothing had changed since her last visit. The music was just as loud, the children just as playful, and the stares from people standing in their doorways equally frank. The house to which the bouncer—whose name, she had just discovered, was Vince—had pointed was a mere few yards away from the bar where they'd begun their search. She half expected to see Austin, the laconic dominoes player who had denied knowledge of Eric's existence, still lounging in the dirt yard, sucking on a frosty bottle. They had been so close and had not even known it! The irony boggled her mind. "Are you sure?" she insisted, even though she knew he was not likely to make a mistake. "We were here, my . . . friend and I. A few days ago. They said they had never heard of him. The people in the bar, right there!" She pointed.

He tried to muster a smile, but the lines around his eyes told her that he longed only to see her on her way and to seek the refuge of his own bed. "Positive. I've dropped him here a few times. And if you asked them, and they told you otherwise, well"—he lifted his shoulders expressively—"we look out for each other. We don't like strangers here. You understand?"

She did. Sure that she had taken up far too much of his time, she stepped out of the car, ignoring the ache in her tired body as she did so. "I understand. Thank you." She fished in the pocket of her jeans for her wallet, wanting to compensate him for his time, but he recognized the movement and waved it away. Instead, he offered his hand, and she shook it, reiterating her thanks. "No problem." He dismissed the issue with a shake of his head and pulled the door shut with these parting words, "You take care."

"I will," she said to the cloud of dust left behind by his speeding vehicle. And then, she was alone—or at least, as alone as she could be with dozens of curious eyes focused on her.

Courage, she reminded herself. *You're an actress; you're used to having people looking at you. Ignore them, and do what you came here for.* Repeating her own advice over and over again like a mantra, she walked across the dry, barren, unfenced lawn of Eric Reese's house and knocked on the door.

It opened before she could knock a second time. There stood Eric, stripped to the waist, wearing nothing but a pair of jeans, seeming to take up much of the doorway in spite of his small stature. Without a word of greeting, he stepped aside to allow her inside.

She hesitated only briefly. She was streetwise enough to know that walking into a strange man's home had its risks, but she had resolved to see it through, and see it through, she would. She willed herself inside.

Eric read her hesitation and correctly guessed at its reason. "I promise you, I'm perfectly harmless. Don't you trust your own flesh and blood?" His lips pulled back in a smile that was calculated to put her at ease but did no such thing.

Just as Vince had done earlier, Eric looked over her shoulder. "Where's your watchdog? Saint Rose?"

Again, she missed Damon sharply, even though she knew that the only way to get Eric to talk was to come alone. She wished that he were with her if only in spirit; that would have made her feel so much less alone, but if ever there had been a connection between her and Damon, she had made sure to sever it that morning.

"Did you two break up?" Eric asked, squinting astutely at the flush on her face.

"No," she said hastily. "We were never . . . not really . . . It wasn't like that."

"Uh-huh." Cynicism dripped.

She didn't like where this was going. "Like he told you, he was my . . . bodyguard," she insisted. "It didn't work out, so I, uh, we parted ways."

"Right," Eric replied dryly. "Well, I'm sure he'd be happy to know that you'll be okay with me. I didn't get you all the way out here to do you any harm."

Kenya decided that she needed to take control of this conversation right now. "What did you bring me here for, then?"

Eric gave her a long look and then graciously got down to business. He beckoned to her, leading her from the short hallway into a living room that was surprisingly well kept. From the furniture and small throw cushions to the artificial flowers and knickknacks, everything bore the traces of an older woman's hand. Eric's mother, she assumed. Her father's wife.

"I'd offer you something to drink," Eric said, "but I'm sure you wouldn't accept it. And I'd ask you how you've been enjoying Carnival so far, but I'm sure I'd just be wasting your time. Correct?"

She nodded, digging deep within herself in search of strength and finding it. "Correct. You brought me here for a reason. You made a claim against my father, but I can't say you've submitted proof. Let's get on with it."

She didn't bother to sit, so neither did he. Instead, he rummaged through the drawers of an old desk, withdrew a large folder, and spread it out on the coffee table, pushing aside little figurines and hand-embroidered doilies as he did so. "My mother's stuff," he explained as he set down a chipped porcelain ballerina. "Since she died last year, I haven't moved a thing." There was genuine grief in his voice, and in that moment he seemed almost vulnerable.

"I'm sorry to hear that," she murmured sincerely.

He lifted his thin shoulders. "She was all I had. All my life, it was only her and me. She raised me single-handedly." He gave Kenya a meaningful look.

He looked so bereft that Kenya felt a pang of guilt at her own full, happy childhood, in the bosom of not one, but *two*, loving, nurturing parents. It was a rarity among black children in her own neighborhood, much less in one as touched by poverty as this. How could her father have done this, she wondered. How could the man she knew, loved, and respected so much have abandoned his son? "I'm sorry," she apologized, even though it was in no way her fault. "I wish—"

He cut her off. "Forget it. It wasn't something within your control. I didn't choose this, and neither did you." He held out some papers to her, enumerating them as he placed them in her hands. "Here. Marriage certificate, my birth certificate, and our father's. Isaac's. Land deeds, receipts. Bills he paid, letters he wrote to my mother."

Kenya sifted through them slowly, beginning with the official documents. Some of them she had seen before; they were the ones Eric had faxed to her in New York. Others were new to her. So engrossing were they that she sank onto the aging, velvet-covered couch. Although she was no expert, the official documents were undoubtedly real. The love letters embarrassed her; she felt like a Peeping Tom prying into a couple's intimate affairs. They were full of emotion, sweet words, and promises, and each word was like a blade. They were her father's words, professing his undying love to a woman who was not her mother. A woman he had left behind with an infant son when he had gone to seek his fortune.

Eric sat beside her, leaned forward a little, and folded his arms across his knees. He didn't look triumphant, only sympathetic. "Believe me now?"

Instead of answering in the affirmative, she asked, "And you say they never divorced?"

"Not according to my mother." He changed the subject a little, indicating the wall before them with a jerk of his chin. "There used to be a big wedding picture up there, hanging on the wall. The only one she had. It wasn't even in a frame: we couldn't afford to get it framed. I remember her tearing it up one day, when I was little. Now the only image I have of him is the memory of that picture."

He took the documents from her cold hands, placed them gently back into the folder, and set it down. "How is he?"

"Very sick. Multiple sclerosis. He's dying." Her eyes burned at the thought. "My mother's looking after him." She turned her head to look at Eric. "She can't hear about this. She won't be able to handle it. So please, whatever it is you want, however much you want, just tell me. Tell me now, and I'll find a way." She didn't have that much; her career had barely begun. But a daughter's love would compel her to spend whatever he wanted. Whatever it took to buy his silence.

When he placed his hand on her arm, she nearly leaped out of her skin. "I'm not a bad person, Kenya. I'm not after your money."

She found that hard to believe. "You don't think sending me threatening letters was dishonest? You don't think that making me drop everything, including rehearsals for the biggest job of my life, was a horrible thing to do? And if you're not after my money, what could you possibly want?" This was confusing. This was bad. Blackmail for money was one thing. You heard about it all the time. Her mind could cope with that. But if he didn't want money . . . Her skin crawled.

"No money. Not from you, anyway. All I want is a chance. The same chance you had." He pointed vaguely toward the window behind them. "You see those streets outside? I've had to walk through them every day to get to and from work. See those people? They're good people, poor people, and I've had to struggle beside them every single day. I've got to go from nightclub to nightclub, singing for next to nothing, and that's just in the Carnival season. When that's over, it gets worse. There's not much work around once the tourists go home."

He took a deep breath and then went on. "My mother was a sales clerk at a shoe store for almost thirty years. She never had much of an opportunity to do anything else. This little house that our father built has just five rooms in it. A kitchen, a bathroom, two bedrooms, and this room we're sitting in. That's all."

She still couldn't imagine what he was getting at. "I'm sorry. I'm sorry about that. But I didn't do it to you. What—"

"When Isaac Reese left for America, he promised to send for us. He promised to take my mother and me up there when he could, so we could have the same chances you got. He never did." Eric paused and looked at her hard. "Obviously, something got in the way."

Surely he wasn't blaming her! She protested. "But

that's not my fault! I never had any say in this! How could you possibly—"

"It doesn't matter. Whose fault it is doesn't matter. All I want now is for you to fix things."

"How?" Fix things? He was acting as though she could turn back the clock and set things right with his family again.

"You've heard me sing."

"Yes."

"I'm good." There was not a note of boasting in his declaration.

"Yes, you are." Even through the shock at seeing him, she had heard real talent in him.

"So I want to be big. I'm meant to be big. And you're going to help me. You owe it to me. Show business is a members-only club, and you're a member. I need you to get me in."

Understanding was quick in coming. What he wanted was not money, but a mentor. A guide along a thorny, winding pathway that led nowhere for most who trod it, and to success for a select few. "But I'm not a singer. I'm an actress."

"That'll do. I just need you to introduce me to someone, someone who matters. That's all. Make it happen for me. You have to." There was an impassioned plea in his voice that could not be ignored.

Kenya found herself feeling more sorry for him than she was for herself, now that her awful suspicions about her parentage were confirmed. She was moved to help, not just as a means of shielding her mother from his threat to tell, but out of compassion, almost a sense of kinship. "I don't know . . . ," she began.

"You *have* to know!" He was becoming agitated. He leaped to his feet and began to pace about within the confines of the small room. "Help me, please!"

"Well, to start, you have to have an agent. You can't do anything without one. I have an agent, Ryan Carey, but he's . . ."

He whirled around. "Introduce me to him. That's all I ask."

"He's a film agent," she was obliged to point out. "Not a music agent."

"But he'll *know* music agents."

"He probably does," she agreed hesitantly. "I could talk to him when I get back."

Eric was smiling now. "Good. Do that. Talk to him; talk to anybody. Just help me get a foot in the door. Then I'll let you be."

That was all. Kenya was so relieved, she almost laughed. It was so ridiculous: she had flown out to this island in a panic, fearing her unseen nemesis, tortured by the idea of being extorted out of money she didn't have, and all Eric wanted was a chance. She could do this for him, buy his silence, and the nightmare would be over. She got up from the couch. "I'll do what I can," she promised.

She made for the door. He snatched a slip of paper and a pen from the drawer and scurried to keep up with her. "Here's my address and number. When you get back to New York, when you know something, when you have a meeting set up, you call me. Call me, and I'll be there. I've been saving for this a long time."

She took the slip of paper, looked at it, and then pushed it deep into her pocket. They were standing in the doorway. "Can you make it back to your hotel okay? Do you want me to—"

Suddenly, she needed to be by herself. "I'll make it back okay," she tried to convince both him and herself. "I've got to go now."

"You don't know what this means to me," he told her.

Now that he had secured her promise, his eyes were glowing with anticipation.

Kenya was sure she did. She knew what it felt like, that urgent desire to perform. To practice one's art. To be *somebody.* "I think I do," she murmured.

He persisted. "And I'll never be able to thank you enough."

She gave him a sharp, meaningful look. She wasn't doing him a favor unsolicited. This was still blackmail; she hadn't forgotten. Her mother must never know. "You *know* how to thank me."

He understood the meaning of her words and looked so embarrassed that something clicked within her. An understanding. Eric had never meant to carry out his threat. In his desperation to succeed, he'd cast his fishing line out blindly, making wild threats in the hope that she would bite . . . and she had. Again, she had to suppress an urge to laugh incredulously. All this fear, all these sleepless nights! The jeopardy in which she'd put her career! All in the face of empty threats! "You never meant to tell her, did you?" she asked him softly.

He would not meet her eyes. Instead, he poked at a clump of grass just outside his doorstep with his sneakered foot. "I told you: I'm not a bad person. I'd never have hurt your mother." His hand came up to grab her upper arm. "You'll still help me, won't you? Your flesh and blood?"

Flesh and blood. After years of growing up an only child, she had a sibling, half or otherwise. Wasn't blood supposed to help blood? "I'll help you," she promised. She pulled her arm from his grasp and left him.

Chapter 20

The worst part of it all was the quiet. Try as she could, Kenya could not hear a single note coming from the room next door. Not a footfall, not the clink of a glass being set down on a tabletop, not the jingle of room keys in the lock. Damon's room was as silent as a tomb, and she didn't like it one bit.

At first, she'd struggled to remain awake, just in case he did make a sound, so that she would hear him. But exhaustion had claimed her, and she'd eventually succumbed, sleeping, albeit fitfully, throughout that evening and most of the night. In the early hours of the next morning, she'd lain in bed and listened to all the many tiny noises around her. Frogs and crickets waking up outside, hotel staff going about their rounds, and some of her fellow guests getting an early start on the festivities that came with Carnival Tuesday, Mardi Gras.

When it was fully day, she'd had breakfast on her balcony, unable to bear the thought of eating alone in the restaurant, surrounded by so many happy, smiling people. She then returned to her room and sat for a few listless hours in front of the television, halfheartedly watching the Carnival parade. Today the festival had changed dramatically from the muddy, reckless revelry of the day before. Sequins, shimmery fabrics, high heels, and beaten brass ornaments had taken the place of clay and body paint. Glad for the two-day respite from the quotidian routine, which normally imposed much stricter conventions upon them, the women outnumbered the men easily by twenty to one as they paraded across the main stage at the Savannah, their bare skin gleaming under the sun, arms outstretched to embrace the world, smiles of delight on every face.

At any other time, Kenya would have been entranced, but her heart was heavy, and eventually, the joy that fueled every masquerader's dancing feet was too much to bear. She turned the television off and surrounded herself once again by quiet.

If Damon wasn't gone, he was very good at keeping silent. God, she missed him! Over and over again, images played out in her mind, like snippets of film badly spliced into a disjointed record of their few short days together. So many contrasts, light against shadow. The way he'd put his arms around her when she cried versus the starker image of him defending her jealously. The way he'd made love to her right next door, in his extra large bed, and his panicked demand that she explain her whereabouts when he'd woken to find her gone.

What a conundrum. How could one man show so many faces? And, more puzzling still, how could she long for him, even that peculiarly pained side of him, so much? That strange sensation that had taken her by surprise out in the crowded park, when she was held aloft in his arms and looking down into his smiling face, assailed her once again. Unexpected love. The anger that had caused her to send him away had dissipated, but that love still remained, distilled, concentrated, after all else had worn off. But at the bottom of that crucible lay the dregs of doubt.

What had caused him to behave the way he had? He was protective to a point that was almost frightening. Why? What scared him so much that he was afraid to lose sight of her, even for a second? Now, after endless rewinds of that mental videotape, her record of that senseless confrontation with her chocolate-covered dance partner of yesterday morning, she knew that what she had seen in his eyes when he'd thrust himself between them had not been anger, not jealousy, but fear.

Of what?

If only she could know. If only he would tell her. If she thought that he would, she would look for him. Even if he was long gone, back to New York, she could find him. Ryan Carey had hired him: he would know where he was. She'd find him and ask him to help her understand, and then everything would be all right. Then, maybe . . .

The tap on her door scared her. She hadn't ordered anything, and there was no reason for her to expect a visit from hotel staff. Damon was gone, and it couldn't be Eric. So who? She hesitated before nervously approaching the door. "Yes?"

"Kenya." The voice she knew so well was low, somber.

She wrenched open the door, unable to contain her delight. "You're here! I thought you'd gone!"

Damon stood in the doorway, hands squeezing a rolled-up scroll of paper in front of him. He looked apologetic. "I'm sorry. I should have left, but it was impossible to get a flight out until tonight. The airport is a madhouse, I'm told. It was a miracle I managed to book something. But don't worry; you can tell your manager that there will be no additional charges for last night's hotel stay." He was stiff, formal, like a man discussing a business contract in the strictest terms. "As a matter of fact, I'm prepared to refund my fee, less travel expenses, for this entire trip. I think that would be fairest for all concerned."

His formality scared her. His eyes were carefully hooded, and there was no ease in the way he held his body, as she would have expected from a man speaking to a woman he had known so intimately. She might just as well have been a stranger, just another client seeking redress for a job gone wrong. He looked anxious to get away, so much so that he was willing to give up his fee in order to make a clean break. That didn't seem fair, not to him, at least. "Why?"

For the first time he lifted his eyes and engaged hers. "Because I can't say I have been particularly useful. If my services were not satisfactory, well. . . ." He shrugged expressively, letting his shoulders finish the sentence for him.

"But you saved my life! You lifted me out of the way when I could have gotten hit by that car, don't you remember? If it weren't for you . . ."

He gave a wry smile that pulled on the corner of his lips but made his eyes seem even more sad. "That wasn't about me being paid to protect you. That was about me being human. Anyone else near enough to respond in time would have done the same. Forget it."

This wasn't right. He was standing just a few feet before her, and yet there was a yawning distance between them. "Come in, at least." She stood aside for him to pass.

He looked as if he was about to decline but then entered. He didn't seem prepared to sit, so she didn't either. She waited for him to explain his presence. If he had severed ties and was leaving that very night, what had brought him back to her room? She didn't dare hope it was her.

She felt her tongue flick out and wet her lips. "Then why . . . why did you come?"

He held out the rolled-up sheaf of papers. "Something I thought you should know about Eric and your father."

She didn't take the papers. "I went to see him. Eric. We talked yesterday."

He looked wearily resigned. "I thought you might have. Was everything okay?"

"He didn't hurt me, if that's what you're asking. He showed me documents. Marriage certificate, bills, love letters signed by my dad. Proof enough, I think." She rubbed thoughtfully at the painfully bunched muscles between her shoulder blades and laughed ruefully. "You know, I thought I would have been devastated to know for sure that what he was alleging was the truth. But really, it's not that bad. If my parents aren't married, at least they love each other; that I know. That doesn't change who they are, or who I am. And if my father made a mistake when he was a young man—"

Damon interrupted, waving his rolled-up documents before her. "Look at these first, please."

She went on as though he hadn't spoken. "That doesn't matter, either. Maybe he regretted it. Maybe back then, he had no choice. He's in no fit state to change things right now. So, you know what? As long as my mother never finds out, as long as her heart isn't broken, I can live with that. And whatever it takes to keep her ignorant—"

"Whatever Eric's demanding from you, don't pay it," Damon insisted. Then a shadow of concern crossed his face. "You haven't paid him anything yet, have you?"

She felt obliged to defend her newfound relative. "He didn't ask for money. That wasn't what he was after at all. All he wanted was a shot at the big time. He wanted an opening, a way to sing in the States. He asked me to help him. I promised I would. That's all. And if I can do this for him, my brother, well—"

"He's not your brother, Kenya. If you'd only let me explain . . ." Damon looked as if his patience was exhausted. He unrolled the documents and fanned them out on her bed. "Read these, please. Just take a look."

The urgency of his command registered with her. She stared at the papers as though she feared they would bite. "What are they?"

"Proof. Proof that Eric Reese is not your brother. He's your cousin."

She stared at Damon as if he were mad. "Come again?"

Patiently, he explained. "Your father had a brother. That brother immigrated to the States at the same time your father did . . . and he left behind a wife and a baby son, named Eric."

This couldn't be right. She protested. "But I saw the documents! The letters!"

"I know you did."

"You mean they were fakes?"

He shook his head. "No, I have no doubt they were real. But—"

"They were from my father. He signed them!"

"No, he didn't." Damon touched her, placing his hands on each arm in an effort to steady her. And, for the first time since he'd walked in, she caught a glimpse of the gentleness that she had known in him before. He was preparing her for something, and she wasn't sure that she would like hearing it.

"Your father is guilty of something, but that something isn't bigamy and child abandonment. The marriage certificate that you saw was real, but it wasn't his. Isaac Reese isn't your father."

She was aghast. "What?"

"No, no, let me say that over. That came out all wrong.

Your father, the man you know as your father, really did marry your mother, and he really is your father. But his name is Canaan, not Isaac. Isaac was his brother, younger than him by eleven months. The two of them travelled to America together, as I told you. The only thing was, Isaac was more successful at finding work and at getting his immigration documents straightened out. It might not have been your father's fault. This was over thirty years ago; times were difficult, especially for poor, black immigrants. It got so bad that your father was facing deportation. And then Isaac, your uncle, died. Tuberculosis, from what I can ascertain."

Kenya felt a buzzing deep in her head, like a trapped insect that just would not quit. She had an eerie knowledge of what he was going to say next, and she shrank back from hearing it, but she couldn't turn away.

Damon continued. "Your father was faced with one tough choice. It was either go back home a failure, back to the poverty he had tried so hard to evade, or seize the only option open to him."

"He took his brother's name."

Damon nodded gravely. "Yes."

"And his documents. Everything."

"Yes."

The buzzing insect grew louder. "How can you know this?"

"Research. Just another tool of my trade."

"But how could you do research? Everything is closed down. Nothing's open again until tomorrow, Ash Wednesday. You said so yourself."

"Everything *here* is closed. All my sources back in the States are open for business. My cousin and business partner made a few calls and got back to me."

Her mind was whirling. This was all happening so fast! Yesterday she had been forced to accept one version of her father's past, and now, today, she was being presented with another. She knew that it had to be true. She didn't even need to read the papers that Damon had brought her. Her father wasn't a bigamist—he was an identity thief. Worse, he'd allowed a woman and child—his sister-in-law and nephew—to believe that they had been abandoned by a man who had, in fact, died. "He never told anyone about it! Not even his family!"

"He was afraid that his cover would be blown," Damon rationalized. "I'm sure he wanted to, but he felt he couldn't. Then, after a while, when things cooled down, he was afraid to go back and stir things all up again."

Her distress must have showed. Damon peered at her. "You okay?"

She considered the question for a moment and then said, "I guess so. Just a little confused, that's all. I knew my father was no god, but this . . ."

"We all have clay feet, sweetheart. Every one of us has something in our past we'd rather not share. Even with those we love. Even if it would be the right thing to do." He got up and went to the minibar and, after briefly examining its shelves, returned with a tiny, shot-sized bottle. He poured its contents in a glass and held it out to her. "Here. Steady your nerves."

She wasn't sure that even the bitter taste of alcohol could do such a thing, but she complied without protest.

"It'll take time," he comforted, "but you're strong. You'll get used to it; I promise. And as for Eric, well, now that he has no hold on you, you can decide for yourself whether you still want to help him or not."

"He's not really so bad," she said hastily, leaping to her cousin's defense. After all, blood is blood.

"I'm sure he's not," he replied without a trace of sarcasm.

"I'll have to tell him the truth." She took a look at the

documents he had brought her. "I'll have to show these to him. He has a right to know."

"That's your call. I hope it works out for you." There was a worrying note of finality in his voice. He confirmed it by saying, "I'll get out of your hair now. I just have to pack up a few things and get some rest before I head back to the airport." As he turned, his gait was ponderous, his limp quite noticeable. He looked as though he bore a terrible weight on his shoulders.

Leaving her all alone? He couldn't! "Don't!" she all but shouted.

He paused. His eyes were depthless. "What?"

"You can't go. I . . ." What could she say? "I haven't thanked you. You did all this work, and yet you're waiving your fee. Why? If Ryan doesn't pay you, at least I should."

He couldn't hide his disappointment. "Compliments of the house," he said shortly. "Don't worry about it."

That wasn't why she had stopped him, but if it delayed him, even for a few moments, it was good enough. "That's no way to run a business," she persisted lamely.

"It's my business, and that's just how I choose to run it. Believe me, it didn't take much effort. In fact, maybe if you'd had someone make those few calls for you before you left, you probably wouldn't have had to come all the way here in the first place."

And then I wouldn't have met you, she thought. The possibility of that was frightening. But he was right: if she had done what now seemed to be the obvious thing and delved into her father's background before even leaving home, she might never have come to know him and might never have felt what she was feeling now. If the forces, including her own neglect in taking action, had brought them together, then maybe that was a sign that what they'd had so very, very briefly was worth fighting for.

Kenya knew that if there was one time to be honest, this was it. A few more seconds and he would be out the door, and then she would never be able to work up the courage to approach him again. "That's not why I stopped you!" she blurted.

His expression was unreadable. "Why did you stop me, then?"

There was nothing in his demeanor that gave her hope, but she took a leap and said, "I didn't want you to go. I want you to stay here with me."

"Why?" he asked again. His face still betrayed nothing.

There was nothing to do but rush to the truth. "Because it's so lonely here. I can't stand it. I'm in this beautiful place with so many people around me, and I feel all alone."

"So, is that what you want? Company?"

He wasn't making this easy for her! "Your company," she clarified. "You. Stay with me. We had something before, and I know it's not dead. Crushed, maybe. Battered. But not dead. I want us to try this again."

He'd halted his progress toward the door, and that was a good sign. "Why do you want to try again?"

"Because I think . . ." If she said it, and he still turned away, the pain and humiliation of it would kill her, but love and courage were one and the same word, so she swallowed both pride and fear and confessed, "Because I love you. I don't know how it happened, and I wasn't asking for it. But it happened all the same, and now I can't get you out of my—"

She never had a chance to finish speaking. She felt herself being lifted up, spun around the room, and then plunked unceremoniously on the bed. As Damon threw himself down next to her, the bed sagged dangerously. "Don't break it!" she gasped.

He ignored her warning, raising himself onto his

elbows and throwing a leg over her hips, trapping her under him. "Do you mean that?"

"Yes!" He was so huge, and so heavy that if she hadn't known from experience just how adept he was at keeping the brunt of his weight off her body, she would have been afraid of being flattened.

A broad smile transformed his face. It was as though the stiffly formal business man who had been in her room before had walked out the door, and his warmer, friendlier twin had walked in and taken his place. "My God, Kenya! You'll never know how much that means to me! I never thought I'd hear you say that! I thought I'd mucked it up and spoiled everything!"

"You didn't." She tried to shake her head, but then he started kissing her, and everything else flew out of her mind. From light and sweet to hard, savage, and hungry, his kisses made a mockery of logical thought. She lifted her arms and wound them around his neck, pressing him to her to make sure that he didn't get the chance to leave. She traded him kiss for kiss, cherishing the wonderful feel of him.

When he pulled at her top, she complied, turning her body to make it easier for him to get it off. Her light, shimmery bra soon joined it, and he buried his face between her breasts, inhaling deeply, sucking in her scent.

"Not fair," she managed to mutter.

He lifted his head. "What?"

"I'm nearly naked, and you have everything on. Strip. Now!"

It was exhilarating to see him meekly follow her command. As he shucked off his shirt, she was surprised to note that there was no sign of his gun. He met her quizzical gaze with an explanation. "I know how much you hate it, so I locked it away in the safe in my room before I came to see you."

She was impressed that he had made this concession, just for her. "That must have taken a lot out of you."

"It did. You're worth it."

He was naked to the waist, and that was enough to distract her once more from mundane considerations, such as conversation. She reached up and stroked his hard chest, letting her fingertips linger over the scar that had been gouged into his flesh by that Surinamese arrowhead before moving down to his small, tight nipples. "Mmmm," she murmured. "So nice." She pressed her lips against his, running her tongue along the ridge of his front teeth. One hand snaked down over his belly and insinuated itself into the waistband of his jeans, and farther. His whole body rocked.

"Wait," he managed to gasp. "I have to tell you—"

"Don't talk," she objected. His flesh was so hot in her hand! She yanked impatiently on the buttons of his jeans, cursing the inventor of the button fly to damnation and back. Whatever happened to the good old-fashioned down-in-two-seconds zipper? "Not now. No time. Just let me touch you. I need you!"

He almost gave in but resisted long enough to tell her, "No, I have to say this, or it won't be the same. It won't be just right. You said it to me, but I haven't said it to you."

That was enough to give her pause. Her roaming fingers ceased their caresses.

His eyes, half closed with pleasure when she had touched him, were open now and held hers steadily. "I love you. I thought it was too sudden to be real. And believe me, I tried every way possible to talk myself out of it, but it's not going away. When you told me to leave, you gutted me. I wanted so badly to come running after you. I didn't care if I looked like a fool doing it. I had no pride left. There was nothing to stop me. Except you. The way you looked at me. Like I made you sick. I felt so small and ashamed. I felt like I wasn't a man anymore. At least, not enough of a man for you. That's why I left you there."

She felt truly awful to have caused him so much pain. "I'm sorry. I sent you away, and I shouldn't have. You have to understand, I spent so many years being controlled by another man, I just couldn't stand it—"

"I wasn't trying to control you. I was trying to protect you."

"I know that *now*. But back then, you scared me."

"I'm sorry. I won't do it again. At least, I'll try my best. I'm not perfect. I make my share of mistakes. But I'll try, I promise . . ."

A promise from him was good, but there was much she still needed to know. The only way to find out was with a direct question. "Why'd you do it?"

"Do what?"

"Flip out like that. More than once. It's like there's this huge blind spot where I'm concerned, and every time you think I'm threatened or out of your sight, you turn into somebody I don't know. If only I knew why, if only I understood, then maybe I could . . ."

He ran his fingers gently through her hair. "Oh, honey, it's not about you. It's nothing you have to worry about. As I told you before, there is something, but I'm going to have to work it out alone. There's nothing you can do."

He shouldn't have to go through that alone. There had to be some way that she could help him. "Maybe there is—"

"No. Nothing." His abruptness was like a slap. He shifted and rose to a seated position, leaving her prone on the bed before him, breasts now exposed.

A chill ran through her, and she brought her hands up to cover herself. "Damon?" she called his name anxiously.

His smile was gone. His warmth was gone. He was a stranger once again.

"I'm telling you again, Kenya, to leave it alone. I did what I did, and I take all the blame for it. But you don't need to know all the details. That's history long dead, and I don't want to go over it again, not even with you."

Slam, slam, slam. Metal doors clanged into place between them, leaving her out in the cold again. She fought against them desperately. "Did something happen? Something awful happened, didn't it, Damon? Please, if you only tell me, I can help you deal with it. Don't try to do this on your own. I love you. Let me help you."

When he rose to his feet, she knew that there would be no loving in her room today, and that made her nudity ludicrous. She looked for something to cover herself with and found only a towel draped over the back of a chair. She wrapped herself in that, and it afforded her a small sense of modesty.

"It's private," he said gruffly. "Leave it alone, for God's sake!"

Oh no, he wasn't going to do this to her! He wasn't leaving her on the other side of his silence! She tried to let him see reason. "Damon, I need to know you! I need to know who you are, and what you're about. I can't love you in a vacuum. . . ."

"Can't you love me just for me?"

He was making her trip on her own words, using her own pleadings against her. She stuttered to clarify her words. "I can! I do! But there's so much more to you than what I know, and it's what I don't know that frightens me. What could be so awful, so dark, that you can't share it with me? And how do I know that one day you won't wake and find I've left the room, or see me across the way talking to a stranger, and come charging in, demanding that I stay where you can keep an eye on me? *What if you hit someone again?*"

"You'll know because I promised," he said tightly. He looked offended that she would question his determination.

"I know you promised, and I believe that you mean it. But if this thing, whatever it is, is stronger than you, then your will alone isn't enough. You can't just fight against it and hope that brute force will let you hold up the sky all on your own. You have to let me help. We have to work on this together or else—" She sucked in her breath, afraid to speak her next thought out loud.

He heard it all the same, unspoken though it was. His face was hard and shuttered, and he seemed to be holding his breath. "Or else, what?"

She was trembling, and there was nothing she could hold on to to steady herself. "Don't ask that."

"Or else what, Kenya?" He didn't exert any pressure on her to answer but cringed like a man waiting for an ax to fall.

Heart pounding, she weighed her own options, as daunted by her own unspoken ultimatum as he was. She was standing on the edge of a fine blade, and what she said next would decide which way their lives would turn. She could choose to do as he begged her and let the matter drop. It would mean trusting him to handle his dark secret on his own, and hoping that he would manage to get the better of it, rather than the other way around. On the other hand, she could demand what she saw as her right: to know more about him, know what made him who he was, and to have information that would impact upon her—upon them, in a fundamental way.

Which could she choose? Either course of action would bring pain. If she let the matter drop, that nagging question would gnaw at her, little by little, until she was sure she wouldn't be able to stand it. If she insisted . . . she could lose him.

Either way, it's over, she realized, *before it's even begun.* It all came down to trust. He didn't trust her enough to share with her what was going on in his heart. She couldn't trust him enough if he couldn't confide in her.

Her hesitation gave him her answer, but he still wanted to hear it from her. "Say it." He was both daring her to say what was on the tip of her tongue and pleading with her not to. "I'm not leaving until you say *something,* whatever it is. I need to hear it from you."

She didn't want to put those thoughts into words, so she tried to stave off the inevitable. "It doesn't have to be like this! You can stop it! You can make a difference!"

"I can't." His breath was ragged, his face full of grief. "I've told you that. Why can't you understand?"

Her heart was pulled toward him in his pain, but good sense told her that compassion would only act as a tiny bandage on a huge wound. It wouldn't be enough. Only honesty would bring true healing. She shook her head, unable even to lift her eyes to look at him. Her throat had seized, spasms brought on by suppressed tears choking her so much that she couldn't say another word.

She didn't have to. The unspoken was real enough; they both understood. Without looking at her again, he picked up his shirt but didn't bother to put it on. Instead, he slung it over his shoulder and stepped into the corridor, closing her door carefully behind him.

It took all her strength to keep herself from running behind him.

Chapter 21

Full circle. It was funny, Damon thought, how life sometimes went around in circles. Just one week ago, he was standing right here in his cousin's hallway, travel weary, heartsick, and alone. Now, here he was, besieged by déjà vu, more weary than before, more heartsick than before, and more alone than he had ever been in his life. He set his bag down and took his coat off, much as he had done the last time he was here. If it had not been for the gaping hole inside of him, filled only with longing for Kenya, he would have sworn that he'd fallen into some crack in the space-time continuum and landed exactly where he had started, and that the past week had simply never happened.

"Come, on! Come on!" Leshawn's wife, Marilee, was beckoning to him, urging him into the sitting room. His niece squirmed in her arms, squalling like an indignant cat, begging to be put down on the floor. "Leshawn will be out in just a second. Sit down! Take some weight off your feet. You look terrible!"

"Thanks," he murmured dryly, although he knew she was telling nothing but the truth. He didn't even want to catch a glimpse of himself in the mirror; he was sure he looked ghastly.

He submitted to Marilee's fussing, allowing her to push him down into Leshawn's big armchair and brush away the melting flakes of snow from his head. The baby tried to follow suit, reaching forward with both arms to grab at his face. In spite of himself, he managed a chuckle, not even minding when the tiny, sharp fingernails scratched him.

"She's grabbing at everything." Marilee rolled her eyes pretending frustration, but her smile betrayed her maternal pride. "We don't know what to do with her."

"She's not bothering me a bit," he assured her, although if he were honest, surrounding himself with such overwhelming familial bliss was both bitter and sweet to him. He wondered vaguely if he had made a mistake in coming directly from the airport. Maybe what he really needed was to go back home, pull the covers over his head, and hibernate for a long, long time.

But before he could consider that option, Leshawn entered, going straight to him. They embraced like brothers. "Damon! Good to see you!"

"Same here, man," was his heartfelt reply. Leshawn's home was one of the few places where he felt completely at ease. The warmth that enveloped him told him that he had, in fact, made the right decision in coming.

The two men sat, and Marilee set the baby down on the carpet at their feet, scurrying into the kitchen with the cheery promise to bring back something "to thaw their bones."

The two men sat in silence, watching the baby play for some time, and then Leshawn asked carefully, "You okay?"

Damon never even considered a polite social lie. He and Leshawn were far too close for that. "No."

"I thought so. You're really in love with her?"

"Really, honestly, truly," he confirmed miserably. The admission brought him no joy.

"So what went wrong? Did she give you a hard time? Did she think you're not good enough for her?"

"No, it wasn't that."

"What, then?"

Before he could answer, Marilee sailed back in with a smile on her face, bearing a tray with two steaming mugs. "Irish coffee," she told them and added, with a telling wink, "*very* Irish, if you get my drift. Damon looks like he needs it."

Damon took a sip of his and winced. She had put enough whisky in there to strip rust off nails. It hit his chest with a soothing heat.

"So, Damon, I hear that movie star fired you," she said breezily, oblivious. "Was she a real diva? Did she push you around, send you out in the rain to get her favorite brand of bottled water?"

Damon shook his head loyally. "No, nothing like that. She was very nice."

"I hear she's got an eye for her male employees. I read something about that just last month, in one of those supermarket rags. Is it true? Did she molest you?" Her eyes were shining, eager for gossip.

"No, she didn't." Damon's answer was unintentionally sharp. He apologized at once, but his answer was enough of a warning. Marilee dropped the subject graciously. "Sorry. Sorry, sweetie. I didn't mean anything by it."

"I know you didn't. And I'm sorry for being such a bear. It's just that I've had a rough flight. A little rest will straighten me out; you'll see."

She scooped up her daughter, planted a sisterly kiss on Damon's forehead, and said, "Look, guys, I realize you've got stuff to talk about. I'll leave you be, okay? If you need anything, the human tornado and I will be upstairs, wrecking the joint. Be sure you stay for dinner, hear?"

He kissed her back on her cheek, still feeling lousy for his moodiness. "I will, I promise. I wouldn't turn down one of your home cooked meals for anything in the world."

She was mollified by his genuine enthusiasm. "Good. Because there's way too much roast lamb for just us." She whisked out of the room, babe in arms.

Alone with his cousin, Damon felt more comfortable about opening up. "I blew it," he confessed.

Leshawn was unsurprised. "I sort of guessed, but how?"

"She asked questions I couldn't answer."

"Couldn't, or wouldn't?" Leshawn asked shrewdly.

There seemed no point in sidestepping his own guilt. "Wouldn't would be closer to the truth."

"What kind of questions?"

"I came on too strong with the whole protection thing. I guess I crowded her. I know I scared her. She wanted to know why. I couldn't bear to answer."

Leshawn didn't even need to guess. "Jewel."

"Yes."

"You never told her."

"No, nothing. Kenya doesn't even know that Jewel existed. And I couldn't bear to talk about her. About how I let her down."

Leshawn popped out of his seat. "For God's sake, Damon, how many times do you have to hear it? You didn't let her down! What happened was horrible. It was a tragedy, but it wasn't your fault. You couldn't have stopped it."

"I could have, if I had only—"

"If you'd only what? Followed her around all day, every day, for the rest of your lives? Been joined at the hip until the end of time? Was that what Jewel wanted from you?"

"No, she'd have hated it."

"And so would Kenya, I'm sure. A woman wants a lover, not a full-time personal bodyguard. You aren't anybody's guardian angel. Nobody assigned you the job. And who's to say that if you'd gone with Jewel to the grocery store, that what happened to her wouldn't have happened the next day? Or if you'd gone instead of her, who's to say that the men that killed her wouldn't have broken into the apartment and attacked her while you were gone? What if it was simply her time to go? Suppose that was her destiny?"

That was nonsense. He dismissed the idea. "I don't believe in destiny. I don't believe that there's anything beyond our control. I believe in vigilance, and I believe in strength. We are our own destiny." He thumped his chest with his open palm. "*We're* the ones in charge here. What happens in our lives is up to us. We don't have to bow to every whim and fancy of some perverse universe—"

Leshawn pointed a victorious finger at Damon's face. "That's it! That's just it! There's your problem. You don't believe in destiny, because it's one thing you have no control over, and God forbid there's something that you can't control. You're not suffering from guilt, Damon. Or grief. You're suffering from an extreme case of arrogance."

"What?" Damon sputtered incredulously.

"You think you're supposed to be in charge of everything. You think everything is supposed to go just the way you want it to, or else. I know you loved Jewel, and I know you miss her, but what's killing you is the thought that *you* failed. That *you* were weak. That's what you can't stand. You know all your nightmares? All your sleepless nights? They aren't about loss. They're about ego."

Rage engulfed his body and his mind. His hands clenched into fists. "If you were anybody else . . ." he ground out threateningly.

Leshawn didn't even flinch. "I'm not afraid of you, Damon. We've been to the mat way too often for that; half the time you kicked my butt, and the other half I kicked yours. So don't even bother. I'm speaking my mind. I'm sick and tired of holding my tongue and letting you wallow in your own misery. If there was any better time to tell you what I think, well, I don't know what it is. You let a beautiful woman, whom you claim to love—"

"I do love her!"

"—walk away from you because you don't have the guts to suck it up and admit to what you think was *your* failure."

He didn't want to believe what he was hearing. Leshawn had it all wrong. His grief was real. All those nights when the ghost of Jewel had drifted into and out of his mind—that pain was real. "That's not true. I wanted to keep Jewel to myself. I couldn't stand the idea of sharing the memory of her with anyone else—"

Leshawn spat in contempt. "Aw, come on! Don't feed me that! You're better than that." He got close enough to poke Damon in the shoulder, punctuating his remarks with a hard index finger. It was only respect and love for Leshawn that prevented Damon from shoving the accusing finger away. "You're just a man, Damon. You're not a superhero. Jewel never thought you were, and she never wanted you to be."

Damon's chest hurt so much he was afraid to inhale. Could Leshawn be right? Could ego really be the fly in the ointment that was preventing his wounds from healing? Ironically, it was ego that made that question difficult to examine. How could he admit to himself that self-recrimination and pity had taken the place of genuine grief?

Leshawn saw the slumping of his shoulders, which

signalled that Damon's fighting spirit had oozed out of
him. His next words were gentler. "What you need, my
man, is some time off. You need to sit and think hard
about all that poison you've been carrying around
inside you. And about what happened over the past
week. Because I'm telling you, if you don't do something, if you don't do some serious mental housekeep-
ing, you're going to lose that girl."

"I've already lost her," Damon reminded him. He saw
in his mind once again that last glimpse he had had of
Kenya's face as he'd shut the door to her hotel room. If
ever there had been a final answer, it had been there in
her eyes.

Leshawn snorted. "That's what a coward would say.
What happened to you? What happened to your spine?
Did you bury your courage with Jewel?"

That taunt was too much to stand. If there was anything that could have made him feel smaller at this
moment, he didn't know what that was. He hung his
head, opening himself to his cousin's words.

Realizing that he was finally getting through, Leshawn
eased up on the pressure. "All I'm saying is, give it some
thought. Take some time off. You've been too hard on
yourself lately. Get some rest, and renew your mind.
You'll be better able to think your way through this once
you're rested." He waved his arm in the direction of the
upper floor. "Come stay with us for a while. You won't
have to worry about food or anything. Let Marilee fatten
you up. You won't have to worry about shopping or
cooking or laundry, either. And I promise to keep the
baby out of your hair. You can get some real rest."

Damon pressed his fingers to the base of his skull,
where a tight throbbing was threatening to make him
mad. Maybe Leshawn was right. He'd been running in
overdrive for far too long, and had run out of fuel. He

did need to regroup. But not here. As much as he loved his cousin and his family, what he needed to do could only be done in solitude. "That's a really kind offer," he began.

"It's not an offer. It's a demand."

He shook his head. "Thank you. I'm grateful, I truly am, but what I need to do, I can't do here. I love you all, but I need to be alone."

Leshawn looked as though he was going to protest further but thought better of it and gave in graciously. "Okay. You're right, I guess."

Damon drained the last of his coffee and got up. He needed to leave. "Listen, I really have to—"

"You aren't leaving! Marilee has plans to stuff you this evening. We've got loads of food, honest!"

He would have loved to stay, but his need for solitude overwhelmed his desire for food and company. "You know that at any other time I would never say no to one of Marilee's dinners. Or to spending time with you three. But I've really got to go." He didn't even wait for Leshawn to acquiesce but set about getting his jacket and bag. "You'll explain to her, right?"

Leshawn let the matter drop. "That's fine." He produced Damon's car keys and turned them over. "Here. Kept her running smoothly for you, as usual."

"Thanks, man." He scooped up his duffel bag before Leshawn could make a move toward it and headed for the door. On the threshold, he paused. "And look, I'm sorry about my reaction back there. You just stepped on a few corns, that's all."

Leshawn laughed heartily. "Yeah. For a moment there, I thought you were going to belt me."

"For a moment there," Damon agreed, "I thought I might."

Leshawn shrugged with the ease that could only have

come about after years of boyhood tussles with his
cousin. "That's okay. I'd have taken you."

Damon gave him a playful parting punch on the
shoulder. "In your dreams," he laughed, and left.

"Love you, too, Momma," Kenya whispered into the
phone moments before the line went dead. "Both of
you," she added softly into thin air. She shut off her cel-
lular phone and put it away. Even though she called her
mother faithfully every night when she returned to her
hotel from a day of shooting, she was unable to resist
giving her the occasional call from her trailer on the set
between sessions, even though her schedule barely gave
her time to catch her breath, much less chat on the
phone. With the knowledge that her father was slipping
farther and farther away day by day, she ached to make
contact as much as possible.

At least, in the relative chaos of the set, her small
trailer provided an oasis of quiet. Not that that was necessarily a good thing. When things were quiet, when she
wasn't concentrating on her lines or the endless har-
rowing hours of repetitive work, she had time on her
hands to think, and often, thinking brought pain.

Three weeks after returning from Trinidad, her sense
of loss was as fresh as it had been on the day she had left.
It was uncanny how, after spending an entire lifetime not
even knowing someone, having met them, one could
miss them so utterly once they were gone again. She
missed Damon's constant presence, and even the caring
vigilance that had become too much to bear.

How she loved him still! Separation hadn't dulled the
edge of that vicious blade. Being in the same city as he
didn't help, either. She'd even gotten Damon's address
from Ryan, but that was as far as she had been able to

take it. While her heart insisted that she could still find him and try again, and forget that stupid incident that had sparked their breakup, common sense told her that sooner or later, his demons would come charging out of the proverbial closet, and they would be back to square one. Whatever they were, if he couldn't face them even long enough to share them with her, they would always be too strong for him. She knew better than to allow herself to enter any relationship with an auto destruct timer already counting down.

She took her shoes off and then carefully removed her costume. The film she was working on was a period piece, set in the era just before the start of World War I. The quaint but feminine dress she wore was festooned with clasps and buttons. Her close-clipped hair was hidden by an elaborately styled black wig. Sometimes, in the afternoons, it amused her to keep it on, as it kept her connected to the role she was playing. She left it on even as she flopped into the trailer's only armchair and put her sore feet up on the small bunk against the facing wall. Those six-inch high patent leather pumps would be the death of her, she was sure.

A knock on her door startled and perplexed her. Apart from Ryan, the director, or a handful of assistants and wardrobe personnel, hardly anyone ever sought her out when she was in her trailer. Whatever needed to be discussed was usually talked about at length on the set. She asked tentatively, "Yes?"

"It's me."

Those two words made her whole body tense. Surely she must be hearing things! That voice couldn't belong to the man she thought it did, because she'd given Damon a choice, and he'd chosen to walk away. Her longing for him must have done worse things to her imagination than she had feared.

The voice came again. "Kenya? It's me, Damon. Open up."

With questions buzzing furiously through her head, she opened the door. He looked wonderful: freshly shaven, carefully dressed in a cream sweater and dark chocolate pants, a far cry from the rugged jeans and denim shirts she had known him to wear in Trinidad. In spite of the cool March weather, he wasn't wearing a jacket. It was his way of letting her know that he wasn't armed. It touched her that he remembered how much she hated his gun.

His hair was newly cut, the razor marks at his temple and nape probably no more than a day old. He looked rested, peaceful, and relaxed. Even standing a foot or two away, he smelled wonderful. She had to resist the urge to lean forward, bury her face in his nape, and inhale deeply.

She felt his gaze directed at a spot above her forehead, and realizing that he was staring at her wig, she whipped it off, holding it nervously in both hands like a sleeping kitten. This was the second time he'd seen her with a ridiculous hairpiece on her head. He, too, seemed to have remembered the bad disguise she'd been wearing at the airport on the evening they had met, and he half smiled. To hide her embarrassment, she stepped back inside, letting the door slam shut on its hinges. She hurriedly arranged the wig on its stand and returned to open the door once again, much of her composure having crumbled. "Sorry," she muttered, an all-purpose apology that she hoped would cover her appearance as well as her bad manners at having shut the door on him.

He hadn't moved an inch and didn't seem the slightest bit perturbed at her lapse. He held a glass bowl between both hands. It seemed to be filled with water. He held it out to her. "I don't even know if you like flowers, or what kind of flowers you like. So I got you this."

In spite of her shock at seeing him turn up on her doorstep like an apparition, curiosity got the better of her, and she peered into the bowl. "A fish?" she asked in puzzlement.

"It's an angelfish. They are hardly any trouble at all. And they're really pretty. See?" To confirm his words, the black-and-white fish fanned its fins for her, glittering in the crystal clear water. She was too surprised by the gesture to take it from him.

"It's yours," he insisted. "I bought it for you."

Humoring him, she took the bowl, found a level surface, and placed it carefully down. When she turned to face him again, he was proffering a small, red tube. "Fish food." He shook it, and there was a muffled rattle.

Given the way they had parted, this meeting was all too surreal, like the setup for a bad joke. *A man walks into a girl's trailer with a fish. . . .* She had to ask. "Damon, what's this about?"

"I thought you might like a little company in your trailer, when you're stuck here between scenes. I don't know much about the movie business, but I'm sure it must get lonely in here sometimes."

"It does," she murmured. *Lonely at the hotel, too,* she could have added. *Lonelier than anything I could have imagined, since you walked away.*

He looked expectantly behind her into the trailer. "Can I come in?"

No, she wanted to tell him. *No, you can't, because I'm tired and my guard is down. I still want you, and I'm afraid I'm too weak to—* "Of course," she heard herself say. To her own surprise, she let him enter.

He stepped in, making the confined space seem even smaller by his mere presence. He was so tall that he had to dip his head slightly to fit. She was sure that if he stretched out his arms, he could touch both walls at the same time. He put his hands in his pockets and looked gravely around the room. "I've been trying to imagine what this would be like. What this wonderful opportunity would be like for you."

She was a little embarrassed by the lack of luxury around her. It wasn't exactly as glamorous as most people expected a movie trailer to be. "I'm afraid the wonderful opportunity doesn't exactly come with the plushest accommodations. I'm not exactly the leading lady. I'm lucky I don't have to share, like some of the other actors are doing."

"You'll be a leading lady soon," he assured her. "That big role is out there waiting for you. I know it in my bones."

She nodded her thanks for his words of encouragement, but when he didn't say any more, she filled the awkward pause by busying herself with the fish, dusting a few grains of fish food onto the surface of the water. The creature didn't seem all that interested, so she let it be. When she couldn't stand the quiet anymore, she asked, "Why are you here, Damon?"

He looked resigned to the inevitability of her question and produced a small, folded envelope from his back pocket. She recognized the handwriting on it as her own. She knew that inside, there would be her check, uncashed. "To return this, for starters." When she didn't take it, he set it down on her bunk. "I told you, you don't owe me anything. You didn't need to send me money."

"You did work for me, and you didn't have to. You found out the truth about my father and about Eric Reese. You told me my father's real name. You deserve something for it."

He shrugged. "I did it as a favor for a friend. As I told you before, forget about it."

She nodded her thanks. There was no sense arguing the point. Damon was not the type of man to back down once he'd made up his mind about something like that.

"Have you spoken to Eric again?"

"I have. Ryan's trying to hook him up with a good agent. He'll probably fly over in a few months to see what he can do for himself." It had taken a lot of thought for her to do that much. After all, Eric had tried to blackmail her and had caused her much distress. But as far as she could see, he had only been trying to get for himself the success that he believed all his life had been denied him because of what he'd thought was his father's abandonment.

"Did you tell him what I'd learned? About who his real father was?"

"Right away. It was hard on him, finding out after all these years that things aren't as he had always believed them to be. But I think what hurt him most was what his mother went through, believing that her husband had never come back to her. Not knowing that he was dead."

If Damon didn't share her sympathy toward Eric, he didn't let it show. "Planning on seeing him?"

"I don't know. I haven't decided yet. He is my cousin, after all." She braced herself for a warning to be careful, but he just looked accepting.

"Family is important," he said evenly.

She could have let the small talk continue, but she had to ask, "You came all the way from Brooklyn to return a check to me? You could have mailed it."

"I could have," he agreed gravely. "But I needed to tell you something."

"You could have phoned," she insisted stubbornly. "E-mail, telegram, carrier pigeon. Anything." She could have added, *and spared me the heartache of seeing you again, looking so good.*

He shook his head vehemently. "No. That wouldn't do. What I have to tell you, I have to tell you in person."

Butterflies fluttered just under her heart, but she refused to let him see her weaken. "Go ahead. What do you have to tell me about?"

"Jewel," he said simply.

She looked confused. "What jewel? Whose jewel? I don't understand."

"No, not an object, a person. A woman. My former client. My fiancée."

Under other circumstances, her shock would have been comical. "You were engaged?" A pinprick of jealousy skittered across her skin.

"Yes."

"Married?"

Pain flickered across his face. "No, we never had that chance. She was killed a week or so before our wedding."

"Killed . . . how?"

"Murdered. Knifed in the street by a couple of drugged-out thugs. Killed for the ring I gave her. Police never even found a suspect." His delivery of the information was dry, almost as though he was talking about a case he'd heard about from a colleague rather than about his own lover, but she wasn't fooled. She knew that his detachment was a mask to his hurt.

Compassion sent any reservations she may have held about touching him clean out of the window. She squeezed his arm, partly to convey her sincerity and partly to comfort him. "I'm so sorry, Damon."

He grimaced. "Thank you. But I didn't come for your sympathy. I came here to offer you an explanation. The last time we were . . . together, you asked my why I am the way I am. Why I made you feel so suffocated. I didn't answer you then, to my everlasting regret, because I didn't want to violate Jewel's memory, even if only by mentioning her. Or, at least, that was the reason I gave myself. I've had the past few weeks to think that over, and I realize now that that wasn't the real reason at all. It wasn't about her. It was about me."

She frowned, puzzled. "How?"

"The morning she died, I was with her. Or, at least, I had been. She left our apartment, left our bed, while I was still asleep. I never heard her go. She went out to buy me groceries for a special breakfast. She never came back."

"I'm so—" she opened her mouth to commiserate once again, but he cut her off abruptly.

"Ever since then, nothing and nobody could convince me that if I had only been able to stop her from leaving somehow, or if I had gone with her, or instead of her, she would still be alive. That ate me up. I couldn't stand it. I played the whole scenario over and over in my mind, every day, every night, for years. Falling asleep next to her, and waking up alone. And panicking. Knowing something was wrong."

This time she had to say something. "Damon, there's no way that could be your fault. You had no way of knowing what was going to happen. Nobody could have, not even her. And what if you had gone with her? Maybe you'd have been—"

"I'd rather have taken that knife. Anything would have been better than the hell I've been living in since I lost her. But looking back, the worst part of it wasn't losing her. It was the way I came to hate myself for my own failure. I'd made a mistake bigger than any fumble I'd ever made on the football field, and I was angry and humiliated. It got to be less and less about her and more and more about me. I've always liked to think that I was in charge. I liked to think that I had everything under control: my life, my relationships, my job, everything. And then I realized that I don't, and that there was a force out there bigger than me, which could make a mockery of my plans in a heartbeat. If there was one thing I couldn't stand, it was that."

Understanding was coming—first, in tiny trickles that became rivulets, and then, in rivulets that became streams. "So you decided it would never happen again."

"You bet. I buried myself deeper and deeper into my work. I took the longer assignments, the ones that kept me far from home, and the people and places I loved, for months at a time. And just to cut the odds of ever making another such mistake, I never accepted another female client after that."

"You accepted me," she reminded him.

He half smiled. "No, I didn't. My cousin and business partner did. As a favor for his old buddy from the force, remember?"

"Ryan. Yes, I remember."

"I was livid. The last thing I wanted was this assignment."

"That you made very clear," she said wryly.

"But that wasn't about you. It was about . . . stage fright. I was afraid I'd be tried and found wanting. I was terrified that something would happen to you on my watch. It worried me so deeply, I couldn't sleep for fear that something might have happened to you while my eyes were closed."

"I was never in any danger," she asserted earnestly.

"In my mind, there were shadows lurking behind every bush. I'm ashamed to admit that I was as afraid of my own potential for another failure as I was for your own personal safety. So I came down hard on you. I was overbearing, I got on your nerves, and I embarrassed you more than once. And I'm sorry."

"But you saved my life, too," she reminded him. "I

could have gotten hit by that car, and you put yourself in danger to help me."

He wasn't accepting any such comfort. "You stepped into the path of that car because you were mad at me," he reminded her. "Because I was making an ass of myself with your cousin. He wanted to be alone with you to talk, and I wouldn't leave. Remember?"

As true as that might have been, she wouldn't allow him to beat his breast about it any longer. She'd asked for an explanation, and she'd received one, even though it was long in coming. She supposed she would have to be content with that. "Thank you for telling me."

He was on a roll; once he'd begun his confession, he couldn't be stopped. "And what I did to that man during the J'Ouvert, the little man who was trying to dance with you, was unforgivable. I scared the pants off him. I could have hurt him—badly. It was only because I know my own strength, because I'm careful enough to pull my punches when I need to, that I didn't do worse. But it was bad enough, and I'll always be ashamed of that."

She ached to see him in such deep self-recrimination. She tried again to cut off the flow of anguished words. "Damon, it's over. I'm sure he's forgotten—"

"He may have, but I won't. Not for a long time." He stopped and breathed in deeply, fueling up for more. "All I can do now is ask you to forgive me."

It was such a simple thing, to forgive. She could have held onto her resentment and mistrust, but all it took to be able to let it go was want to do so. Her words came easily to her lips. "I can. I have."

He examined her face hard for evidence that she was telling an untruth but, finding none, sighed in relief. "Thank you. Thank you so very much."

"It's nothing. It's really not that big a deal, now that I understand—"

He cut her off. "Not just for that, although your forgiveness means the world to me. Thank you for the peace you've brought me. For letting me sleep at night."

She gaped. "For . . . ? How do I . . . ?"

He seemed suddenly weary of standing and fell heavily onto her bunk, rubbing his chin with one hand. "What would you say if I told you that for four years, I hadn't had a single night in which I've slept the whole night through? What if I told you that there have been times when I've gone four or five nights without more than three consecutive hours of sleep?"

No wonder he'd always looked so exhausted! "Why?"

"My nights were always filled with monsters. Fears. Guilt. And Jewel."

"Jewel?"

He nodded without embarrassment. "She came often. In my dreams. When I was awake. When I was tired or sad, she was there. No matter how much I tried to control my mind, and no matter how hard I talked myself out of it, whenever I let my mind slip in the smallest way, she was there. And there was nothing I could do to stop it."

Pity made her sit next to him and put her arms around his shoulders. How horrible it must be for you to constantly be plagued with memories of your lost love! No wonder he couldn't sleep. She asked tentatively, "Was she . . . mad at you?"

He shook his head vehemently. "No. Never. Always sweet, always understanding. In a way, that made it worse. I could deal with anger. But this—"

"And is she . . . still there?" An eerie shiver ran down her back. She didn't believe in ghosts, but yet . . .

"No. No, she's gone. It's over. My apartment is so quiet now, it's almost strange. I go to bed and sleep the whole night through. No nightmares. No visions. I'd become so used to the disturbances that I thought they'd be with me until the day I died. And then . . ."

She was almost unable to breathe. "Then . . . ?"

When he turned to look at her, his eyes were so deep, so full of emotion, that she was almost afraid. "Then I found you."

Could she have done that? Could she have changed his life so radically, brought him sleep, and chased his ghosts away? It was unbelievable. "Maybe it was just a matter of the fullness of time. Maybe it was just time for you to heal."

He wasn't hearing it. "No. No. Trust me, Kenya, I know myself. I know how deeply I had let myself be buried. I was willing to stay there, stuck in the mire I created, and die slowly. I knew I was dying, and I didn't care. And then you changed something. You did it so fast I barely knew it was happening. And how you did it, I'll never know. But you set me free, and I'll always be beholden to you for that. I'll always love you for that."

She wasn't even aware that she was crying until she felt him stroke a tear away from her cheek with his forefinger. She'd been so wrong about him! She'd branded him a bully, when in fact all he had been was a prisoner of his own guilt and fear. And to think that she had done something to change that! She was so overwhelmed that more tears joined the stray one that had fallen.

"I didn't mean to make you cry," he whispered. "I promised you once that I'd make sure you never cried again."

"It's not you," she protested. "It's . . ."

"It is me," he insisted. "You were fine, going about your business in that funny-looking wig—"

She had to suppress a laugh at that.

"And then I turn up like a schoolboy with that stupid fish and a long story. I'm sorry I disturbed you. I'm sorry for making you cry. But I had to tell you. You asked me a question, and I didn't have the guts to answer it before. I had to let you know."

To her horror, he looked like he was about to get up. "Where are you going?"

"I'm leaving. You have your answer. I didn't come here to force myself back into your life. I know I was overbearing, and there's no proof I won't be again. I'm forever thankful to you for how you've changed me." He looked around. "You've got a good thing going here for yourself. You've got what you've dreamed of all your life. I'm happy for you. Good luck, Kenya."

Good luck? Was she hearing correctly? He'd come back into her life, set her heart aching for him again, dropped off his depth charge, and now he was wishing her good luck? Where there had been tears, there was now outrage. "Don't you dare!" Her shout was so vehement that he froze, half risen, and then fell back onto the bed again.

He was too perplexed to do anything but ask, "What?"

"Where do you think you're going? How dare you do this to me?"

He began to explain, "I told you I—" Then he cut himself off with another thought. "Do what to you?"

She put her hands on her hips, looking so forbidding that if he had been contemplating making a run for it, he wouldn't have had the courage to see it through. "You've got a lot of gumption! You walk in here, spill your guts, get me all churned up, and then walk out again? Here I am, pining for you, going *nuts* over you, and then you turn up on my doorstep and put my heart in the wringer all over again, and now you want to leave? Well, you know what? You're going to have to make it through me first!"

Just when she thought he'd been knocked speechless, he asked chokingly, "Why don't you want me to go?"

What a stupid question? Did he really need to ask? Her response was far from gentle. "Because I love you, you stupid . . . *jerk!*"

Another long silence, and then he said very softly, "Don't say that if you don't mean it."

"Which part? The first part, or the second part?"

"The first part." He was smiling tentatively. "The second part is a given."

That small curve of his lips was enough to cool her ire somewhat. "I meant it. I wouldn't say it if I didn't."

The smile broadened. "Then say it again. *Without* the second part."

"I love you."

She felt herself being lifted onto his lap and pulled against him. She felt the next question vibrate deep in his chest, against her breasts. "You sure?"

"Positive." Her voice was muffled against the collar of his shirt. "I told you once before, remember?"

"Did you think I'd forget? But I thought I'd ruined it by the way I behaved. It was so new, and so fragile, like a tiny blossom, and I—"

"Like a blossom! That's exactly what *I* thought!" She lifted her head to look him in the eye. Even their mental images were the same.

"I thought I'd crushed it." He shook his head sadly.

"You did, but maybe it was a hardier little plant than either of us ever imagined. Because it's still alive, and stronger than before." She put her hands on either side of his face. "I've been longing to see you. I got your number and address from Ryan, and every day I've wanted to call. I've considered turning up on your doorstep a dozen times. I was even willing to forget the questions I'd asked you, and let you keep your secrets to yourself—"

"Wouldn't have worked," he cut in ruefully. "We might have tried, but unless I had gotten to a place where I was able to confront myself, I'd have kept on hurting you. Maybe even someone else. That's why I let so much time pass. I needed to work my way through this long, dark tunnel, and I needed to do it on my own."

Her heartfelt response was a deep, intense kiss, and the taste of his mouth almost distracted her from saying vehemently, "I'm glad you did."

"I'm glad I did, too." Unwilling to let their kiss be broken for too long, he placed his hand at the back of her head, his fingers deep in the wisps of her hair. His tongue traced the outline of her lips before grazing her lower front teeth. As their kiss intensified, his hands slipped down to her back, along her hips, and then moved to grasp her bottom. He leaned back awkwardly, trying to stretch out on her tiny bunk and pull her down on him. "Where'd they get this bunk?" he griped when he found he couldn't fit. "Who'd they get it for? A munchkin?"

"Fits me just fine," she teased him.

He came right back at her. "Mine would fit us both. With tons of room to spare. It's only a short ride across town. And my chariot is just a two-minute sprint to the parking lot. Less, if I carry you."

She was shocked at the speed at which her body grew hot. She was tingling from her scalp to her toes, which curled in anticipation. It was as if her core had turned to warm liquid. She laid her palm down flat against his hard chest, and under the fabric of his shirt, she felt his racing heart, made even more evident by the fact that he seemed to be holding his breath, waiting for an answer. To feel him again! The anticipation of his weight pressing down upon her, and the delirium brought on by his invading body, mingled with the delicious fear that she would be crushed by his hugeness! It never entered her mind to say no.

But first, there was one small matter to be addressed. "Password," she managed to gasp.

His fingers, busy toying with the two small indentations on her back that embraced the base of her spine like quotation marks, stalled. "What?" he puffed.

"What's the password?"

Understanding dawned. "Please?" His smirk told her he was playing games with her.

She swatted him playfully on the arm. "Not *that* password! The other one. You know what I mean."

His smirk transformed into a broad grin. "Or no dice, huh?"

"Or no dice." She shook her head in fake regret. "And that would be a pity. I was *so* looking forward to touching you here"—she let her fingers encircle one nipple, visible in its hardness as a pucker in his shirt—"and here. . . ." She danced her fingers lower, sliding the same digit into the space between two of his shirt buttons and into the indentation of his navel. "And this," she pulled on the large metal buckle of his belt, "would definitely have to go."

He was done playing. "I love you," he gasped. He captured her roving hand in his. "Stop, stop, I need to think straight. I need to *talk* straight."

She let her hand go quiet and listened attentively.

"I love you," he said again.

She mimicked his earlier question, "Sure?"

"Positive. I've never been surer of anything."

"It was, uh, a whirlwind romance," she reminded him. She needed to know that what he felt was not a whim, a passing fancy. She *had* to know.

"Yes, a whirlwind that sucked us both in and hasn't spit

us out yet. And I don't ever want to set foot on solid ground again if it means being away from you."

It was vitally important that they both understand what they were up against, so she persisted. "There's so much we don't know about each other. What we like and don't like, where we stand on things like politics and religion and . . ." She hesitated, feeling almost foolish. "And . . . kids."

He kissed her, both to reassure and to hush her so that he could speak. "We have so much time to discover one another. We have all the time in the world to talk. I'll tell you everything. I'll tell you where I went to school, and what food I hate the most, and the name of my first dog. But not now. Right now, I only need to tell you one thing: I love you. That's all we need tonight. Okay?"

She felt any anxiety that she might have had drain from her, and then she was soft and pliant in his arms again. "Okay."

"Good."

She felt the sash of her dressing gown come loose. "What are you doing?"

"What does it look like?" He lifted her easily, just enough to peel the gown off her shoulders. "I'm stripping you naked." He rolled his eyes, as though pained to have to state the obvious.

She was puzzled. "But I thought . . . your bed . . . and your chariot outside." Her words were disjointed, as his kisses peppered her mouth and face.

"Later," he breathed.

Surely he wasn't dangling before her eyes the promise of an evening of love and then snatching it away! She protested. "But I'm hungry for you! And you said yourself, this bunk is too small!"

"And *I'm* ravenous for *you*," he countered. "But we can have the main course across town. This is just an appetizer—and what I intend to do to you doesn't take up a whole lot of space."

He knelt before her. Just before he lowered his head, the wicked look on his face told her all she needed to know about his intentions. She felt her panties slide down her willing thighs, and then her body went rigid with shock as his lips made contact with her soft belly. "Oh! Mmm," she breathed.

"Oh, yes," he agreed.

She leaned back, closed her eyes, and gave in to pleasure.

BOOK YOUR PLACE ON OUR WEBSITE AND MAKE THE ARABESQUE ROMANCE CONNECTION!

We've created a customized website just for our very special Arabesque readers, where you can get the inside scoop on everything that's going on with Arabesque romance novels.

When you come online, you'll have the exciting opportunity to:

- View covers of upcoming books

- Learn about our future publishing schedule (listed by publication month and author)

- Find out when your favorite authors will be visiting a city near you

- Search for and order backlist books

- Check out author bios and background information

- Send e-mail to your favorite authors

- Join us in weekly chats with authors, readers and other guests

- Get writing guidelines

- AND MUCH MORE!

Visit our website at
http://www.arabesquebooks.com